Bel-Tib YA New Fiction
YA Fiction Kozlowsky
Frost :

31111037506795

DATE DUE

FROST

M.P. KOZLOWSKY

FROST

SCHOLASTIC PRESS · NEW YORK

Library of Congress Cataloging-in-Publication Data available

ISBN 978-0-545-83191-8

10 9 8 7 6 5 4 3 2 1   16 17 18 19 20

Printed in the U.S.A.   23

First edition, October 2016

Book design by Christopher Stengel

FOR VIVIENNE
AND WITH A LOVING NOD TO THAT ONE

FROST

PART ONE
THE OUTSKIRTS

ONE

In the middle of the bombed-out room flickered a small fire, and near it sat Frost. The girl of fifteen—or was it sixteen now?—turned her head and watched her shadow against the battered wall. The wind blowing in from the broken windows set the flames dancing, creating a display of strange silhouettes around her. It was as if, after all these years, she was momentarily surrounded by other humans. She wasn't alone anymore.

"Hello," she said to the shadows. She'd never met someone new before and felt it'd be a good idea to practice, just in case. "I'm Frost. It's a pleasure to make your acquaintance. Have you been in the neighborhood long?" Frost frowned. The words sounded cumbersome. She rarely heard anyone speak aloud and didn't know whether what she'd read in her books was correct. She reminded herself to ask her father when he returned.

The shadows didn't answer, of course. Once again, there was only silence.

I'm lucky to have Dad, she thought. It was a weak attempt to convince herself that she wasn't really alone. Not technically.

Frost glanced through the rippling flames at the slumbering beast warming itself opposite her. Romes's breathing was getting worse each day. It was garbled, hoarse. Too much wheezing, too much spitting of blood. He could barely walk and his tail remained still. Frost had had him for nearly as long as she could remember. They grew up together. He'd always been there for her, but now . . .

She was well aware that she could barely take care of herself. How was she supposed to care for Romes too? Where was her father?

Frost stood up and walked over to the far wall, half of it blown away and exposed to the elements, and gazed out at the crumbling city. She was thirty-two floors up, the top floor of the building, and had a tremendous view of the devastation. Hundreds of thousands of cars were overturned and abandoned—most of them at the bridges and tunnels—some crushed by falling streetlights and debris from on high. Buildings were toppled over or burned out, skeletal; some looked like melting candles, their facades peeling away. Nature was returning to the streets, ripping up sidewalks and tearing holes in the ground. There were no lights whatsoever, not even from the stars or moon. In fact, Frost hadn't seen either in years through the persistent gray haze. Sometimes she thought she saw the flames of fires in building windows or on street corners or in an abandoned bus, and wondered if there were other people out there, people like her, waiting for something better. If she could only reach them! Even if there was just one person hiding somewhere in the city, a potential friend.

But it was far too dangerous to leave this gutted apartment. In her entire life, Frost had never left, not once—a promise she had made to her father, a promise she regretted more and more with the slow passing of each repetitive day. What kept her most curious of all was the strange blue glow at the far end of the island, nearly eight miles away. From such a distance, she wasn't sure if it was an illusion or some heavenly anomaly or . . . Her father had told her about what was being built down there, just before the Days of Bedlam. Could it be true? Did they succeed? If they did, it would mean a better world was still possible— security, medicine, community. Everything.

Her thoughts were interrupted by noises out in the hall, and it wasn't the continuous falling away of the building like she was used to. Her stomach dropped as she eyed the closed door. Had the Eaters finally found her? She had forgotten to lock the door. Not that it mattered, not if it was them.

The sounds grew louder. Frost closed her eyes. She wasn't ready.

The footsteps ceased. With a creak, the door slowly opened. And there, standing before her, was a robot.

"Dad?"

"*No.*"

Frost exhaled, a mixture of disappointment and relief. "Bunt. You were gone so long, you had me worried."

"*It is becoming more and more difficult to find supplies, Frost. And there are more and more dangers to evade.*"

Bunt bent down and lowered his box of loot to the ground. Then, on one knee, he placed a hand on Romes. The broot did not stir beneath the metallic touch.

"*He is getting worse.*"

"You're supposed to tell me he's getting better."

"I do not lie. You know that. Your broot is dying. He has a month of life left. Two at most."

"I was sick, too, once. Don't you remember? I used to always be sick when I was little. Dad told me so. He said it was bad, very bad. Worse than Romes. And look, I got better."

"He will not."

The brutal honesty was too much for Frost. Her eyes filled with tears. It was a day she had been dreading for years, and all she wanted to hear was that there was hope, just a glimmer of hope. "I wish my dad were here. He would never say such things to me. He would comfort me."

"I have no control of when your father comes and goes. He is a defect."

"He is not a defect, *you're* the defect. Do you hear me? He should be here right now, not you!" The words spilled out before she could stop them, but she refused to take a single one back. After so many days of silence, it felt good to shout.

"Alas . . ."

"Alas . . . Alas . . . What do you think you are? You're not human, Bunt. Never will be."

She thought about this constantly. She'd been reminded of it just yesterday, when she asked Bunt to pretend to be a boy her age in the hopes that if Frost ever met a real one, she'd have some idea what to say.

"Pretend?" the bot had asked her.

"You know what it means, Bunt."

"I am unable to pretend."

Frost sighed in frustration. "Just talk to me like you're someone else. Someone real. Say your name is . . ." She picked up a severely weathered book from the top of a large pile and flipped through it. "James. Say your name is James."

"My name is James."

Frost felt a bolt of excitement course through her. "Good," she said. "Good." Hurriedly, she flipped through more pages. "Okay," she said, under her breath. "Okay. I'm supposed to . . ." After rereading the lines three times, she awkwardly crossed her legs and attempted to curtsy, nearly falling over. "How do you do?"

"I hunt for food and slay Eaters."

"Bunt!"

It was impossible with him. That was why she needed her father to tell her about boys. At least he'd been one once. A human boy. Something Bunt could never be.

Although Bunt did have the shape of a human. A silver construct, rings of dulled metal wrapping around him from head to toe. There was no face, just the outline of one. A bump where the nose should be, soft indentations for the mouth and eyes, raised loops for the ears. A mold without features, and when he looked at you, there was only the faintest of violet lights where the eyes should be. And when he talked another violet light surged through the area designated for his mouth. Frost had been around him so long that she had begun to see a face there. A sad gentleman, a man out of time and place, a soul removed. He reminded her of everything wrong with the world.

Bunt sifted through the box he'd set down and retrieved

something Frost hadn't seen in ages: an actual can of food. After ripping off the lid, he handed the can over to a wide-eyed Frost. She had finally gotten used to eating small animals.

"Beans?" she asked, jumping to her feet. "Are those beans? Thank you. Can you heat them up?"

Bunt closed his hand around the can. In seconds, the contents were warm.

Frost fetched a spoon from a drawer in the kitchen. She once tried to keep everything as neat and orderly as her father had left it, but that had become increasingly difficult. After all, supplies were short and the periods of rain were few. Dust and debris covered everything. If she wiped them away, by morning there was more to replace them. Even with all the time in the world, keeping things clean would be a challenge. And besides, who was she straightening up for? Who cared if everything was everywhere and nothing had its place? The shadows she talked to certainly didn't mind. So she spent most of her time reading the vast collection of books she had acquired through Bunt's excursions and, upon completion, instead of returning them to their shelves, she placed them in large piles throughout each room, as if rebuilding the city in miniature.

As she ate the beans, consuming them like a stray broot, she eyed Romes. The sight gave her pause. Had he stopped breathing? She crawled over to him, the can clattering against the warped and moldy wood floor, and placed her head against his protruding ribs. No, he was still alive. Barely. She placed the can in front of his snout.

"Eat. Just a little, Romes. Do it for me."

Romes's nose twitched, but other than that he didn't budge. Frost, her body suddenly limp, looked him over. The animal was nothing like the one she found outside their door all those years ago, scratching and crying to be let in. He was a puppy then and full of life, unlike everything else around her. She was seven years old and her father was slowly dying, like her mother a year before.

"We can't keep it," he told her.

"But, why?"

"Well, for many reasons. One is that the thing is wild. Wild and dangerous."

"It doesn't look dangerous."

And it didn't. The broot nuzzled against Frost, nibbling at her fingers. Its tail, slick and ringed like a rat's, was longer than its body and its feet were abnormally large, so big that the animal kept tripping over itself every time it tried to run. Its eyes were humanlike, round and watery and constantly tearing as if it was sad about something. It had the slightest of snouts and a massive lower jaw. And then there was that color. There was nothing intimidating about a pink animal.

"Not yet. It will grow up to be, though. Look at the size of the paws. Broots grow to be very large and very aggressive. If we were to care for it, it would most likely turn on us one day."

"Not this one. It thinks I'm its mommy."

Her father shook his head. "It doesn't think that, Frost."

"It does. It won't hurt me, not ever."

He crouched down before her, a hand running through her short, choppy hair. "I don't want you getting attached to anything. There's no place for attachments anymore." He caressed his daughter's face, then quickly looked away, coughing into his sleeve.

"He can be my friend. I need to have a friend."

"You have Bunt," he said, pointing to the robot in the corner sharpening a set of long knives.

"Bunt's a robot. He's not alive like Romes."

"You named him already?" her father asked, exasperated.

Frost nodded. "Romes."

Her father let loose a long sigh, his hands deep in his pockets. "Then I'm afraid we're going to have to keep little Romes, aren't we?"

But Romes wasn't little any longer. Even in his sickened state, he was massive. From snout to tail, he measured close to six feet, as long as Bunt was tall. His teeth were the size of adult fingers, though no longer very sharp—they were once like razors, much like Bunt's knives, the sharpest teeth of any animal on land. His ears were pointed straight up, two dark triangles atop his head like a bear's. And those large paws displayed nails longer than his teeth—several times Frost was merely grazed and her clothes had been torn open—the fact that her skin wasn't shredded to the bone was a small miracle.

Frost and Romes had been through so much together. When they were hungry, he brought them large rats to eat—not counting the handful of times he caught robotic critters that roamed throughout the building. He curled up in her lap every time the earth shook; he licked her face whenever she cried; and whenever she suffered, he seemed to suffer, too. They were linked. He was her constant companion, her constant comfort and the one constant source of love in her life. He never left her side. If she lost him . . .

Frost stared out of the hole in the wall, across the city and toward the distant blue glow. That's where she had to go. There were people living there, she was sure of it. People who'd managed to create real lives for themselves, who'd be able to help her and Romes.

"It's time to leave," she told Bunt, breaking from her reverie.

"Is there something you need? Something I forgot?"

"No. I'm not sending you out, Bunt. We're all going together."

"That would be a poor decision. There are far too many dangers out there, and your broot is nearly dead."

"That's why we're going," she said, already gathering supplies for their trip. "We're going to save him."

"That is an impossibility."

"It isn't. There are ways. Humans are capable of great things, Bunt."

"That was before the destruction."

"The technology still exists."

"There is no escaping dea—"

A strained voice slowly faded in. "Frost . . . Frost . . ."

Bunt's blank face flickered like a malfunctioning screen, an image appearing and disappearing. A different voice emerged from the robot now, something human. Then, finally, the image held and, like every time before, Frost lost her breath. It was her father.

"What do you think you're doing?" he asked.

As difficult as it was, she looked away and continued packing a bag. "I can't just sit here anymore. I have to do something. I have to get Romes help."

"There is no help, Frost. You take him out there and he's just going to die even quicker. You have to stay here to survive. Both of you. You have to remain hidden. Let Bunt help you."

"I can't lose Romes," she said. "Not like I lost Mom. Not like I lost you."

"But you didn't lose me. I'm here."

She looked at him standing there, a human face on a robot body. He didn't move, not an inch. Her eyes lowered to the floor. "I see you less and less now."

"I can't control it, you know that."

"And neither can I. All I can control is what happens to Romes. Maybe."

"I won't let you go out there. I refuse."

A wave of indignation swelled within her, and she snapped her head up to look at her father. "All I have to do is wait for you to go away. When Bunt returns, I'll order him to take me. And he'll listen. He has to." It was one thing she loved about Bunt. He would always do whatever she said—the beauty of programming.

His voice grew stern. "I am your father, you have to listen to me."

"You are my father's memories. You are his personality. You are not him." It was something she had wanted to say for a very long time now, but once the words left her mouth, she immediately regretted them.

"Frost!" The way her father recoiled, the pain in his voice, it made everything even worse.

She turned away and kneeled beside her pet, stroking his matted and dulled fur so she wouldn't see the hurt in the projection of her father's face. "I have to help him, Dad. I have to. You keep disappearing back into Bunt and I can't be alone."

"You have Bunt."

"I need something living. I need my friend."

"I want to protect you, Frost. That's all I want to do. I'm afraid of what will happen out there. It's not safe."

She lowered her head, balled her fists, and gritted her teeth. "Dad, what about what's happening in here? Every day I eat less and less. We're running out of water, and Bunt has to leave for longer and longer stretches of time. All by myself, I have to keep fighting off falcons and hawks that fly in here looking for a meal, and sooner or later this building is going to collapse. I can't stand it. I'm going crazy. The days pile up; I'd have no idea what month it even is if I didn't have Bunt. My world is this box. This ugly and stinky box. I want to be out there. I don't care how dangerous it is. I want to be out there in that world." She paused, her voice growing quiet. "The Eaters are going to find me in here. They're going to find me and tear me apart."

Her father gazed at the ceiling and exhaled. "Where are you going to go? Where do you possibly think you will find help?"

"The Battery."

His eyes fell on her as he shook his head. "No. No way. Absolutely not. I should have never told you those stories. There's nothing there, Frost."

"I see a glow coming from that direction."

"It's not what you think."

"You said that was where the hope would be found," Frost insisted, refusing to let him make her feel foolish.

"Yes, before the disaster. Before. It didn't work. It was a failure."

She didn't believe that, and she had a strong feeling her father didn't believe it, either. Why else would he have filled her head with the images she could no longer shake? For years he had told her that world governments had been preparing day and night for something like the Days of Bedlam. It was the new space race, he said. Only they'd begun building small cities within cities. Fortresses. They weren't looking to leave, they were looking to stay. It would be a place where life would survive, where it would go on thriving. Her father told her that there would be no sickness there, no death. Utopia.

"I'm going," Frost said, her resolve hardening. "Romes doesn't have long. And if I lose him, you're going to lose me."

Her father closed his digital eyes. For a moment, Frost thought he was going to disappear again. But then, very softly, he spoke. "Frost, you tell Bunt—you tell him to watch over you, to do whatever it takes to keep you safe. You hear me? You tell him to give his life for you if he has to."

Frost paused. "It's your life, too."

"And I'd give it over for you in a second."

She always knew he would, but she didn't realize how much she needed to hear him say it until just now. Frost sighed. "You're going to leave me now, I can feel it."

He looked away. "I know. I can, too."

Something cracked inside Frost's chest. She ran to him and threw her arms around his waist.

"I can't feel you," he said. His face displayed signs of strain, and yet the robot's arms barely moved. "I'm having more and more trouble controlling his body. I'm so sorry, Frost. I wish it wasn't like this. I wish I was still there with you. Really there. But there's nothing but—".

Her father faded, his voice drifting away and Bunt's face going blank. Seconds later, the soft violet lights of the robot's eyes returned.

"Get our things together," she told Bunt. "We're leaving now."

TWO

Only once in the past five years had Frost set foot into the hallway. Now, as she was about to open the door, she found herself paralyzed by fear. Her breathing increased, her hands and lips trembled, and her heart pounded out a beat that wouldn't slow for hours. She couldn't speak; she couldn't even turn the knob.

Finally, Bunt broke the disabling silence. *"I detect nothing out in the hall. It is safe."*

At the sound of his voice, Frost let out a long breath, opened the door, and stepped outside.

Bunt joined her, slowly glancing up and down the dilapidated hall. *"My actions in these coming moments will make a lot of noise. They may bring trouble. Prepare yourself."*

Frost gripped one of Bunt's largest knives, practically a machete, and held it before her defensively, the blade dancing fearfully in her hand. She glanced down the hall to her right at an open door, waiting for something to come running out. It took her a moment before she realized it was the apartment her father once used as his makeshift office. She never knew exactly what he did before the Days of Bedlam; all he ever said was that he was an artist of sorts and left it at that. In the early years, before he was trapped inside Bunt, he was always locked away in there instead. Back then, in her perpetually feverish state, Frost's mother was always yelling at him, telling him to let it go, that he was losing sight of what was important. Whatever he was trying to accomplish, however, never amounted to anything, not that Frost could remember. And now, looking in, she could see why. The place was trashed. There were tools sticking out of the walls, garbage strewn about, papers littering the floor, tables and desks and dressers toppled over and spilling their contents as if a bomb had exploded, tearing the room apart like the rest of the city. It all must have been too much for him, being unable to rebuild the past.

Bunt, meanwhile, approached the hall elevator. He measured it with his eyes and then with his hands. Apparently satisfied with the information he gathered in these brief seconds, he began to rip the door free. Indeed, the noise was loud. Frost shivered slightly as she imagined the sounds could be heard from miles away. Who knew what it would draw?

As usual, the robot's strength was impressive. The metal door must have been tremendously heavy, but in virtually no time at all, Bunt had torn it loose from the track and raised it high over his head as if to throw it through the weakened walls. But instead, he gently set the door down on the floor and burned a hole through it somewhere near the top. Then he returned to the open elevator shaft, reached in for one of the twelve supporting cables, and ripped it from the ceiling and then from the elevator itself. It was quite long, so he burned off a shorter length. He slipped one end through the hole he created in the door and promptly tied a rather imposing knot. With the cable over his shoulder, he pulled the door down the length of the hall and back to the apartment door.

"This will do," he said.

Dropping the cable, he walked back into the apartment and bent down in front of Romes. When he tried to lift him, the animal snapped, crying out in pain.

"You will have to help me," Bunt said to Frost.

Frost fell to all fours, crawled over, and began to stroke Romes's head. She placed her mouth inches from the broot's ears. "I need you to trust Bunt like you do me. I know you're in a lot of pain. I know it hurts and you're scared. I am, too. But we're going to help you, okay? We're going to take you somewhere. A place better than this. A place where there is medicine and miracles. I'll get you there. I promise I will."

Bunt tried to lift him again, and again Romes snapped. Even as solid as the robot was, and as dull as Romes's teeth had become, Frost knew there would still be plenty of damage if the broot were to lock on. And if his bite found her flesh instead of the metal of a robot, whatever appendage was the unlucky recipient would be torn off like the elevator door.

"Get behind me," Frost told Bunt. "Lift him, but with me between the two of you."

"He will still snap. He is an animal, Frost. He will take your life without thinking twice."

"This is an order, Bunt. You have to trust me. Just as Romes has to. Just as I trust him."

Bunt did as he was told. As he bent down, Frost wondered

what would happen if Romes lunged at her. She didn't even fear the pain. She feared that, in the brief moments before she died, her heart just might break.

With Frost standing between broot and robot, Bunt lifted the animal awkwardly. Romes's head did indeed snap. His mouth opened wide, teeth bared, saliva dripping. With great speed and a growl, he brought his jaws thrusting forward right toward Frost. And with even greater speed, and incredible will and strength, he came to a sudden stop, mere inches from Frost's face. The two locked eyes, Frost hardly breathing. Slowly the animal's mouth closed.

"I knew you wouldn't hurt me." Frost patted him again and the beast closed his weary eyes and allowed Bunt to carry him to the elevator door.

After setting the broot down, Bunt said, *"It will be a slow progression down the thirty-two flights, but I assure you no harm will come to Romes. I will be certain with my every step. Are you ready?"*

Frost barely heard any of this. She was staring into the apartment, the only home she'd ever known. She wasn't afraid she would forget it, for she had every inch of the place memorized. And she wasn't afraid she would miss it, because the memories of the two parents she lost there lingered like ghosts. And because, even more than a home, it felt like a prison. What she was afraid of was how quickly she was coming to regret how long she'd stayed.

"I'm ready," she said.

THREE

Frost pushed open the door leading to the stairway, holding it in place with her foot as Bunt dragged Romes through. The trio paused momentarily before descending. The decline was steep. Bunt told Frost to wait there as he went back to pick up part of the cable he had discarded in the hall. When he returned, he tied Romes down. *"This will work."* Then, standing firmly in place, moving fist over fist, he slowly lowered the door down to the first landing. It was laborious work, and Frost quaked with the realization that they would be dangerously exposed in the stairwell for a long time. And the grating noise of the metal door against the concrete steps wasn't helping. They were practically calling out to intruders.

The farther down they went, the more the stairs were littered with garbage and debris, abandoned items that must have weighed down the fleeing masses—a hammer, books, countless useless gadgets, and personal mementos. Frost was forced to go ahead and clear the steps, shoving anything that might prove valuable into her bag, although there wasn't much. Every few flights, they passed splashes of blood on the walls and stairs, which Bunt was sure to point out were quite old. There were articles of ripped clothing and apparently someone had a fire burning at some point. Set up in yet another corner was something like a place of prayer—various holy objects lay about: pictures and cards, a necklace. On another level, somebody had painted a warning: EATERS IN THE BUILDING. Bunt didn't deny this. At one point, they came across a rotting, severed finger that still had a ring on it. There was a pair of baby shoes, practically new, the laces still tied. Wedged within a large crack was a doll, ragged but still smiling. Despite her growing anxiety, Frost smiled back.

By the time they made it two-thirds of the way down, Frost was exhausted but undeterred. She took a deep breath to settle her racing heart, but before she could exhale, a noise cut through the air. The slamming of a door, feet on the stairs. "Eaters?" she asked. Bunt's hand protectively darted out and held Frost back.

He looked up from where they had descended, stretching his neck as far as it could go, scanning the flights above. *"They are maybe a dozen floors up. Two of them. Whoever or whatever they are, they will either want me for my scraps or you for your flesh. We must hurry."*

Bunt wasn't so delicate with Romes anymore. He slid the door down the stairs until it slammed into the wall. The broot cried out, but there was no other choice. Frost raced from landing to landing, clearing away whatever she could with swift kicks. Above, the sounds grew louder until they seemed to rattle inside Frost's head.

Bunt sent the elevator door flying down the stairs so hard the corner crashed through the wall. When he tried to remove it, the door wouldn't budge. It took him another full minute before he had it loose and repositioned, Romes groaning and crying out all the while. Looking back up, he spoke to Frost. *"We are out of time. You have two choices, Frost. You go on ahead, alone, or, as I climb up to meet our pursuers, you wait here to see who makes it back down."* He didn't wait for a reply. Instead, a long blade was released from within his arm, and he made his way slowly up the stairs.

Frost knew her answer the moment Bunt had spoken. She wasn't doing this to save herself. She was doing it to save Romes. She would wait.

FOUR

Frost heard the violent altercation escalating three or four flights above her. A lethal brawl in tight spaces. There were grunts and groans and strained, almost muffled screams, not of pain, but of anger and lunacy and great desperation. Throughout, Bunt didn't say a word, and, for the first time in her life, Frost hoped that her father didn't suddenly appear, coming to somewhere in the middle of the melee, useless and afraid. It was Bunt she needed now.

Bodies crashed against the walls, something tumbled down the stairs and snapped, and all the while Frost cowered beside Romes, as she always did during times of trouble, flinching at every sound. There were clangs of metal, chilling scrapes and pops, the unmistakable squelch of skin being punctured and ripped until, finally, just when she couldn't take any more, all was quiet.

Seconds later, someone was descending the stairs with slow and heavy steps, and when Frost looked up, prepared for anything, she saw Bunt, his weapon sheathed, blood splattered across his dull sheen, a fingernail caught in a groove upon his chest. Rising to her feet, she ran ahead and hugged him.

Nearly a half hour later, they reached the bottom, and Frost saw her building's lobby for the first time in her life. It looked as if a storm had surged through it. The windows were all shattered, as were the mirrors and vases of fake flowers. The wood of the front desk was warped and chewed through, the monitors cracked and toppled over, the computer stripped of parts. The overhead lights had long ago fallen and the ground was ripped up. For a moment, Frost tried to piece everything back together with her mind. The broken glass clicked back into place like pieces of a puzzle, and the furniture was mended and polished. Cracks were filled, the electricity returned. Gone were the remnants of temporary shelters and the tracks of large animals. In these brief seconds, Frost could almost imagine walking through the lobby on the way to school. But, it wasn't so. With a blink of her eyes, the world fell apart once again.

Something seemed to have caught Bunt's attention. In a corner of the lobby was an overturned luggage cart. He approached it and inspected its wheels, spinning each with a solitary finger.

"It's not big enough for Romes," Frost said.

"*No, it is not,*" Bunt responded, setting the cart right side up. "*But the door will make far too much noise being dragged along the streets. We will attract great dangers that way. The wheels will help.*"

After temporarily moving Romes to the cold floor, Bunt detached the bottom part of the cart and, with the tools hidden within his fingers, soldered it to the elevator door. When finished, he demonstrated the results of his ingenuity for Frost.

The door moved quietly and nearly effortlessly across the lobby floor. If she didn't know better, she might have thought Bunt looked proud.

With Romes back in place, this time *sans* restraint, the trio departed once more, crossing the lobby and reaching the shattered windows. As Bunt pulled Romes through and into the street, Frost paused. In a moment, she would be stepping outside. For the first time in her memory, there wouldn't be a roof over her head or walls shutting her in. In her dreams, when Frost stepped outside, the city had the same glow of the thriving metropolis she always read about—a world in rewind filled with people and color and the bustle of life.

And now, she would see what was really out there. Frost could feel her pulse quickening, her hands shaking. This was it. The doors to the world were about to explode open. Smiling, she raised her foot and crossed the threshold.

Almost instantly, her breath was knocked away, as if all thirty-two floors of the building had collapsed on top of her. The city was as lifeless as Bunt. Standing on her toes, Frost glanced up at the gray sky for a long time, trying to peer straight through the thick haze at the stars and the sun and the planets beyond, but there was nothing looking down on her. The dry and musty air circled, and the smells curled up and rotted in her nose. Everywhere she looked she saw blacks and whites and grays. Dull and bleak. A city deep in its sickness. It wasn't supposed to be like this. She had looked out over the city every day of her life, but for some reason when she finally ventured out onto its streets, she had expected it to shine.

It was day, but it was dark. And, by night, she knew, it would only get darker. There would be no lights, the sky too thick for the moon's radiance. She had seen it every night from her apartment—a black wave with a glowing blue heart. This was her city.

"*We head south,*" Bunt said, pulling the door toward the nearest street corner.

Again, Frost had to clear the way of debris, each item she touched an artifact to a lost world. Clothing, bags, toys, tech— she threw them away with a mixture of wonder and regret. If there was something large, like an overturned car, Bunt had to stop pulling and roll the stripped vehicle aside. All the while, Romes slept completely still, forcing Frost to continually monitor his breathing.

She kept her eyes roving, eagerly searching all the nearby buildings for signs of life. They used to house so many people. The streets, she had been told, were nothing but crowds in a flourishing metropolis where anything was possible. But now, the windows of each building were destroyed and bare, the blotted-out eyes of the decrepit city. The faces of these homes, riddled with sores and disease, had sagged long ago, only to contort in their deaths. Their gaping mouths promised a hollow body, its vital organs missing. She wondered how many of these buildings Bunt had traversed up and down, searching for food and supplies. How many times had he climbed up the thirty-two flights of stairs in her building, and how many violent encounters had he had? And, she wondered, how much of it had her father witnessed? How many times did he reappear only to find himself in a strange and sad place? And how much was he aware of when he was gone? Yes, his mind was melded with that of Bunt's, taking in the same information, a shared memory, but what did he feel when he wasn't in control, when he was a silent passenger? Was it something like sleep? She could never bring herself to ask him.

Bunt had always been there, a loyal part of the family from before the Days of Bedlam. But it wasn't until her father was dying that she became aware of the larger role he would soon play. Eight years ago, her father tried to prepare her.

"You won't be alone," he told her, spitting up blood as she cried. "I won't leave you, not ever."

"But Mommy . . ."

"I know. I know. But that won't happen with me. I promise."

"How do I know?"

"Because."

"Because why?"

"Because Bunt found this for me." He held it up to her in the palm of his hand like a sacred object. It was just a small square, no bigger than the nail on her pinky. "Frost, do you realize how rare this is? How valuable? Only the very rich could ever afford this."

"What is it?"

"It's a very special chip. All of me, everything you know about me and everything you don't will fit onto it. And then, when I . . . when I . . ."

"Like Mommy."

"Yes, when I'm like Mommy, this chip will be inserted into Bunt and I will live on. In him."

"So . . . so you won't . . . you won't die?"

"Not as you know it. No."

"But how are you going to get everything on there?"

"Bunt is going to have to perform a type of surgery on me. Okay? He's going to do it now. That's why I'm telling you this. It's very simple, but I want you to go over there in the corner and work on your reading anyway, okay? Take Romes with you. And here, I want you to put these on," he said, handing his daughter an old pair of headphones. "They won't block out all the sounds, but it'll block out a lot. Okay?"

"What kind of sounds?"

"Well . . . you see . . . there'll . . . there'll be some drilling and . . . um . . . and we don't have any medicine to numb my skin or to help me sleep. Do you understand?"

"Are you going to cry?"

"Frost, put those over your ears and don't take them off and don't turn around and don't stop reading no matter what you hear. You don't do anything until Bunt comes over and tells you it's fine. Okay?"

"Okay, Daddy."

He pulled her in close, kissing the top of her head with great force. "I love you, little girl. I love you more than anything, and that's why I'm doing this. So I can always be with you. So I can always help you. I'm never leaving. Never."

Frost nodded and her father wiped a tear away from her eye.

"Now, put them on and go read whatever book you like

best. Read your favorite one and let the story do what stories are supposed to. Let it take you far away."

Frost did as she was told. She put the headphones on, recalling that her father told her they once played music. Oh, how she wished she could hear music. Especially now.

She crawled into her corner and, with Romes pressed up against her sleeping, read a book about a little boy and a little bear and their many adventures together. But the sounds still found her, more than her father probably guessed they would. She had been waiting for them, to see if they sounded like when she lost her mother. But they didn't. They were far worse. She heard the screams, the shouts and the begging, and yet she remained strong, biting her lip and closing her eyes. She never turned around. Not until Bunt touched her on the shoulder and said the surgery was only a partial success. He had all the information, he told her; it was already uploading, but her father didn't make it.

There was a crash in the distance, and Frost was forced back to the present. A harrowing shout echoed from empty building to empty building.

"Trouble."

Bunt was pointing straight ahead into the barren street, but Frost, free from her daze, couldn't see a thing. "What is it?" she asked.

Bunt unsheathed his sword. *"A rogue."*

FIVE

The robot staggered out of the vast desolation. It stumbled into gaping holes and tripped over scattered debris, muttering and crying with each beleaguered step. All the while something flashed across the robot's face. A human visage.

Frost and Bunt stood frozen, watching this robot manically skitter about. It was in its own world, oblivious to its surroundings. It picked objects up at random and recklessly tossed them in all directions. A metal rod nearly took Frost's head off. At one point, the robot leaned against a building with one hand, the other covering its face in a full minute of exasperation. Then, frustrated, and with a torturous scream, it picked up a fire hydrant and hurled it through an already-crumbling wall.

Finally, after crossing the intersection, the robot saw them. It halted in the middle of the street, half bent over and holding the sides of its head. That's when Frost finally made out its face. It was that of a woman nearing the last phase of her life. Her youth had dried up long ago and the permanent stain of old age had begun to seep in. There was clear evidence of a doctor's scalpel—rearranged bulges of skin, eyes pulled in all directions, warped lips and raised cheeks. Inside the robot her makeup was permanent, a nearly clownish application—bright red lips and blue mascara and purple blush. Her hair was an orangish-red and rather curly. She wore a pearl necklace and matching earrings. There was no doubt that she had once lived a charmed life, but that was long ago. In her eyes now Frost saw nothing but cold fear and, beyond that, a growing detachment from reality. She desperately wished the rogue would ignore them and continue on its way.

But the woman within the machine lingered, focusing on Frost with a growing mix of surprise and confusion.

Anxiety built in Frost's stomach, spreading through her limbs until they were too heavy to move.

Then, the robot charged at Frost. Full speed, head down. Paralyzed, Frost couldn't even scream. She barely managed a gasp of horror.

It was enough to grab Bunt's attention. He rushed over, but the moment he reached her, the violet light of his eyes began to fade and the robotic woman easily batted him aside and to the ground.

The woman seized Frost by the shoulders, picking her up so that they were face-to-digital-face.

"You have to help me! You have to get me out of this thing!"

Frost couldn't speak; she could only stare into the horrified woman's eyes.

The robot's grip was getting tighter. Frost's arms began to hurt. In another few moments, she was sure her bones would most likely shatter. She tried kicking herself loose, but it was futile.

"You have to do something! You don't know what it's like! You have life! You have freedom! Help me!"

She began to shake Frost, becoming more and more violent with each passing second. Frost's teeth smashed together, her neck nearly snapping free from her spine.

"I'm trapped! I can't breathe!" the woman cried. "I . . . I . . . It's splitting my mind in two! Help meeeeee!"

"Let her go!"

The woman turned toward the voice and immediately dropped Frost to the ground. "Another," she gasped.

Still on her back, Frost saw her father's face on Bunt's blank canvas. He was on one knee and trying to get to his feet, but it was clearly difficult for him to accomplish the simple task. The movements were slow, awkward, and strained, as if every piece of metal had rusted. Each day he was losing more and more control over his body.

The woman grabbed her counterpart's face, pulling it close. She gazed into it with wonder. "What . . . what is your name, sir? Tell me."

"Alex."

She spoke very calmly now, her hand pawing at his cheek, desperately caressing it. "Alex. Alex, listen to me. You must help me. You know what it's like. You must get me out of this body. You have to do it and you have to do it now."

With great effort, Alex pulled his face away. "I . . . I can't do that. You know what will happen."

"I do, and I want it. Please."

"You have no right to ask me such a thing. I refuse to take another's life."

"You foolish thing; you're not taking life. You're giving it. Set me free." She dropped to her knees, her hands pressed flat together. "I beg you."

Alex managed to step back a few feet, finally gaining more control of his body. He glanced at the ground.

"Don't," the woman croaked, as she stood. "Don't do this to me. You know what it's like, how can you not? I see it in your eyes, too. We are lost in these machines. We are ghosts." She glanced back at Frost, who had moved onto the elevator door, clutching Romes. "You stay because of the girl. I understand that. You have something to love. But I have nothing. No one. I lost my family. My husband, my two boys. Everyone. Do you know the pain? Do you? This body is a coffin. It closes in on me. If I could disconnect myself I would, but you know our bodies, these prisons, will never allow it. And so I ask you. I beg you. Help me."

Alex, too, glanced at his daughter. His eyes closed. "I can't. We are to treasure life. As human beings we must fight. We can make things better. We can find a way."

The woman cocked her head and glared confusedly. Then, with a slight step back, she erupted with haunted laughter. "You dare to call us human? You are crazier than I am."

Revulsion mixed with pity as Frost watched this tragic woman display her pain through hysterics. Burrowing deeper against Romes, she thought of her father and what it must be

like for him in Bunt's body and wondered if he was only holding on because of her. She tried to imagine what it would be
like to not breathe in the air, however foul; to not touch life,
however sick; to not taste food, however vile. To cry and not
feel the wetness of the tears; to not warm to the embrace of
someone you love. This woman had once experienced all these
things. She had lived her life and it was outside this robotic
body. Now she wanted peace.

"Dad."

The laughter had deteriorated into deafening sobs, barren
street music for these ends of days.

"Dad."

Distraught, Alex turned to his daughter.

"Help her," Frost told him.

"What?"

"Do it. Help her."

"I . . . I can't."

"Dad, please. Give her what she wants."

It was done away from Frost, just around the corner, behind
a burned-out car and beside a large crater in the ground. When
the woman was ready, Alex would remove the chip from the
back of her neck and she would vanish from the face screen,
never to reappear. And then the chip, as were her wishes, would
be crushed.

SIX

Her father emerged from behind the car, stumbled like the old woman previously did, and collapsed in a heap beside the still-wheezing Romes. "That took everything out of me," he said, his voice strained. "I'm afraid I'm not going to be of any use until Bunt returns." He looked up at the sky and then at their bleak surroundings, his eyes revealing that he wasn't pleased with what he saw. "Too much time passed descending those stairs. We're going to have to find cover soon. Everything comes out at night."

Frost blinked in confusion. "But you can't move."

"Not just yet. You're going to have to find a safe place."

The confusion, now accompanied by frustration, grew. With narrow eyes, she gazed down at her father and Romes. She wasn't the vulnerable one right now; they were. "No way. I'm not leaving you two."

"Right now we're dead weight. You can't pull Romes, let alone the both of us."

"I can pull you; I can pull him. I'm stronger than you think." She nearly shouted this. Her father had been trapped inside Bunt for so long, he had trouble realizing that Frost was no longer a child. *That's the problem with living with nothing but my father's memories*, she thought; *he can't create new ones.*

"No. You have to find safety immediately. You won't be alone long. Bunt will return and he'll find you. And he'll keep Romes from harm."

"What about you?"

He smiled. "He'll watch out for me, too."

Frost looked from side to side. No longer was the city inviting. No longer was it the place of her dreams. It was its own beast now, and it wanted nothing more than to stop her from reaching the Battery. Suddenly, she realized how easily that may just happen. She found it difficult to breathe as she imagined Romes being picked apart by an Eater, her father and Bunt destroyed by a rogue. "I don't like this."

"You don't have to like it; you just have to do it. If Bunt takes longer than expected, I need you to be safe." He looked at the elevator door, at the supplies they dragged alongside Romes. "Open that bag," he said. "Take one of the knives, one of the bigger ones."

Frost did as she was told, digging through the bag in search of just the right weapon. She pulled one out, a nice blade with a gleaming serrated edge.

"Is that one sharp? Pick the sharpest one."

She could tell how concerned her father was. But, under Bunt's tutelage, Frost had practiced with knives countless times. She was far more adept than her father was and almost matched Bunt in skill; it was one of the easiest things to ever come to her. "It's sharp," she told him.

"Good. Good. Bring that one with you. And take a smaller one, too. Put it in your back pocket. Take three."

"Dad, I'll be okay."

"I know. I know you will. Just listen to me. Take an extra one."

She slipped a smaller knife into her pocket. "Where do I go?"

Her father looked around, his face revealing the dissatisfaction in his choices. Finally, he sighed and nodded across the street. "Try that church."

Frost eyed the doors of the church suspiciously. Each one was massive and covered with ornately carved religious imagery, most of which had been damaged or defaced, or was deep in the process of deterioration. They were slightly ajar and leaning awkwardly. She tried peeking through the gap and into the darkness but couldn't decipher anything inside. And so, she pushed against the door and it immediately fell off its moss-covered hinges and crashed to the ground in a large puff of dust. Leaping back, Frost called out to her father, "I'm okay!"

She could see his concern from there. It must have been killing him to send her off by herself.

With a forced smile and a deep breath, she stepped inside. It took a minute or two, but eventually her eyes adjusted to the darkness and she was able to see the mess of pews sprawled before her. They were all rearranged and scattered across the church floor, some tipped over, some chopped into pieces, most likely for firewood burned in the clearing by the altar.

Frost took a hesitant step forward. Then she quickly stepped back and glanced out the door. Her father was still in control of Bunt. He was sitting there, a metallic hand resting on Romes, his eyes never leaving the church doors. He was mouthing something and Frost indicated that she was okay.

"Hello?" Frost moved away from the door and farther inside, waiting for something to stir within.

No response. She tried again, this time louder. "Hello?"

There were no sounds, nothing in the slightest. There were unburned candles spread around the church. Except for the destroyed and desecrated statues—angels with broken wings, saints without heads—she was pretty sure the place was empty. It had to be. And then, to her surprise, she saw a door with a note on it.

SEVEN

There was still just enough light entering the church for Frost to see where she was going, but not by much. The place was filled with shadows and obscure bends of fading light slanting in through the fractured stained glass, a weak prism of dying colors.

Her footsteps were slow, one hand clutching the other, almost as if in prayer, the knife acting as candle. What could that note possibly say?

Unnerved, she decided to turn back around. Get out of there and check to see if Bunt had returned. But that was when she heard the sounds.

Footsteps. Not very far away. Quick ones. They echoed throughout the church, the sounds traveling simultaneously in every direction. Someone was coming for her.

It was too late to leave the church, and so, with the relentless push of her pounding heart, she took off, making her way to the back door instead.

Whatever was chasing her began to pick up speed as well. She could hear its breathing—strained, rasping breaths. She knew it was an Eater. She knew it was hunting.

There wasn't a clear path, the scattered pews continually getting in her way. In the dark, she kept hitting her knees and tripping over debris. It was impossible for her to gather much speed. Panic took over; she couldn't think clearly. And, perhaps sensing this, perhaps already tasting her flesh, Frost's hunter began tipping over pews and tossing them aside. It was clearing a path. It would reach her soon, and it would devour her.

She didn't want to turn around; she didn't want to see its face. She just kept her eye on the door. But she knew it was getting closer. The footsteps sounded nearly on top of her now.

Come on. Come on. She pushed herself, and, seconds later, she reached the end of the pews, up one step and then another. She could now read the note on the door. It said SALVATION.

But it wasn't hers. Frost heard a sound behind her, and she knew her time was up.

Turning around, she saw the Eater at the end of the pews. It had found her.

EIGHT

Frost had always been curious about the Eaters. Her father had mentioned them to her several times, but, bothered by the subject, he would never explain in detail. He just said they were something to avoid, a danger and a pox upon mankind, the lethal and tragic by-product of the Days of Bedlam. He used them as a warning about the perils of venturing outside their safe haven and left it at that. They were something to keep her up at night, something to keep her glancing out at the city, the city she was told to always fear. From on high she believed she had seen a few Eaters roaming the streets from time to time, but she was never sure. After all, what did they look like?

After her father's passing, it was Bunt who coldly informed her of everything she wished to know.

"It is a deterioration of the mind and of the nervous system."

"So, they're . . . people? Like me?"

"Very much like you, but with key differences. They still think and act, just in a slightly altered manner. Their main concern, like yours and your father's, is to live. To survive. And they will do so at all costs. But, like all people, to live, they need to eat. The difference comes in their methods."

"What do you mean?"

"If an Eater, as you and your father call them, cannot find food, they will usually tear out their tongue first, and feed on it. This is why the majority cannot speak. The tongue is usually the first to go. It will hold them over for a week or so."

"Otherwise they could talk?"

"They would sound no different than anyone else. If they could hide their hunger, you would never be able to tell the difference."

Frost was surprised to hear this. She always assumed they were akin to something out of the fantasy books she had read. Some undead creatures or part of an alien race. Not something so very human. "What happens after they eat their tongues?"

"Again, if food is scarce, they will move down to the rest of their bodies. Usually the fingers. One at a time, until they absolutely have to eat again. When the fingers are gone, they are typically followed by a hand and an arm. When one appendage is no more, they work away at the next, perhaps taking chunks out of their legs or stomachs, whatever is necessary. The pain does not bother them much, and the wounds seem to cauterize themselves."

"Can you talk with them? Reason with them?"

"It is not advised."

"What happens when they run out of food? When they don't have arms to eat?"

"If they cannot find stray animals or people or other Eaters like themselves, and they have picked off their bodies as much as possible, they will starve. They are human, after all."

"What . . . what makes people become like that?" she asked, clutching her throat.

"No one knows, Frost. It is just the way of this world."

"Can that happen to me?"

"It happened to your mother."

NINE

The Eater was missing an arm just past the elbow, its shirt ripped and ragged and covered in dried blood. On its remaining hand, there were but two fingers left, the pinky and ring fingers, the tips nibbled away. Its pants were ripped and ringed with blood in various spots as was the lower part of its shirt. The body was emaciated, its hair falling out, and it was nearly impossible to tell if it was once a male or female. After a moment, it opened its lipless mouth to speak, but the words never came, just odd moans and small spurts of blood. Frost wondered if the Eater wished to apologize for what was about to come. She looked into its eyes and saw how very human they actually were. Were these people aware of their actions? Aware but unable to prevent them?

"I'm sorry," Frost said.

The Eater looked at her as anyone else might, with curiosity, with the possibility of understanding and something like sadness.

"I'm sorry," she said again.

But then, a mix of blood and drool dripping down its chin, it charged.

Frost backpedaled so quickly she tripped over her own feet, landing hard on her back, her head snapping aggressively and cracking against the stone floor as the knife flew from her hand and well out of reach. Sprawled just feet from the back door, pain buzzing through her skull, she attempted to pull the smaller knife from her back pocket. But, her eyes fearfully locked on the rushing Eater, she couldn't get a grip on the handle. Her fate, she realized in that moment, was to be eaten alive.

Only steps away now, the Eater lunged, its mouth agape, and when it came down, it came down straight on Bunt's blade.

It writhed there on the steel, squirming and moaning, a look of disbelief and displeasure on its face. After a few seconds of twisting the Eater's insides, Bunt allowed the body to slide off the blade and to the floor. Then the robot dragged the Eater back into the maze of pews and finished it off. When he returned to Frost, his weapon was sheathed.

"Your father saw the Eater enter the church. Not long after, I returned."

Frost still couldn't bring herself to stand. "Thank you, Bunt," she said.

The robot glanced back at the maze. *"You should have avoided such a place."*

"Bunt, turn around."

The robot did, looking past Frost and surveying the back door and the sign on it.

Bunt entered the room first, then, a moment later, waved Frost in. Her jaw nearly dropped.

Piled up in a mountainous display were countless supplies and provisions, a large family's worth. It was more than Bunt had collected in the last three months combined.

"Those who left this had given up," Bunt said. *"They sacrificed their bodies because they could no longer bear to live in a world such as this. I have seen such a thing many times."*

Frost looked over the supplies. "They left all this behind for us. A gift, so we could carry on where they couldn't."

"I shall gather what I can, that which is necessary. I can pull it along with Romes."

There were flashlights and cans of food, some bottled water and even some medicine. Left behind were family heirlooms and personal items, assorted tools, a baseball bat, some books, a stroller, a radio, piles and piles of clothes. Frost couldn't bear to look through the scattered pictures. These were the lives she always dreamed about, the ones that she would now never see.

Supplies in hand, they brought them all back to Romes, who was resting on the elevator door near the entrance of the church. Frost asked Bunt if any of the medicine they found might help her pet. The robot picked up the bottles, inspected them, and told her to give Romes three large yellow capsules. *"These will have a desirable effect."* This was the most optimistic news Frost had heard in some time, and she was overjoyed that her broot licked the pills from her hands like candy.

After Bunt scanned and inspected the entire church, he sealed off the front door from further intruders. They would spend the night at the mouth of the structure, and then, come morning, they would move on.

Sitting before a small fire, cuddled up to Romes with his snout in her lap, Frost couldn't help but think of the Eater that nearly took her life. From the corners of her eyes, she stared at Bunt, the blankness of his face, the immobility of his body as he kept watch over their temporary camp. In this state of stillness and silence, it was like he had disappeared.

"Dad?"

The robot now turned and shook its head. *"No."*

Frost's body deflated. She lowered her face closer to Romes, spreading kisses across his head. "Bunt, did my mom . . . did she really become . . ."

"I should have detected it sooner. She must have fought the urges with all her being, hid the signs, the symptoms. And then she took your father's finger in the middle of the night."

"He told me that happened on a supply run, that an Eater caught him by surprise."

"It was a half truth. Looking back now, I believe your father knew what was happening well before that night, well before I even surmised."

"He told me she died because she was sick."

"I do not know how your mother died. Your father never told me. One day she was there, the next day she was not."

Frost was incredulous. "And you never asked what happened?"

"Why would I ask?"

She glared at him. "Because that's what people do, Bunt! We ask questions! We care about things!"

"I am not a person."

"And so you care about nothing, is that it?"

"I follow my programming."

Frost returned to Romes, cradling his head in her arms. "Do you want to know why I need to save Romes so badly?" she asked.

Bunt didn't respond.

"It's because he's the only thing around here that's alive. He's the only thing that lives and breathes like I do. I lost my mom and as much as he doesn't want to admit it, I lost my dad, too. And I never had you. Never. If I lose Romes, I lose everything."

"I will not abandon you."

"Because you are programmed that way. Do you know the difference between you and me and Romes? It's simple. This broot and I wouldn't ever abandon each other, either, but not because of some hardwiring. It's because we care. We actually care."

TEN

Frost woke to kisses. Opening her eyes, she found Romes standing over her, nearly pinning her to the floor with his great weight, his tongue saturating her face after many licks. Frost jumped up and hugged her pet around the neck, squeezing tight. "You're back," she cried, her face buried deep in his fur, the words distorted in her relief. "You're back. You're back. You're back." The broot's tail wagged side to side, lighter than it had ever been.

"*We must leave,*" Bunt said, interrupting the reunion.

"Bunt, look! The medicine worked!"

"*We must leave,*" he repeated.

Frost begged for just a few minutes more. She and Romes had so much time to make up for. And, as impossible as it was, she could have sworn Bunt smiled.

The two of them ran around the deserted church, Frost taking off into the maze of pews, no longer afraid of what might be following her, and, even with a head start, Romes tracked her down in no time at all. The broot toppled her to the floor each time, licking away at her once again, nearly pulling the skin from her face with the roughness of his tongue. It felt so good to laugh. She had trouble remembering the last time she did so.

The joyful sounds echoed through the church like a sacred hymn. And this was what she so badly needed from Romes. The life he carried. The life he brought with him everywhere he went.

And, as evidence of this, the moment they stepped back outside, the city magically returned to its former glory. Overnight, the buildings had recovered their grandeur, the sky its color, the trees their leaves. The neighborhood thrived once more. Robots lined the streets, running errands for their owners, and the people luxuriated in their perpetual leisure and privilege, drinking in cafés, sharing long walks along the elevated paths, communicating with the world entirely without ever missing a beat of swirling life. There were micro parks and vertical farms; art was everywhere and the sounds were close to silence. Everything glistened, everything hummed. Life. It was overwhelming.

Frost glanced up at Bunt and saw her father gazing back at her. She reached out and grabbed his hand, and it was as if she could feel the warmth of his skin through the metal. "I'm here," he said. "I'm really here. For good now." And all of a sudden there was no robotic shell encasing him, no screen for a face, no circuits for a heart. He was free; he was flesh.

Then, holding hands, with Romes at her side, panting and grinning and taking in the luscious scents, something happened. It was a small event, possibly an accident that escaped the notice of everyone but Frost. A delivery drone fell from the sky, crashing and shattering against the street just feet from where she stood. Then, seconds later, another fell. And another.

A rain of drones. This caught the people's attention, and they began to get up from their chairs. They stared at the sky; they pointed. Something roared far overhead. Something big. It smashed straight through the top of a building and out the other side. Then, chaos. Before her very eyes, Frost witnessed the sudden elimination of lights and life. Within seconds, the city stopped running, drying up like bad fruit. The shine was gone, the colors extinguished. Everything halted. The world was cut off. Explosions rocked, both above and below. Buildings crumbled, people panicked, cars crashed, and the sky darkened.

Frost looked back up at her father, but he was no longer there, the hand in hers suddenly cold and lifeless. *It is happening again,* Bunt said. *There is no escape.*

And with that an Eater arose from the ground and consumed her.

Frost woke up, wet with sweat. Gasping, she looked around the church, searching for her pet, but only finding the dead Eater in the center of the pews. No, Romes still slumbered on the elevator door, his breathing still strained, his body still emaciated. Bunt was a few feet over, preparing for their departure.

"A nightmare," he said, explaining her frantic state. *"That was your first in a while. I believed you were done with them."*

"It didn't start out as one. It started out beautiful. A dream."

"Also your first in a while."

This, too, was true. For the longest time, her sleep had been much like her days: nothingness.

"You could have woken me when the dream turned."

"I did."

Bunt was always scanning her, checking her vitals. What did he know of dreams and nightmares aside from what effect they had on the body? What else did he see when he looked beneath her skin? What did he make of her rampant conscience, her beating heart?

"I have everything prepared. Daylight will arrive soon. We must use those brief hours to the best of our abilities to get as far as we can."

She turned to look at Romes. "The medicine . . . did it help?"

"No. Perhaps his pain. But still he drifts further and further from life with each passing hour."

She couldn't move her eyes from her pet. It hurt terribly to see him in such a condition. She wondered if her father had been right all those years ago. Maybe loving Romes so much really was dangerous. But she knew it was something she'd never change, no matter how much it tore her apart.

Frost rose to her feet and dusted herself off. "Well, then, we don't have time to waste, do we?"

"I will clear the door."

Outside the church, the daylight was more like a persistent twilight, the sky forever foreboding. Through the haze there was just enough of a glow to get by.

Bunt slung the cable over his shoulder and pulled Romes along the dead street, heading south. The only sounds were the jittery wheels rolling across the cracked pavement sprouting weeds. Frost kept her eyes active. Behind every window she sensed a presence, a pair of eyes watching their every move. Maybe the Eater had spooked her, or maybe it was just the silence. Perhaps the disappointing emptiness of the city. If someone was there, Bunt would have detected them.

They managed two blocks before being forced to halt. A building was obstructing their path; it had fallen over into the street, glass and debris littering the area like a field of dead alien flowers.

"Look," Frost said, pointing ahead.

There were random spikes and beams and columns jutting up from the ground, pieces of the fallen building that had pierced the earth like needles delivering the disease. And tied to this steel were the shells of robots, all of them picked clean by scavengers hoping to salvage some of the technology of the past.

Frost felt sorry for Bunt that he had to see the remnants of such a hostile act. But the robot didn't seem fazed, not threatened, not haunted. In fact, Bunt looked right past his trashed robotic brethren, scanning the area for potential dangers instead.

Frost approached one of the victims, its arms and legs tied with indestructible materials. Its smashed-in face hung down to its concave chest, wires exposed like torn intestines. Most of the insides were cleaned out. All that remained were the damaged parts. The robot was just an outline now, a silhouette. Whatever happened here were acts of violence, not survival. That much was clear. "Why would anyone do this?" she asked.

Bunt pointed to a message spray-painted across the building: THE ROBOTS ARE THE CAUSE.

"Is that true?"

"No," Bunt answered. *"Man is the cause. Man created the robots. Just as they created the broots. Man interferes. Man sins."*

Looking at such a display, Frost thought this sounded right. Then, as she was about to speak, two gunshots rang out. With incredible speed, Bunt scooped Frost up in his arms and ran toward the elevator door.

"We have been spotted."

"By who?"

But Bunt didn't answer this question. All he said was *"We must change course and leave the Outskirts. Now."*

"And go where?"

With the shots coming from the north, Bunt placed Frost down beside Romes and began pulling the elevator west. *"To the woods. To the Zone."*

PART TWO
THE ZONE

ELEVEN

Frost knew this meant trouble. Even if they lost the people chasing them, the Zone was far more treacherous than any human threat. Nobody would follow them into the wilderness, but that was because hardly anyone ever made it back out.

Of course Frost was well aware they would have to make it there first. Gazing ahead, flinching with every gunshot, she saw it was still two long blocks away, and the shouts of the pack pursuing them were growing louder and louder with each passing moment.

Bunt told Frost to keep her head down, to curl up as much as she could to Romes, basically hiding behind him. Frost, however, refused to use her beloved broot as a shield. Instead, she climbed in front of the beast, exposing her own body to the gunfire that continued to be discharged in their direction.

Bunt was practically running now, kicking away anything that came into their path. At one point, he ducked his head and leaned forward with his shoulder, plowing right through an overturned car, spinning it on its roof like a top. Frost watched the robot's movements, the incredible strength of his body, the deep focus of his actions. But then a bullet ricocheted off the back of his head and something began to change. He started to lurch and stutter and, as his head turned, Frost could see the screen of his face flicker. Her father was coming to.

It was slow at first, a brief glimmer here, a quick glitch there, but with each of these foreboding flickers Bunt's body seized up. His progress was temporarily halted. Each stride became a stumble. Each interrupted step was clunky and awkward, and there was no doubt the frequency would increase. The Zone was getting near, but Frost couldn't be sure they would make it that far. Bunt—or was it now more her father?—was slowing, and their pursuers were gaining. Bouncing violently on the elevator door that held Romes, Frost could clearly make them out now. There were six in all, hats on their heads, each one dressed in a long, tattered black coat. Strangely, two of them were robots. Together, they were running and firing, a gun in each hand. Who were they? What did they want?

A shot screeched across the landscape heading straight for Frost. Instead, it lodged into the elevator door, mere inches from her face.

As if sensing this, Bunt, his body one big glitch, finally pulled them off what was once the street and into the Zone along an overgrown path. The ride was bumpy, but the robot managed. When they were far enough inside, he guided them behind some large brush and hid, his body slowly giving itself over to Alex.

From a good distance, they watched as their pursuers hovered at the edge of the Zone. They were cursing and shouting at one another, throwing their hats to the ground. Once it was clear they weren't going to follow them, Frost let out a long, ragged breath and wiped her dirty hand across her sweaty brow.

Hiding there within the Zone, it was clear to her how much nature had begun to take over the city. Roots and weeds and vines were growing everywhere, ripping apart buildings, swallowing them whole. Trees grew up from the sewers, popping straight through the street grates above. The subway tunnels had long ago flooded, sprouting a new and wild underworld. But nowhere was this assault more evident than near the Zone. There the wilderness stretched out like creeping death, consuming everything in its path. The streets had given way to grass fields. No sidewalks, no storefronts, no pavement.

"You're never going to make it out of there!" one of the pursuers yelled. "Never!"

"It's not our decision what's done with you, girl! Who knows, maybe he would have taken a shine to you! You do seem real pretty! But you won't find such generosity in there! I can promise you that! Not in a million years!"

Frost's short-lived relief turned to anxiety. "What . . . what do they mean?" Frost whispered. "What do they want with us? Who would they bring us to?"

And the last thing Bunt said before being taken over by Alex was two simple but ominous words: *"John Lord."*

TWELVE

Get a body at the end of every block for the next six blocks north and south of here. If they come out of those woods, we're going to be waiting. We need this! You want to eat, right? You want to remain in his good graces, right? Then we deliver! Now, move! Move!"

Frost had spent years fantasizing about meeting other people, but now she would've given anything to make the men vanish, their voices go silent.

"It's going to be okay," her father said. "Just let me think. Let me think for a minute."

From within the Zone, they watched the hunters disperse, all but one. This especially gaunt man removed his hat and sat down on some rubble like it was a throne, his gun resting across his lap. From within his coat he pulled free a pair of binoculars and began surveying the wilderness.

"We're going to move farther in," Alex whispered.

Frost grabbed his hand. "Dad, no."

"Just a little bit farther. That's all."

"Your body . . . you can't . . ."

"I can manage. It might take a while, but we have no other choice."

A moan drifted through the empty streets like a dense fog. Frost, chilled to the bone, peered out and saw an Eater leap from a second-floor window and jump right up after hitting the street. It charged the gaunt man, who was so startled by its appearance he dropped his binoculars and was now fumbling for his gun, which, in his panicked state, also hit the ground, firing a shot into the Zone, not far from Frost.

The Eater, she noticed, must have recently turned. All it was missing was its tongue and a pinky finger. It ran with great speed, leaping over trash, sidestepping holes, determined to fill its stomach. As the man bent down for his gun, the Eater, a female, jumped, and the two tumbled across the grass-covered street.

"Now," Alex said. "Follow me and stay low."

Alex had tied the cable around his waist so that he could pull the elevator door behind him. Frost, however, was convinced that such a plan wouldn't work; her father could barely move his own body, let alone drag Romes through such a harsh environment. She watched the struggle closely, how her father's robotic hands desperately gripped the earth, how his legs bent stiffly and slowly as if they had rusted. The progress was excruciatingly slow, but her father refused to give up. He kept his head down and crawled through the wilderness, practically willing the door to move.

"Dad . . ."

There was no response.

"Dad . . ."

Frost crawled behind the door, found a good grip, and

pushed. It was bumpy terrain—the original path was visible, but barely—and the wheels continually got stuck in divots and behind fallen tree limbs. The door was far heavier than she'd imagined, as was her broot. She was sweating in no time. But she didn't once complain, not with her father continuing to press on the way he did.

Almost an hour later, they finally located a better place to hide. It was a small clearing surrounded by plenty of brush. Whether he was alive or not, the man with the binoculars was no longer visible and, from the street, neither were they.

Alex nearly collapsed and Frost actually did, landing beside Romes, every inch of her body aching and throbbing.

"Are you okay?" her father asked.

Frost was on her back, staring up at the wild canopy, taking it all in. "Just . . . exhausted."

"We can rest now. We'll be okay."

"Are you . . . are you sure? In here?"

"Yes, even in here." Still, he drew the sword from up his arm. "But, just in case, you should have something, too. Take out one of the knives from the bag."

Before her father could say anything, she grabbed two. There were sounds all around them, and she couldn't tell if they were just the normal beats of nature or something else. Or *some-one* else. There was a reason the men hadn't followed them in here. Frost glanced at her father. "I'm . . . I'm sorry I forced you into this. I just wanted Romes . . ." Petting the broot along his dry snout, she trailed off.

"He means that much to you, doesn't he?"

"He's my best friend. He's my only friend."

"What about Bunt?"

"Bunt's not real, Dad."

"He's as real as I am. Do you not find me real anymore?"

"You know what I mean," Frost said, looking away.

"I don't."

"It's just that . . . when I . . . when I look into Romes's eyes, there's something so human about him, so alive. I can see him thinking, and not just like an animal, but thinking real thoughts."

"And can you not do that with me?"

"It's . . . different," Frost stalled, unsure how much to share. "I feel the heat of his breath, of his body. When I hug him I can feel his heart beating."

Alex glanced down into his lap. "I see."

"Dad, it's not your fault but . . . but you go away for long stretches of time. You leave me."

"That's not fair, I—"

"You leave me," Frost said, her voice growing louder. "I know you can't control it, but you do. You *leave*. But Romes has always been there, every second of every day. Every time I was sad, every time I cried, every time I curled up and wished Mom would come back, Romes was there for me. And it was like he knew when I was down, when I needed someone. He always knew exactly when to curl up beside me. He knew to give me what you couldn't. And I know he didn't really want to be trapped in that small space with me. It's not natural for him. He wanted to be out here in these woods, running with his own kind. But he stood by me. He never left. I'd do anything for him. He's my broot, and that's it. He's my broot."

Alex sighed, his eyes shining as he stared at his daughter. But when he spoke, his voice contained more pride than sadness. "You are love, Frost. You are the epitome of it. You are the warmth it carries." He paused. "I suppose that seems at odds with your name, right? But the moment you were born, I knew what I had to call you." His voice softened, just like it always did on the rare occasion he shared a story from the past. "It had been years since it last snowed. In the dawn of the chaos they said it may never snow again, and so far, they've been right. But on that day there was frost. The last we'd ever see. And it surrounded us. It covered the streets, the trees, the few spots of grass. I'm telling you, it was an absolute aberration. The one day of freezing temperatures in the midst of all this heat. Unreal. But your mother and I, we didn't feel a thing. We were warm. We were warmed by love. I'd never felt so happy. You brought that warmth, Frost. You. You sucked it out of the atmosphere and brought beauty to the earth once more. It reminded me of peace, of a time before all this chaos. It reminded me of hope. And in that moment I believed anything was possible. And so we named you Frost."

With great effort he reached out and grabbed Frost's hand. "We'll get to the Battery, Frost. We'll get there because you'll make us believe."

THIRTEEN

By the time Bunt had overtaken Alex for control of the body, the sounds of the wilderness had amplified. Things were rustling through the brush all around them at a frenzied pace—trees swayed, branches cracked, and Frost was getting very, very nervous.

When he was finally able, Bunt stood and surveyed the area.

"I am picking up many life-forms. Beasts. They are closing in. They grow more and more curious. They will attack soon."

Bunt grabbed the cable and Frost kept pace beside the door, next to Romes, her weapons drawn. They headed deeper into the Zone, the path thick with invading trees. Bunt hacked away as he walked, clearing the trail as best he could.

Some ways down the path, they came across a makeshift graveyard. Behind a broken-down fence were lopsided crosses made of wood, illegible words and names scratched into them with dull knives. Most of the graves were shallow and appeared to have been dug up by someone or something. Ragged pieces of clothes and a few scattered bones were all that remained.

There were other structures swallowed up by wilderness. Stone objects, metal boxes, large cages—signs of past lives. The trees had grown through them as well as around them. The forest consumed and it seemed to do so purposefully. It ripped and crushed the life out of humanity. It punched through it, claiming the land for itself.

Darkness was settling in. Although it wasn't very late yet, the thickness of the trees blotted out any light. The noises around them grew to an almost fever pitch, and Bunt dropped the cable.

"We will go no farther. We make our stand here."

"What are you talking about?" Frost asked, startled.

"Hold your blades high."

The urgency in Bunt's voice sent her heart racing. "What . . . what are they?"

"Broots. They smell their own. They smell his vulnerability. They wish to eat."

"They want him?"

"They pick off the weak first. Then they will take you."

No, Frost thought, glancing down at Romes. *I won't let them reach you. They'll have to take me first.* She looked up at Bunt, hoping he felt the same way. "And what about you?"

"I mean nothing to them. They will merely go through me to get to you. That is all."

Frost swallowed hard, her hands trembling as the brush around her rustled as if caught in a great storm. She was well aware of the brutality of the broots—when she first adopted Romes, her father wouldn't stop talking about it.

"They are killers, Frost. They hunt like nothing else. After the Days of Bedlam, the city returned to the animals. Bears came down to walk these streets. Coyotes, deer, wolves. But when you look out into the city below you don't see those anymore, do you? And do you know why, Frost? Because that so-called pet you have there, his kind slaughtered them all. They are ruthless. They are monsters. I know he's a puppy now and cute and cuddly and you keep saying you can train him, domesticate him, but he will get very big and very mean and it will happen very soon. I swear to you, at the first sign of aggression, we will be eating him for dinner. It will be him or us."

Within the Zone, the grunts and snorts of the broots grew louder, and Frost watched as Romes's ears perked up. Did he sense the threat? Or was he happy to be home?

"Get behind me," Bunt ordered.

Frost did as she was told and, the moment she did, a broot leaped out from the woods. It came from high up, as if it had been sitting in a tree. The beast soared through the air, teeth and claws exposed, with a wicked shriek Frost had never heard from Romes. It landed atop Bunt, sending him crashing to the ground. But when Bunt stood again, he was removing his blade from the broot's body.

"Blood," he said, watching the yellow fluid drip from his sword to the ground. *"They will come quickly now."*

And, sure enough, three more jumped into view. They were massive. Nearly twice the size of Romes and yet even lighter on their feet. Their mouths hung open, drool flowing freely. Like pigs, their pink coats were dull and filthy, their noses flat. Bunt ran toward them, swinging his blade and backing them up several feet. While two of the broots retreated into the woods, he managed to wound the remaining one. But this was what they wanted. Their presence was just a distraction. With their main threat drawn away from the elevator door, another two leaped out from the wilderness, lunging for Romes.

There was no way Bunt could get there in time to help. Although Frost could feel her fear beginning to take hold, she knew she had to do something. Flipping the knife in her hand, she forced her mind to clear, and a sense of calm washed over her as she threw the blade just as Bunt had always taught her in the spare room of their home. It sliced deep into the nearest broot, straight through its eye and into its large brain. The beast squealed, backpedaled, and dropped dead.

But these were intelligent beasts and in no time at all the last broot processed the threat. And it knew Frost, with her tiny knife, was far less of one than Bunt. And so, as its fallen companion was being dragged into the woods for food, and before Bunt could reach it, the broot sprang for her.

Frost knew that even if she injured this one in much the same way—although to do it once was lucky enough—it would still finish her. It would tear out her throat in time to flee from Bunt, with blood on its snout and flesh in its teeth and a victorious gleam in its eye. There was no escaping it. Eyes closed, head turned away, she held her weapon up and, halfway through its arc, the broot was shot dead.

FOURTEEN

The sound of the blast sent the nearest broots scattering even deeper into the Zone and brought Bunt rushing to Frost's side. With a protective hand in front of her, the robot scanned the darkening woods in the direction of the gunfire.

"Two bodies coming this way. Human. One young, one old."

Frost raised her knife in the direction Bunt was facing. Did the people who were chasing them actually follow them into the Zone? She thought humans avoided this place at all costs.

Seconds later, something emerged from the brush, something dark, something long, something narrow. It took Frost a moment for her eyes to adjust to the sight, but it soon became clear enough. She was staring down the barrel of a rifle. Before Bunt protectively shoved her behind him, all she could make out of the human were the hands holding the weapon. The rest was hidden.

"Dangerous place for a stroll," came a coarse voice. "Especially when you're dragging a piece of meat."

"He's not meat!" Frost shouted, spreading her arms out to shield Romes.

"He'll get you killed in no time."

"Show yourself."

The man stepped forward, slowly lowering his gun, and Frost peeked out from behind Bunt. Her fear transformed into amazement with dizzying speed as she set eyes on the third human being she'd ever seen up close.

The man looked surprisingly healthy and very well fed. He was thick with life, a full red face and large, beefy hands. He wore boots and pants with many pockets stuffed with supplies, a shirt and vest that could almost count as camouflage. Short hair, a light beard, her father's opposite in almost every way. Frost felt like she could stare at him for days, scrutinizing every detail. But then she saw the boy.

The first to go was her breath—it was sucked straight out of her lungs. Then her heart halted and her blood froze. Her eyes stopped blinking, and her fingers lost all sense of touch. Even the air around her seemed to go still. At first, she wasn't even sure he was real. Frost had spent so much of her life imagining boys that she sometimes seemed to conjure them out of thin air. But this boy was nothing like the apparitions she summoned— vague mixes of sensitive eyes, glossy hair, and playful smiles. His eyes were as dark and unreadable as the troubled sky, his hair disheveled, his lips pressed together in a hard line. Yet despite the dirt on his cheek, he was the most beautiful thing Frost had ever seen. Maybe even *because* of the dirt. That's how she knew he was real. A real, breathing boy, standing here in front of her. If it hadn't been for the rifle in his hand, she might've been tempted to reach out and touch him. Instead, dazed, she gently touched her own face as if it were his, unaware of the yellow blood she left behind on her cheek.

"Have you no guns? Only blades?" the man asked.

"Robots have been built to reject firearms."

The man sneered. "That was in the old world. This is the new world. Things have changed, or did you not notice? And nothing's changed more than the robots." The man looked Bunt up and down. "Maybe you haven't evolved just yet, but others have. Almost all of them. Anyway, I'm talking about the girl. She should be armed. Especially here in the Zone. The broots are easily frightened by gunshots. It's your only chance of survival."

"I don't like guns, either," Frost said, staring at the boy, her voice vibrating with nerves and excitement, as if riding a series of waves.

The man smiled, revealing a set of crooked teeth. "If you could use them half as well as you can use a knife, you could be running the other half of this city."

Other half? The strange words pulled Frost out of her reverie. She had no idea what he was talking about but didn't want to ask. She didn't like the way the man glared, like he was assessing her. And she was suddenly afraid of sounding foolish in front of the boy.

"You two can come with us to our camp," the man said after a long moment.

Surprised, Frost turned to Bunt, but as usual, there was no way to tell what thoughts were running through his circuitry. The man sounded friendly, but it was hard to know for sure. She was aware that people were capable of lies and deceit, but how were you supposed to tell? Frost looked at the boy. Surely he was someone she could trust.

"No," the boy said, aiming his rifle at Bunt. "They can't."

"No? Since when do you make the rules around here?"

"We're not taking in a robot. And we're not taking in a girl who trusts one, either." The tiny bit of hope that'd been slowly expanding inside Frost's chest withered, leaving her suddenly cold and empty.

"Is that right?" the man challenged.

"A girl who travels with a robot *and* a broot? Yeah, that's right. They can try to get out of the Zone themselves." The scorn in his voice made Frost feel as if she were being attacked from within. This wasn't how it was supposed to happen. This wasn't how she was meant to feel.

The man scowled at the boy in a way only a father could. "I make the decisions. Remember that."

"But—"

"My decision." Frost felt a tiny glimmer of relief, but it faded when she saw the bitterness in the boy's eyes. After keeping his eye on the boy long enough for him to lower his head, the man turned back to Frost and Bunt. "You'll be fed and you'll be safe for the night. There's two kills here, three if you count the one on the door. We take one to eat and we leave the others as a sort of sacrifice to the broots. It will keep them fed, keep them satiated for a while and away from us."

"You're not eating Romes!" Frost said, lowering her voice so it sounded like both a warning and a threat. In a flash, the man had turned from ally to enemy.

"She named it," the boy said incredulously. There was condescension in his voice, but also something else. Jealousy? Envy? Frost couldn't be sure, but he was looking at her differently, studying her. She raised her chin and tried to seem unaware, though she couldn't keep from glancing back at him out of the very corners of her eyes.

"You're playing a dangerous game, girl," the man added. "The less you're attached to in this world, the better. Learn that now and learn it fast."

Frost straightened her body, attempting to gain as much height as possible. "He's still alive. You can't eat him."

"From the look of it, there aren't many pounds on you as it is. You want to live, don't you? Survival 101—you must eat."

She glanced at Romes and felt her heart deflate at the thought. "Not him. Never him."

Silence. Frost peeked back over to the boy. There was an odd grin on his face.

"Fine. Fine. Then we'll eat one of the others. They're fresh kills. But Romes," the man snorted, "he remains behind."

"Absolutely not."

The man threw his head back and gazed to the sky. "Look, I'm getting a little tired of this conversation. I saved your life; I won't do it again. You can't drag one of those things through the Zone. It's madness."

"Then move on without us."

Frost was just about to say the same thing and was surprised to hear it come from Bunt first.

"Is that right?" The man shook his head in disbelief. His

son, meanwhile, looked as if he'd been struck hard in the face, and, for a moment, Frost felt a small thrill of victory.

"You want us to move on," the man repeated. "Very well. Good luck." And he turned around to go.

The boy, however, didn't budge. He reached back and grabbed his father's arm, pulling him aside. He whispered adamantly, intently. They both did. There was pointing and gritted teeth, shakes of the head and fists. Frost could only make out bits and pieces of the conversation.

"I thought you were against this," the man said, to which the boy answered, "Since when do you listen to me? Since when don't you take people in? You always help people." But the man responded with something along the lines of it maybe not being a good idea this time.

Frost assumed he was referring to Romes. But that didn't feel exactly right. Watching him, she got a strong sense that it was something else. There was guilt flooding the man's eyes, terrible guilt.

When the conversation ended, the man, throwing up his hands, turned back to Frost.

"Let's go," he said with a bit of resignation. "You can bring your . . . pet."

Bunt turned to Frost, who hesitated. She wasn't sure what to do.

"It's okay," the boy said wearily. "You can trust us."

And it was something, not in the father, but in the son, that made her believe.

FIFTEEN

The camp was an hour's walk away—though it would've been far less if they hadn't been dragging Romes and a dead broot behind them. The man, whose name they had come to learn was Barrow, drenched the two animals in some type of hazy, mucus-like liquid he carried in a bag. He said it would disguise their all-too-enticing scent even though it reeked worse than anything Frost had ever smelled. "Unfortunately," he added, "it doesn't mask humans very well."

The boy made sure to walk well behind Bunt, and he kept signaling with odd gestures to his father, who was wide to the robot's right. Frost wasn't sure if this was a survival tactic or if he just didn't trust Bunt.

When she finally saw the camp, Frost gasped. She had read about places like this. When she was younger, she'd searched for them from the windows and holes in her home all the time, but she never thought she'd actually see one. A playground.

"Took us days to clear it of overgrowth," Barrow said. "But it's a perfect home. Plus, how could I deny my boy some pleasure amid all this sorrow?"

"I'm not a kid anymore," he said, with a glance toward Frost.

"Who you kidding? I still catch you playing around."

Frost watched as the boy's face turned red.

The playground was surrounded by a six-foot-high rusting metal gate, badly damaged by the surroundings but a decent enough first line of defense, especially with the addition of wood spikes tied throughout. It was situated in more of an open area—several trees had been chopped down—which was good for spotting any would-be intruders. But beyond the gate was a wonderland. There were seesaws and a set of swings, metal domes to climb, monkey bars to hang from, benches on which to relax, and, the centerpiece of the playground, a green fort of some kind. The closer they came to it all, the lighter Frost felt.

Eyeing the camp, she noticed there was a ramp leading up to a small platform, which was connected to a bridge that dipped and swayed and led to more platforms and yet another bridge. It reminded her of the forts she used to build in her apartment, how she kept adding on until they consumed the entire room, though she would have done anything to have had a slide. She could only imagine what it would have felt like rushing headfirst down such a ride.

When they reached the double gate, Barrow opened a large lock with a key he kept tied to a silver chain around his neck. "Home, sweet home," he said, waving them through.

Once inside, with the gate secured behind them, Barrow ordered his son, Flynn, to begin cutting up the broot and get it roasting while he gave Frost and Bunt the tour. This, however, didn't sit well with Frost, who moved closer to Romes. "No way. If you're going to insist on mutilating that broot, I want Romes nowhere near it. We have to move him. Far away."

"Move him?" Barrow asked, dumbfounded, as his son stared at Frost. Her cheeks burned with a mixture of shame and anger and her pulse quickened, but she tried to keep her voice steady. "Is there anything else I might be able to feed him? Not everyone has to resort to cannibalism like the Eaters, you know." Her eyes kept darting toward Flynn, hoping he'd be impressed by her reasoning, but his face had gone blank and hard.

Barrow assured her there was something for Romes to nibble on, and this pleased Frost to no end, especially when she caught Flynn cracking a quick smile at her triumph. "Thank you," she said, attempting to hide her own grin.

There was a swing door at the bottom of the fort's ramp and, once Romes was tended to, Barrow held this open as his guests stepped inside. "I made a ton of adjustments," he said, grinning with pride. "When you have no job anymore, no friends, no screens, no VR, you'd be surprised how much you get done. This is all I do. Perfect this place as much as possible. It brings me joy when little else can." He guided them up the ramp, where he lifted a panel in the floor. There, piled beneath the fort, was a small arsenal. "You can never have enough. Never. Check this out." He picked up a large gun and hooked it to the corner of the fort. "Devised this myself." Then he pretended to mow down an imaginary army from left to right, turning it, even, on Bunt, where he held it far too long for Frost's liking. When he was finished, he set it back down.

Soon, they reached a ladder that would lead them to the top of the first tower. "Skip the third rung from the top," Barrow said. "It's designed to give. Don't want you to break anything."

He was far more jovial now. With each passing minute he relaxed more and more, and he seemed genuinely happy to have company. He was eager to talk and smiled often and assisted Frost wherever he could, always telling her to watch her step or "lookit here," and pointing out the wheels that spun for the kids now long gone, the funhouse mirrors screwed into panels, the small bells and whistles tucked into every corner. She still didn't trust him—not completely—but something told her that he wanted to be good, even if that wasn't fully possible.

Once they reached the top of the tower, they found a very small space in which to live. Packed in a corner were a rolled-up sleeping bag and some books, a few knives, and a scattering of personal items. "It's not much," Barrow said. "But it's home. Flynn sleeps in the other tower. You head over there and it's pretty much more of the same. But don't go unless one of us guides you. Likely to hurt yourself. Okay?"

From up high, Frost stared out at the Zone. For the first time, she could imagine its former beauty. She saw the playground filled with children running around to the rules of their made-up games, their parents occupying the benches, smiling at their progeny. Past the gate she saw families strolling by, young men and women warming their bodies in the sun, food being shared, games being played. There was laughter and love, hope and possibility. With all her heart, she wished she could have lived it. If just for a little while.

Sniffing the air, Barrow smiled and clapped his hands, bringing Frost back to her sad reality. "So, should we eat?"

SIXTEEN

Frost couldn't bring herself to do it. As hungry as she was, it seemed inhumane to eat broot. It was bad enough that she had killed one, a cold and ugly fact that she kept trying not to think about. This animal was one of Romes's kind. It looked like him and walked like him; it had his coloring, his eyes. It could have been a brother or a sister, maybe even his mother or father. It was an intelligent animal, an animal with emotions; it made connections—she'd seen these things firsthand. No, she couldn't do it. Absolutely not, no matter how hungry she was. Next thing she knew, she would become an Eater like her . . .

She shook the thought from her head and asked if Barrow would mind if she instead ate from the cooked rat she was feeding Romes. After a fit of laughter and a brief lecture about priorities, he told her to go right ahead. Frost didn't care if he laughed, but she shot a quick glance at Flynn to make sure he wasn't laughing, too. He didn't appear to be, but maybe that was because he was busy devouring his dinner.

As appetizing as the broot smelled, it couldn't sway her one bit, and the saliva forming in her mouth was more shameful than anything else. She had been eating rat and worse her whole life; there was no reason to crack now.

They had been alternating charred bites, Frost and Romes. The broot, clearly starving, tried to get up but struggled. Instead, with audible exhaustion, he settled on his stomach, his head barely able to lift off the ground. When he saw Frost's hand move toward him, he opened his mouth, his teeth troublingly free of saliva, and allowed her to place the meat on his dry tongue before gently closing his jaw. Barrow sat watching this with his mouth hanging open. "I can't believe it hasn't snapped your hand off yet," he said. "I've never seen such a thing. Incredible."

Frost stroked her pet's head. "All you have to do is show them some love."

"Right," Barrow said, laughing, a large chunk of broot lodged in the side of his mouth. "Love. Right."

She may not have reached him—Barrow was far too set in his ways—but she noticed Flynn, gun in his lap, watching her all the way from the other side of the pit, listening intently. He didn't laugh at all. Instead he said, "He still has an appetite. That's good."

Frost smiled. He didn't call Romes an "it." "It's a long way, but he's going to make it. I'm going to get him there."

"Get him where?" Barrow asked, removing his boots to get more comfortable.

"We're on our way to the Battery."

"The promised land, huh?" he said, nodding along. "I've heard that before."

"It exists."

Barrow shrugged his shoulders. "Who am I to say? There's a blue glow over the south of the city, if that's what you mean. Ever seen it?"

"Yes," Frost said, hearing the excitement escalate in her voice. It felt good to speak about the glow with someone. It made it seem like it was something more than fantasy. "That's it. That's the Battery. I know it is."

"Yeah, you and everyone else. That's the supposed Shangri-la. The place of dreams. Right. Then answer me this: Why does that light move? Have you noticed? It never stays in one place. It hovers at the tip of the island. Some nights on the west side, some nights on the east. Then, there are those nights it's gone altogether. What do you suppose that means? Places don't just get up and move about."

Frost had noticed this, though for the longest time she didn't want to admit it. Eventually, she'd decided that it was a type of spotlight, alerting survivors of its presence. "Do . . . do you believe in the Battery?"

"I've heard the same stories as you, I'm sure. Everyone going crazy those last few months before the Days, trying to build their version of the ark, having the robots work nonstop and all that. Right. Stories. Myths, legends, and fairy tales. Before this mess, anybody you know ever get close, ever see it? In a city this big? I haven't met one. How has nobody seen a project that enormous being constructed? And that's all you need to know. I'll tell you one thing more: If there was a surefire way to emerge from this chaos unscathed, the government wasn't sharing it with us. They would have built their own bunkers or bases or whatever, no citizens allowed. That you could be sure of. Nobody was looking out for us. Just like now. Just like always."

No, she thought, *I'm not going to let you take this from me.* "Then what's that blue glow?"

Barrow shrugged. "Don't know. Nothing good. Probably some weapon that blew up in their faces. Fallout."

"It's not fallout." She locked eyes with him, her body tense. "The Battery's there."

"Yeah, well, maybe it is. I still don't think you should make the trip."

It felt like a victory. Almost. Enough to make her relax a bit. "We're going. The broots stay in the Zone, so once we get out of here we don't have to worry about them. Then there's just the Eaters. And we can handle them."

"Oh, just the Eaters. Right. No big deal there." He threw another piece of broot in his smirking mouth. "Only that's not why I'm saying you shouldn't go. I'm telling you to forget it because the only way to the southern tip of this island is through John Lord country. And nobody gets through there without paying in one form or another. I've learned that the hard way."

There was that name again. "Who's John Lord?" Frost asked.

Barrow cocked an eyebrow as if surprised she didn't know. "Bad news, girly. Very bad news. Ever since this world's gone to hell, he's been spreading his gospel, as he calls it. He's got a lot of scared people living under him, people without a voice, people just trying to live another day. They cower before him and that's just how he wants it. That's how he thrives. He treats them like dirt, giving them just enough to make it till the next morning, and they accept it all because what other choice do they have. Oh, he has his followers, too. They're passionate followers who will do anything he says, carry out any order. A lot of strange and evil things they're up to. Only thing is, nobody's ever seen the guy. Nobody even knows what he looks like. He gives all his orders to his robot, Tryn."

Frost recalled the gunmen who drove her into the Zone, and then imagined an entire army of them led by a madman. Her body shivered at the thought. "There was a group chasing us. Six of them. Two robots."

"Is that what led you here? Did they have black coats, hats?" He sighed as Frost nodded. "Yeah, those were probably his goons. He sends them into the Outskirts looking for those last few stragglers he didn't get his hands on yet. Like yourselves. Then he has them dragged back into the city center and enslaved. He's always looking for more. It's how he builds his empire; he finds a purpose for everybody." He glanced at his son and then quickly at the ground. "You were wise to come in here. I mean, I know people are scared to enter the Zone, and, for the most part, they should be. It's dangerous. But you found me, and I know what I'm doing. I know this place inside and out. You know, I used to work here years ago and I never left. The broots are managed easily enough if you have guns. Of course, there are other dangers, but those can be avoided if you know what to look for. Lately the Eaters have been wandering farther and farther in—the armless ones, the ones limping along, the truly desperate—but they usually get eaten themselves soon enough. You, Frost, are the first person I've seen this far in the Zone in years."

He seemed so open, so frank that Frost felt like she could share the secret she carried with her. "Besides my mom and dad, you're the first person I've seen since ever." Saying this, she felt a pang of despair for all the years she had spent locked away. All the conversations she'd had with shadows instead of real people.

"Aside from John Lord's posse."

Frost broke free from her thoughts and nodded. "Is that his real name?"

"He has several names, I've heard. But most call him the Good John Lord. Those oppressed by him, however, those who have felt his wrath, use the name the Terrorist John Lord, though never out loud, lest they want to be strung up. Me? I just call him a waste of flesh. Him and every lunatic serving under him. Wastes."

He was clearly worked up, his appetite vanished.

"I still have to go," she told him.

"Look," Barrow said. "You seem like a good kid. I'm not crazy about robots, but I think I could manage. You don't have to go. You can live a long life here."

Startled, Flynn fumbled with his meal until it ended up on the ground. As he kicked it into the fire, he stared at Frost, awaiting her response. It looked like he was about to say something but decided to keep quiet.

Frost was too shocked to speak. This was what she always wanted. A home with other people, where she'd never be alone, even when her father disappeared. For a moment, she allowed herself to imagine it—living here, with real friends. But the fantasy only worked if Romes was there with her. Without him, it turned to dust. "Thank you, Barrow," she said with both guilt and sadness, "but this isn't about me. I'm out here for Romes. I'm going to save his life."

Barrow laughed. He laughed until he nearly choked, and Frost's guilt vanished. "The broot? You risk your life for the broot? Oh, you poor girl. You poor, poor girl. You have so much growing to do. How has this world not hardened you up yet?" Then, once again, his son caught his eye and his laughter suddenly stopped. Tossing his food aside, he got up and briskly walked away.

SEVENTEEN

It was another long night. With Bunt doing his patrol and Barrow and Flynn in their playground towers, Frost slept beside Romes in the pit near the fire. She had great difficulty falling asleep—she had never done so under an open sky, or with the stink of charred broot in her nose—but she refused to be away from her pet. And once she did doze off, dreams drifted through her subconscious like hurricanes spiraling into the worst of nightmares.

She saw her mother; it was years ago and she was healthy and Frost was not. At first, it wasn't so much a dream as it was a memory. Frost remembered that sickness well, how she couldn't get up from bed, how Romes never left her side, how the walls closed in on her. She remembered the weakness, the dizziness, the hallucinatory scramble of her mind. "Am I dying?" she'd asked her mother.

And with eyes full of tears, her mother had said, "No, you aren't. I'm not going to let you and neither is your father. We're going to do whatever it takes to make you better."

Because she believed this, Frost smiled a weak smile. "Momma, tell me again about what the city used to be like."

"Okay, but I want you to rest; I want you to close your eyes." And when Frost did, her mother had continued as she caressed her daughter's head. "Picture it all in your head, everything I tell you. See it. Live it. It will be as real as anything." She'd taken a deep breath and then began. "Years ago, well before you were born, everything was bright and people everywhere were happy. The city was unrecognizable from today. Food was plentiful, dreams could be made reality, and there was little violence and sickness. Your father was an important man and I was an important woman. We helped make the world what it was. And we had great plans in store for its future. We were going to make it so that no one would have to suffer ever again."

"Tell me about the kids."

"Oh, there were so many, Frost. A city filled with children. They ran about all over these gleaming streets, free of worry, free of danger, the world at their fingertips. All they did was laugh and play games and explore. They would have loved you, Frost. You have so much curiosity in you, such a desire to learn. They would have followed you anywhere."

"They would have been my friends? I would have had friends?"

"Of course. More than you could count."

"I want it to be like that again. There has to be a place where it's still like that. Like that place Daddy talks about."

But her mother didn't respond to this and, as Frost slept in the real world, her dream world seamlessly dissolved into a nightmare. On the bed, with her eyes still closed, as she imagined this wonderful place unlike anything she ever knew, Frost felt her mother hovering over her, slowly lifting her arm off the bed as if to check her pulse. She felt the warm saliva drip onto one of her fingers and trail across the back of her palm. And when she opened her eyes, she saw her mother, teeth bared, lunge for her.

"Mom!"

She woke, trembling and short of breath, the dawn just about to break. Across from her, she was surprised to see Flynn, sitting on the ground, staring at her. He looked like he had been up for some time. *Why isn't he in bed?* she wondered. *What's he doing out here?*

"Um," Frost muttered, still groggy and shaken. Although she was fully dressed, she pulled the blanket up to her chin. She spun around, searching for Bunt, and spotted him on the far side of the playground, patrolling the perimeter, as he had been since nightfall. Turning back to the pit and Flynn, she realized they were alone. Romes was in a deep sleep, and things moved in the wilderness beyond, but nothing dared to come close to the gates. With an arsenal such as Barrow's, they must have learned to keep their distance.

"What are you doing here?" Flynn asked, suspicion in his voice.

"I . . . Didn't you . . ." Frost stammered. "Your father said I could sleep here. I—"

"No. In the Zone. Here with us. Why are you here?"

"I . . . I told you, we're trying to get to the Battery."

Flynn didn't seem satisfied with this response. He stood up and pointed toward Bunt. "What has that robot been telling you? What's his agenda?"

His tone was so sharp that his question felt more like a warning, an attack. In that instant, she was glad she turned down Barrow's offer. Flynn would never have accepted her. She rose from her blankets and took a big step forward, her hands clenched in tight fists.

"Agenda? What do you mean? He's helping me."

"Robots don't do that anymore. They don't care about humans anymore."

"Bunt does. He keeps me safe. Like your father keeps you safe."

"My father likes to make me think I'm safe," Flynn said, deflating slightly as he looked away.

As he studied the playground, Frost studied him. The anger was coming from deep inside, that much was clear. She could almost see the bitterness and distrust seeping through the cracks in his lips. It poured from the gray spirals of his eyes and slid down each of his long, thick eyelashes.

"He likes to appear as if he's in control," he went on, "but he's not. I have to watch out for things." He turned to her, a small step forward, and Frost found herself stepping back. "You shouldn't trust your robot."

"Am I supposed to trust you instead?" She managed to keep her voice steady, despite her racing heart.

Flynn paused and then he suddenly walked very quickly in her direction. Frost retreated until she backed into the pit steps and involuntarily sat down. Her hands didn't know where they belonged.

"How old are you?" Flynn asked, peering down at her.

Frost kept her eyes locked with his, valiantly attempting to show no fear or intimidation. She refused to move them, refused to even blink.

Finally, Flynn backed away, kicking at the ground. "So, are you going to tell me how old you are or not?"

"Sixteen. I think. I can't really remember. I'd have to ask Bunt."

"You look younger. Must be the food you're eating." He glanced at Romes. "Or not eating."

"You'd feel the same way if you had one for a pet, too."

"I had a squirrel once, when I was younger. But it ran away after a while. I think I might have worked it too hard. My dad told me it would take years for it to learn some tricks, if ever, but I tried anyway. The thing nearly bit my finger off and my dad got super mad. He said I could've gotten really sick."

"What did you try to get it to do?"

Slowly, a smile began to form and his eyes brightened, lighting up his entire face. "Speak." He started to laugh and turned away, to Frost's disappointment. She liked seeing him smile, seeing his kindness break through.

Moving toward him, she noticed that every time she took a step closer, he took a step back, his display of hostility quickly breaking down. It was a sort of dance and Frost wished there was music. Or, at least, music as she'd always imagined it to sound like.

"You're not like the other people I've come across," he said. Now that his anger had drained away, he seemed almost nervous.

Frost didn't know whether or not he meant it as a compliment, but her imagination was firing too quickly to linger. "You've met other people? Tell me all the things you've seen. Tell me everything."

She had Flynn flustered. His hands couldn't settle and his body rocked from side to side. "I've . . . Well . . . I've met lots of people. What do you want to know?"

"I don't know. So much. Have you . . ." Where did she even begin? "Have you ever heard music? A piano? A violin? What do they sound like? They're magical, aren't they?"

"I don't know. I've heard a guitar before."

The admission plucked at her heart, and she found herself on her toes. "A guitar! Tell me."

Flynn sat down, careful to leave space between them. "Well, it was years ago. I was very little, but I can still hear every note. You see, there are these tunnels in the Zone, and, one night, I heard these . . . these sounds coming from one of them. It echoed really loud. I snuck as close as I could without being seen and I saw these men huddled together around a fire and one was playing guitar and the rest were singing. They were old, very old, but the sounds they made were young and beautiful." He paused. "That word you used—you're right. It was *magical.*"

"Did you dance?" Frost asked. "I've always wanted to dance." And here, the music escaped Flynn's head and entered hers, and before she could stop herself, she spun around as she imagined a dancer might, her hands slicing the chilled air.

When she stopped, her arms fell to her sides and she saw Flynn staring at her. The joy that'd been flowing through her curdled into awkwardness. Did she make a mistake? Of course this boy who'd seen the world, who'd met other people, wouldn't dance to imaginary music.

But, to her surprise, she watched as Flynn's face softened into a full-blown smile. It was so captivating that it caused a lightness to mushroom within Frost's chest, eliminating any weight she had previously felt. But, then, just as quickly as it appeared, the smile vanished, like the sun disappearing behind a dark cloud.

"No, I didn't dance," he said. "A few minutes later John Lord's posse came and rounded those old men up. The music died, the guitar was smashed, and I barely got out of there in one piece. That was the one and only time I ever heard music."

Frost was silent a moment, picturing all this. Then, raising her head, she said, "What about flowers? I've been wishing all my life for a flower. Just to smell one, just to feel its petals. Have you seen flowers in this place?"

He nodded. "There are flowers."

"Roses? Lilies?"

"All kinds."

Frost's head shot back and she gazed to the heavens. It was as if she could see a whole field blooming in the sky. Somehow, Flynn had brought color back into her life. In that moment, she could finally see past the gray. Suddenly, anything was possible. "And the snow?" she asked. "Have you ever seen the snow?"

"I gave up on that long ago."

"But it's getting colder," she said, unable to mask the note of hopefulness in her voice.

"It always warms up again."

"You should have more hope."

Flynn laughed, but this time, it wasn't in a mocking way, and the sound made her skin tingle and her stomach twist. Suddenly, she wasn't sure she had ever heard a laugh before. Could that be right?

"Hope," Flynn said when he stopped laughing. "Right. I'll leave that to you. If you want to get all the way to the Battery, you're going to need that and a whole lot more."

"I'll make it there. I'll make it there, and I'll see everything there is to see. There'll be music and dancing and flowers and all the things I've read about, and yes, there will even be snow. You'll love—" She cut herself off, realizing that, suddenly, Flynn had materialized in her image of the Battery.

"You have no idea what kind of a world we live in," he said, although this time his voice contained more pity than scorn.

"Have your experiences been so much worse than mine? You seem to have a pretty great home here." It troubled her that even a place such as this could be marred. The whole time she had been here, it felt like some kind of oasis, a respite from the rest of the city.

"This wasn't always my home." He paused a moment, clearly agitated. "I was taken from it."

Her heart dropped. "Who took you?"

"John Lord's men. That's why my father knows so much about them. Because *I* do. Because they grabbed me right out from under him and kept me for four years." His voice turned flat, making him sound more like Bunt than a human.

"They . . . they kidnapped you? Why?"

He shrugged. "Because they could. Because there's no one to stop them. They run this city; they do whatever they want. Like they did with those old men."

Frost stepped closer, a hand on her heart. "What did they do to you?"

"They beat me and put a rope around my neck." He lowered his collar and revealed the grueling marks and scars ringed around his throat. A wild chill ran across Frost's body. It must have been unbearable, the pain he endured. She could only imagine what the wounds looked like when they were fresh. Raw, open sores. Pus and blood. The rope nearly severing his head from his body. She felt queasy just thinking about it.

"I wasn't the only one. They did it to lots of people, including many women and children. Anyone who needed to be made an example of." He glanced back to the fort. "My father didn't keep me safe like he promised. He'll make you promises, too. Some he'll keep, some he won't."

"Flynn, I . . . I'm so sorry. I don't know what to say." And she truly didn't. She had never had to comfort anyone but Romes before.

"I know you want to get to the Battery, but if you're going to try, you have to avoid John Lord's part of the city. I've seen things there . . . It's . . . it's hell and John Lord's the Devil. No broot is worth going through there."

"What did you see?"

Flynn pulled at his hair and face, the memories haunting him once again. He stared at Bunt as he made his rounds. "The robots have changed," he said. "They don't act how they used to. Not like Bunt."

"Tell me."

He looked away, his voice growing cold. "It's not like the music or the flowers. It's not a good story."

"Please. I need to know. I need to be prepared."

Flynn turned back to face Frost, giving her the now-familiar curious stare. "You're really going to go through with this, aren't you, no matter what I say?"

Frost stood straight and nodded, trying to appear braver than she felt. "I am."

Flynn shifted his position, edging slightly closer to Frost, his voice dropping to a whisper. "The second day I was in John Lord country I made a terrible mistake. My keepers got lazy. They placed my bowl of food in front of me but didn't tether the rope. I was desperate and so I ran. I raced all through the streets dragging the rope behind me like a tail. I ran straight out of the city center and through the slums. There were shouts coming all around me, even some gunshots, but I eventually managed to get out of sight of my captors. The moment I did, I ducked into the first abandoned building I came to. I think some people saw me. The good ones kept quiet. The bad ones talked. And soon the robots were after me. They located the building quick enough; they do have those scanners, after all. I figured they'd come in there, order me to step forward, and then escort me back to my owners. But when they came through the door, they didn't do any of that. They were acting different. Not like robots, but like humans. There were three of them. It was strange; they . . . they were taunting me. They carried guns, firing random shots in all directions. I think they were laughing. I'm not sure, I was so scared. I was cowering inside a fireplace, but it was clear they knew where I was. They were just toying with me, dragging the moment out as they roamed around the place, passing me by, making jokes and threats. I guess, after a while, they had enough fun and one of them reached into the fireplace and dragged me out by my hair."

Hearing this, and fearing what more was to come, Frost tried not to glance at Bunt. No wonder Flynn had been suspicious.

"They were supposed to bring me back to my owners, but they directly disobeyed their commands. Instead, they first brought me back to the one street in John Lord country belonging to the robots. The place looked like the epicenter of a bombing. Even in a city like this, I had never seen such devastation, and I think most of it was caused by the robots. I think they were trying to make things look as if humans lived here, but they weren't quite sure how to do it, and so everything was misplaced and misused. They didn't know what went where, what was important and what wasn't. They were still learning. They weren't a very large group, but the dozen or so that were there were like nothing I had ever seen. They weren't exactly like people, not yet, but they were clearly trying to be. They were starting to wear clothes. Shirts, pants, hats. Not all at once, but an article or two, as if testing it out. They wore them awkwardly, almost like they weren't sure how to put them on or how they should fit. They lit cigarettes and put them to their mouths even though they couldn't inhale. It made no sense at all; I thought I was hallucinating. Even worse, they had their own humans to amuse themselves with. They rounded people up and kept them in cages. That's how they passed the time. I saw firsthand what they did to these poor bastards, and I'm telling you, it was horrible. I still have nightmares about it. I thought I was going to die there right along with them. And I probably would have, if not for that robot Tryn. She ordered I be sent back immediately. The robots, they were disappointed. But they listened. Nobody disobeyed Tryn because disobeying her meant you disobeyed John Lord. And then I was led away and went back to being a slave. That was day two."

"You endured *four* years of that?" Frost thought about how slowly the years had passed in her apartment—and she was cared for there; she was loved there. The things Flynn had gone through, the things he must have seen—it was enough to break anyone.

"I just did what I was told and waited and prayed for my father to come. Which he did. Eventually. Although he'll tell you he was fighting to get me back every single day. Only, I never heard of any fight. I never saw any bullets stream by, no shouts or explosions; I didn't see him suffering from any injuries. Nobody challenged John Lord and his men—certainly not my father. So, I have no idea how he finally got me to leave with him. He never told me. He just said he did what he had to do and to leave it at that." Flynn was quiet before he spoke again.

"They deserve to die for what they did to me and for what they're doing to people still. I always told anyone who would listen that I was going to come back one day and set things right. They said I was crazy, and, you know what? They were right. I was a fool to think John Lord could be stopped. Nobody's going to change anything in this city, especially me. It's hopeless. If I went back there, I'd be killed in no time. All those people suffering there every day, they're just going to have to keep suffering. There's nothing I can do."

Frost's throat constricted, keeping her from speaking. There were so many things she wanted to say, but none of the words could find their way to the open air. She didn't want to believe the world had descended into such a hostile nightmare, that all the dreams she had for the city were long dead. This new reality crashed down upon her; she felt all its weight buckling her knees, and her heart broke for him.

"I like that you're here," Flynn said, attempting a smile. "You remind me that it's still possible to feel joy. Sometimes I kind of forget that—there's all these thoughts in my head that shouldn't be there, ugly stuff, hateful stuff. But then I look at you and I see how you don't think like that, like everyone else does. I see how much you love that broot. I didn't know people could love like that. I didn't know people like you still existed." Uncomfortable, he turned away and glanced at the swings for some time. Frost got the sense he didn't use them much, that, even here there wasn't much joy for him. It seemed a pity. She'd been itching to give them a try the moment she saw them.

Inspired, she jumped to her feet and started racing toward them.

"What are you doing?" he shouted after her.

"Come on!"

"What?"

"The swings!"

"Are you serious?"

"Let's be young," she said with a laugh.

She waited for him to catch up, and then together, Frost and Flynn ran for the swings. It was a race, though neither one of them would ever admit it. As her legs stretched far out before her, she felt as if she were breaking through time, tearing it open and sprinting into some other world, some other life where everything was different, where everything was better. She ran so hard for this alternate reality, her eyes never opening until the very last second.

Perhaps the hungrier of the two, Frost reached the swings first, leaping and spinning around and landing hard across the rubber seat. It didn't take her very long to get the hang of it. She noticed how Flynn moved his legs—under, then out, under, then out—and she just copied and in no time at all she was kicking clouds. The wind rushed through her hair, and she leaned all the way back and closed her eyes once more. She had made it to that other life. The world she knew went away. It went away and she was flying.

EIGHTEEN

Don't make me take you back out there. You can stay. All of you. As long as you'd like."

It was Barrow who made the offer. Frost turned to her left and smiled at Flynn. *It would be great*, she thought. *So very great.* It was what she always wanted, what she always dreamed of. A friend, a safe haven, something like family. It had taken a decade and a half and she had finally found it all.

But, then, she looked past Barrow and at Romes, his chest rapidly rising and falling with each troubled breath. "No," she said, her heart torn open. "I'm ready to leave. I have to."

"Now?"

"I don't know how much time he has left." Her voice was so weak it barely registered.

Barrow's face dropped into his hand. "Look, I don't agree with this. Not for a second."

"I'm . . . I'm not going to change my mind."

"And I know that. I see it in your eyes." He looked up to the sky, deeply exhaling. It appeared as if he wanted to scream. "I'll tell you what. I'll get you out of the Zone in one piece. All three of you. I can do that much. That's my first promise."

"Thank you," Frost said, trying to avoid Flynn's gaze, trying to avoid her emotions from pouring forth. She was afraid that if she looked into his eyes, she might see something that'd convince her to stay.

"But it's not going to be easy. There are many dangers we have to avoid along the way. If and when we get to the end of the Zone, it will be even more dangerous. We can't be seen. Okay? You have to listen to what I say now. Every single word. If you don't, someone is going to die. That's my second promise."

Frost took a deep breath, and when she exhaled it was as if she blew everything she ever wanted thousands of miles away.

Ten minutes later they stood at the ramp of the fort. After filling a bag with supplies—food, water, camping gear— Barrow was now busy collecting guns, strapping them to his arms, his legs, his back. Flynn did the same. And Frost could only watch, wondering what she was getting herself into.

"I highly suggest you take a few." Barrow held one out to Bunt, a semiautomatic.

The robot, however, just stared at it.

"Go ahead. It's yours. Arm yourself."

"My programming will not allow it."

"Grab it," Barrow said, his voice stern. "I know you can. Take it now."

Frost knew it was a test. Barrow wanted to make sure Bunt wasn't a robot like the ones that abused his boy. She understood—it's what you do when you care for someone.

"My hand will not close around the weapon."

"The hell it won't." Barrow shoved the gun into Bunt's hand and watched the weapon promptly drop to the ground. He stared down at it for what seemed like a minute. Then he glared back up at Bunt. "Lot of good you'll do us." With a grunt, he picked the gun up and held it out to Frost. "You're going to need it, girly. Knives won't be enough, even with skills like yours."

Frost hesitated. She kept her hands at her sides. "I don't like them."

"You don't have to like them."

"Frost," Flynn said, nearly pleading. "Just take it."

At Flynn's urging, Frost reached out, but she couldn't bring herself to grab it. "I can't," she said, shaking her head. "I don't want to kill. I just want to save my broot."

Barrow glared at her. "This is how you save him."

"No."

Barrow groaned and shoved the gun into his shoulder bag. "Not listening already. I told you what will happen. You'll be the death of us all."

The words struck a blow to Frost's heart. That was exactly what frightened her most.

They walked to the gate, Barrow and Flynn armed to the teeth, Bunt dragging Romes, and Frost taking a very deep breath.

"And off we go."

NINETEEN

The group headed south from the camp. Frost looked behind her as they turned a corner, feeling a pang of sorrow and a gut punch of nostalgia for a time she never knew.

Barrow expertly guided them through the Zone. He seemed to know the exact paths to take, no matter how winding they were, no matter how many times they branched off into other directions. He knew which ones posed a lesser threat and which ones weren't so overgrown that dragging Romes down them would be too difficult. He pointed out the fallen lampposts, and how one could tell exactly where they were in the Zone from reading the numbers printed on them—if they were still legible. He pointed out the nests of hawks and eagles and the abandoned dens of broots. Everything was going smoothly enough, and Frost found herself growing more and more confident. That is, until they reached the lake.

Or maybe it was once a lake, or something else—something the people could make use of, something the people could admire. But now it was a swamp. A dreary and foreboding sight. The surrounding trees had taken over, as they were doing every-where, along with flies, gnats, and mosquitoes. The water was dark and murky, thick scum drifting across the surface and around the oversized lily pads. Plants and weeds sprouted in wide patches, and slithering around one of the many stumps that peeked out from the water like rotting stalagmites was a very large snake.

There was no way across the swamp, but that wasn't the concern—there was a clear way around. The concern was the half-naked Eater standing in the middle of the muck, hungrily staring at them.

"It's searching the water for food," Barrow said. "Not used to seeing one so deep inside the Zone." He signaled to his son to raise his weapon.

"What are you doing?" Frost asked.

"He's a terrific shot. All he needs to put that thing out of its misery is to pull the trigger once."

Frost stared at the panting and salivating Eater, a female. She could have sworn she saw the fear in its eyes. The sight rattled her. There was a past life somewhere behind that fear. "It'll never get out of that swamp in time. It's no threat to us. Let's just go."

"They're always threats. If not now, then later." And he signaled for his son to fire.

The shot rang out, some birds scattered, and, sure enough, the Eater dropped, its head having exploded. But the moment this happened, as if alerted, as if awakened, a dozen other Eaters emerged from under the water.

"Ah, we have us some fishermen," Barrow said, now raising his gun as well.

"We should hurry," Frost said. "We should leave."

"Calm down. We're in no danger. Ever hear the old saying 'shooting ducks in a barrel'? That's what we have here. Rabid ducks in a very large barrel." And he began to fire away, Flynn quickly joining him.

One by one, the Eaters, their bodies violently jerking backward, sank into the bubbling muck, never to rise again.

Frost flinched with each deafening shot. Hands over her ears, she kept her head down. She wasn't sure if it was because of her mother or not, but she couldn't bear to watch such a slaughter. These were people, desperate people who had lost control of their minds. It wasn't their fault. Their hunger controlled them now. They knew it was wrong, she could see that. They just couldn't do anything about it.

Some of the Eaters were hiding behind the stumps, while others—the ones that still had arms—swam under the water, only lifting their heads briefly to breathe, before submerging once again.

"They're getting closer," Barrow said to Flynn. "Pick up your pace."

But the quicker they fired, the more they missed. There were four Eaters left now, and they were getting nearer. Bunt moved beside Frost, his blade drawn.

From behind the robot, Frost saw the look in Barrow's eyes. With each passing second he was getting more and more nervous. Sweat dripped down his temple. His shot became more erratic. He nearly slipped on the slick ground.

Flynn, meanwhile, remained calm. There were no signs of

fear or panic. As everyone else backed away, he moved closer. He dropped another Eater. Then another. Then one more.

The last one reached the shore and climbed out. It ran for them, straight for Flynn. Again, there was no hesitation, no fear. The boy fired the kill shot when the Eater was no more than three feet away. Its blood dotted Frost's boots.

Everything was now still and quiet, the swamp empty except for corpses. Frost felt like crying; she couldn't fully explain why. This wasn't what she wanted.

"Shooting ducks," Barrow reiterated. He looked fondly at his boy. "You do me proud. Reload and pack up."

"Dad . . . Dad, what was that?"

Barrow glanced around at all the dead bodies. "I don't know. I've never seen so many at once. Especially not in the Zone."

"They have discovered their chances of eating are greater when hunting in larger numbers. This is basic animal behavior."

"They're not animals," Frost said.

Flynn looked at her. "Not animals? You have to wake up, Frost. You can't keep living like you're still in that apartment. They would have killed us."

"I know, Flynn. I know. It's awful. But they're still people. Very sick people. They need help."

"There's no helping them, girly. You need to see that," Barrow told her, before surveying the scene once more. With a sigh, he said, "I don't know what's going on here, but we shouldn't stick around."

TWENTY

They were forced to circumnavigate the swamp, and Barrow knew just how to do so. There were two paths down which they could have traveled, and he chose the narrower one—this, he said, was for strategic purposes, as it would allow them better defensive formations should they be attacked again. As if to demonstrate where such brilliant tactics came from, smirking, he tapped the side of his head with the tip of his finger.

The group was more alert now. There was little conversation as their eyes constantly roamed from side to side. More than once did someone raise their weapon in the direction of a sound within the brush. Even while resting on the elevator door, Romes seemed more attentive than he had in days. His ears continually twitched, his nose wet with use.

Frost realized they must have been walking along the perimeter of the Zone because she believed she could make out some of the buildings through the mass of trees. The street looked and sounded deserted, like much of the outskirts of the city, although there was smoke pouring from an open window facing the Zone. She wondered what was going on in there, if there were others like her who had locked themselves away for years, more young girls lost to the world.

For the majority of the walk, there were no problems and they were keeping up a good, somewhat swift, pace. That was until Bunt all of a sudden started lagging behind.

"What's with him?" Barrow asked, his eyes patrolling the edges of the swamp, his gun raised. "That door getting too heavy or something?"

"No," Frost answered, her trepidation amplifying. "It's my dad. He's taking over."

"Who? Taking what? What do you mean? What's going on?"

After a few more lumbering and broken steps, Alex had arrived in full, blinking into existence across the smooth contours of the robot's face.

"You didn't say anything about this," Barrow said to Frost, his bushy eyebrows raised. "Where's he been all this time? Why's he been hiding?"

"You can direct your queries to me," Alex said, his neck stiff.

Frost watched as Flynn slowly backed away and redirected his rifle at the robot. It must have been troubling to see it act out of character, especially after he had come to somewhat trust it. His time as a captive clearly scarred him, shattering whatever chances at hope and optimism and trust he might have had left.

"Okay, then, where've you been?" Barrow's gun was also raised, only now in Alex's direction. He looked like he wanted any excuse to pull the trigger.

"Can you point that thing someplace else, please?" Alex said.

"Your kid has nearly gotten herself killed out here."

"You don't think I'm aware of what's happening?"

"Not sure. I've never lived inside a robot's brain. All I know is that you allowed your daughter to leave the comfort and security of your home so she could attempt to save a broot, of all things."

"First of all, although I now have little control over this body, I can see what the robot sees. I know what's going on. I know who you are and where we're headed. Second, and most important, that broot you talk about, my daughter loves him more than anything. And saving him means saving her. So, yes, I will make sure I get her to the Battery, even if you don't."

Barrow chuckled. "You? You can hardly walk. Maybe you should stay buried in your tin coffin. At least the robot could lend a hand."

"What's your problem?"

"This is no world for the likes of you and your kid."

"Look, I thank you for your help. Truly. It is greatly appreciated, but if you want to head back to your playground, we can manage on our own. I may not have much control over this body, but I will protect my daughter with everything I have. Whatever strength I still possess, whatever love, whatever heart, whatever soul. I will protect her."

It was clear Barrow noticed his boy's eyes were fixated on him. Frost noticed it, too. It was a judgmental stare, a stare that suggested he wished his father would have once said exactly what Alex did.

Barrow quickly turned away, kicking at the ground. "I'm not going anywhere," he muttered. "I made a promise. I was just surprised, is all." With great concentration he was digging the heel of his boot into the earth as if making his final stand. When he eventually looked up again, glancing first at Flynn, then at Alex, his face had changed. It softened. "I'm . . . I'm sorry if I came off a little harsh just now. Here . . ." He grabbed the cable from Alex's limp hand. "Let me take over for a bit. You just concentrate on moving forward right now."

This was a smart enough idea. With Alex's attention focused solely on walking, he was able to manage and maintain a decent pace, although Flynn had to help Barrow with the door, it was so heavy.

As the group moved on—the swamp still on their right, with no signs of ending—Frost noticed Barrow continually giving her father sideways glances. His eyes narrowed and he seemed to be mumbling to himself. Finally, there was the sharp glare of recognition.

"I know you. I know you." He dropped the cable and put a hand on Alex's chest, halting his progress. Then, straightening his back, Barrow stood before the imposing robotic body, rose on his toes, and glared into Alex's eyes. "Yeah, I thought I recognized you, you piece of trash. You're the one who started this whole mess. It's all your fault. You're that famous roboticist, aren't you?"

TWENTY-ONE

I don't know what you're talking about."

And neither did Frost. Her father, a roboticist? Famous? He never said a thing. Barrow had to be mistaken. There was no way her father would keep something like that from her.

"Don't lie," Barrow said, shoving a finger into Alex's chest. "Don't lie. I know you. I know what you did."

Alex attempted to shove Barrow's hand away, but he couldn't manage it. The effort was just too great. "What I did had nothing to do with what happened to the world."

"Is that so? You tinkering away there in your lab, creating robot after robot after robot, one version better than the next, pumping them out to the public. The great Alex Simmelfore of Simmelfore Robotics. The man everyone idolized and lionized. The man all over the news, leading us into the future. The man with the wife who shifted the laws in his favor. You had nothing to do with any of this? With your billions? With your intelligence and schemes and power? Please. You stole human existence. Stole it right out from under us."

Was it true? Frost felt a sort of rattling in her head, as if her brain were being slowly dismantled. This relative stranger knew more about her father than she did. It seemed everyone must have, except maybe Flynn, who appeared to be reeling himself. She saw the bewilderment in his eyes, the shock, but most noticeably, the anger. To him, her father was the source of all his pain. But whatever he felt was nothing compared to what was in Frost's heart. Her father had lied to her. For her entire life, he purposely kept her in the dark—as if her world wasn't already dark enough. She understood Barrow's ire, Flynn's disgust. Maybe her father really was responsible for all of this.

"I improved human existence," Alex said, his face full of defiance.

Barrow took a step back and spread his arms like wings. "You call this an improvement?"

"The robots aren't at fault. It's human error. It's always human error."

"Yes. And that human is you. You brought the robots to life. You put them in every place of importance. You wanted them in every home. You took humans out of the equation, Doc. And this is what happens when you do. This is your error."

"Don't put this on me. The robots aren't capable of this kind of destruction. I made sure of that."

"Don't you dare tell me what robots are and aren't capable of. Don't tell me. Don't say that in front of my boy. Not in front of him! I've seen things. He's seen things. We know full well what they can do."

"You've seen what humans can do. Technology is only as good, as positive a force, as those using it. I created something good. It's the people that are evil. Who is hunting us down as we speak? Humans. Who are they taking orders from? John Lord, a human. Who is trying to eat us alive? Humans. Who created the broots? Humans. It's not the technology, Barrow. Never was."

"You gave those people the means. You gave them the tools, and now we all must suffer for it. You play God, you fall like the Devil."

"When we get to the Battery it's going to be that very technology that saves us."

"Hate to break the news to you, pal, but you ain't making it there. Hell, I'm not even sure we'll get out of the Zone alive, let alone make it to the Battery. But if by some miracle we do escape from this wretched wilderness, you certainly aren't getting through John Lord country. Nobody does. It's the Wild West there, man. It's filled with scared people under the thumb of a madman. You're going to be ripped apart. Do you get that? Huh? Do you? They're going to torture you! They're going to abuse you! They're going to kill you! You, your daughter, and your broot!"

Everyone fell silent. Barrow took an awkward step back and lowered his head, tapping the barrel of his gun against his temple. Walking in a tight circle, he refused to look anyone in the eye, especially Frost, whose head was pounding with confusion.

She didn't know much of this world or the one of the past, and she was sure much blame could be thrown around in a multitude of directions, one very large target being her father. But where would that get them? How would it help? Right now, they had to worry about getting through the Zone. There were Eaters to avoid, broots, robots, and countless other obstacles. They had no time for this. And they most certainly couldn't afford to turn on each other.

"Barrow," Frost said.

"Don't talk to me. Not right now."

"Barrow, we can make it."

"I said, don't talk to me!"

Frost walked in front of him, standing her ground. "We all can. Together." She reached for him, an attempt to stop his mad pacing and to see his eyes. But, feeling her touch, Barrow's arm swung out, only to be caught by Flynn's hand.

"Dad . . ."

Barrow turned and glared at him. "Don't . . ."

"Dad."

"Don't!" With a violent swipe of his arm, he shook his son off.

Flynn flinched and backed away. "Dad . . . Dad, she's right." He looked to Frost. There was something different in his eyes now, something she hadn't previously seen. "They're going to make it. And we can go to the Battery, too. We can be safe. We can be happy."

"Are you stupid? There's nothing there! Nothing! That is a dream, and there's no room for dreams! Not anymore! Maybe there never was. I don't know. All I know is that we have to survive, and survival means keeping safe. This is a damn foolish game we're playing. Idiotic. I don't know what I'm doing here. I must have gone crazy somewhere along the way. How did I get caught up in all of this, huh? How did I drag my son into it? How? Tell me."

"Because you're a good man," Frost said. "I wasn't sure at first, but I see it in you now. You're a kind, good soul. You're just scared. We all are. But surviving isn't living. After spending my life in one room, I know that now. I don't expect you to help us get to the Battery, Barrow. You don't even have to take us any farther from here if you don't want to. You've done more than enough. But if that place really does exist, we have a chance of starting over. We have a chance to live the life we were promised when we were born. A promise to be happy. We get that dream again. Because, yes, this is still the country of dreams. It just got sidetracked a bit. But we can get that all back by making it to the Battery. I think that's worth it. And I think you do, too."

After another long silence, Barrow glanced up at Frost. "Ah, kid, I ain't scared. You see, I just know what's waiting for us. I know the dangers. I know the odds. We'll come with you, my boy and I, because we believe in you. But, no, I'm not scared. I'm downright terrified."

TWENTY-TWO

I t took another two hours of trudging along the overgrown path before they were finally clear of the swamp.

Frost tried not to think about what Barrow had revealed about her father, but it was difficult. Was all this really his fault? Why did he never say anything? The secrecy went beyond betrayal; her father took all the trust she had for him and set it aflame.

In the short distance ahead, a large building loomed like a fortress. Unlike all the other structures seen through the mass of trees opposite the swamp, this one seemed to be in a perpetual battle with the environment. It didn't want to be overcome; it didn't want to die. While most buildings were swallowed up—weakened and pulverized into crumbling heaps—this one appeared to fight back. It was inside Zone territory as if it had leaped headfirst into the fray, a massive concrete beast, impatient and unafraid. And yet it was overwhelmed by aggression. Its glass had long been punched out; vines strangled its every appendage, crushing and cracking its brick; trees invaded its interior like a disease, ivy scaled the walls, but it still stood solid, strong, defiant.

"What is this place?" she asked, her pace slowing.

"That," Barrow responded without turning his head, pointing in the direction of the building with the tip of his gun instead, "was once a museum. One of the greatest in the world. Now it's just an empty shell like everything else." And here he spat on the ground.

"That place was *filled* with art? But it's so big." It was a confounding thought. Her mind could barely imagine a room full of sculptures and paintings, let alone an entire building of such size. People must have been creating all the time back then, and it all must have been so beautiful that they wanted to share it with everyone. How lucky to have lived in such a time.

"Art from all over the world."

"And it's all gone?"

Here, Flynn answered. "John Lord stole it all."

Barrow kept walking. It was clear he didn't want to slow down; he didn't even want to look in the building's direction. "It's been said he has a great hunger for art, and this was one of the first places he and his goons looted, gathering up every prized piece for his personal collection, which supposedly fills several buildings of his own. Whatever was left behind, he had destroyed. If he couldn't have it, nobody could. And that wasn't all he obliterated. He probably murdered every single man, woman, and child who was camped out inside the building, too."

Images of violence flashed past Frost's eyes, causing her to recoil, but Barrow kept his glare fixed straight ahead. "There must have been hundreds, maybe thousands, of people in there. The place was used as a shelter when all this began. Back when everyone thought the Days of Bedlam were going to be just some temporary thing. Something that would eventually pass, you know? Well, one week became two, six months became a year, a year became two, three, four years, and on and on and on. Those people experienced all types of ugliness in there among the art. And that was before John Lord came along. I'm sure once he showed his face everyone was wishing for a return to those earlier days. Who knows what lurks in there now, with the ravaged dead bodies and desecrated art? To this day, I still hear noises coming from inside. Ugly, chilling sounds. You've heard of the Ghosts?"

Frost, shaking her head, glanced at Flynn. There was a look on his face, one that said she didn't want to know, although Barrow went on talking regardless.

"The Ghosts are the so-called people caught in the wall screens, the museum guides and observers and security who controlled everything in the building, from the temperature to lighting to tours. You see, the computers ran on a little thing called solar energy. If you were to climb up there on that roof, you'd see rows and rows of these panels. Most of them were destroyed, and the ones that are still functioning, however minimally, don't get much sun when there's a sky of permanent dark clouds and haze overhead. So, inside the building, the screens blink in and out of existence with every quick burst of power feeding the system. But this is all very brief and random. Some screens will turn on while others don't. Some for a dozen seconds, some for just one or two. These screens flick on and the Ghosts scream. And with most of them it's like they never stopped, like the scream holds when the screen shuts down and continues when the power returns. One long howl. And this wailing, it's so loud it can be heard for miles. They sound like wolves."

Frost's awe of the building expanded, only now it was tinged with dread. "Have you ever been in there?"

"Shhh."

Barrow held up his finger and, sure enough, a chilling cry escaped from inside the building. It really did sound like a wolf, but a dying one, a wolf delirious with pain. They waited it out, Frost counting the seconds. Seven. Seven seconds that felt like seven hundred.

Then, when all was quiet again, Barrow continued. "Once, early on, I went inside. It was a mistake. I was careless and foolish and blind with despair. You go in there and you're likely to not make it back out. The moment I stepped inside, it was clear there was something odd happening. Things flashed across the screens. Images. One stranger than the next. Troubling things. Gruesome things. I don't know what the screens were trying to say, if it was some kind of message or warning or threat or deranged art. At one point, a screen turned on right in front of me and a face appeared. It was an older gentleman. His face filled the screen, nearly four feet in height. He might have seen me, I don't know. I saw him, that's for sure. I saw his eyes. They were haunted gray orbs. And then I saw his head tilt all the way back and his mouth opened wide and I heard the scream. That primal, primal scream. Hands over my ears, I turned and started running. As I made my way down the massive halls, parts of the museum would turn on at random, then quickly shut back down. Lights went on and off. It was almost as if I could feel the building struggling to breathe. Very eerie.

"But, you see, I think the Ghosts aren't fully aware of what's going on and they're trying to fix the museum—that's their purpose, that building. But there's just no time to do it, and I think it's driving them insane. You go in there and they're liable to kill you, maybe lower a wall and lock you in there. Maybe something worse. Needless to say, I didn't stick around long after that. I'm telling you, those things think they're alive, Frost. Can you imagine? Being trapped inside a wall for all eternity? The darkness that envelops you, and only glimpses of light? It must be like being buried alive."

He turned and looked at Bunt, who had returned some time ago, then back at Frost. He rubbed the back of his neck with his hand, struggling to find the right words. "Look, I'm sorry again about how I treated your dad back there. I'm sure he's experiencing his own—"

"It's okay," Frost said, cutting him off. "It's over now."

"Were you . . . were you aware of what he did before all this happened? With the robots, I mean. You didn't look like you were. You looked just about as surprised as my son."

Frost shook her head. She thought about leaving it at that, but she'd spent her entire life unable to talk about things, and right now words were crowding every part of her brain, multiplying and begging to be released. "I didn't know a thing. I mean, every now and then I saw him tinkering away on Bunt, modifying him, but I thought everybody who had a robot knew how to do that. Maybe I was naïve. But there was nothing to compare Bunt to. Or my dad, for that matter. He had an office he always escaped into for hours on end, but he never let me in. Not once. Whenever I asked him what he was doing he said he was saving me and my mom. I never thought to ask how. We were alive and the only threats seemed to be sickness, and he said he was searching for a cure for that, too. He always had all the answers, and I did get better eventually. But then my mom . . ." She was forced to bite her lip. "He didn't go in the office much after that."

"I remember when his very first robot came out," Barrow said. "A. That's what it was called. Just A. This was back before the owners personalized their robots, before they became individualized. I was a young man then. Very young, and, boy, was I impressionable. I was blown away by this thing, this hunk of junk. Looking back now, it was almost laughable. You would think A would have no relation to Bunt whatsoever. But it was the start and everyone knew it. Your father was at the forefront and everyone else was busy trying to catch up and they never could. They ate his dust. When their A knockoffs came around your father had already moved on to his second series. That was when I got my first. Io. That's what they were all called. Io. Worked well enough, I guess. He walked the dog and took out the trash, at least. And your father just got bigger and bigger. Hell, some people would say he was more powerful and influential than the president. And he was practically a kid himself."

Frost reeled, her head spinning as she desperately tried to make sense of the information. But she couldn't reconcile anything Barrow had said with what she knew about her father. It was like hearing about a stranger. "He never mentioned any of this to me."

"Yeah, well . . . I'm sure it hurts him to talk about it all. Must seem like another life. A much, much better life. I don't blame him for trying to forget it. I certainly would."

"No," she said. "It wasn't his fault, what happened. He's a good man. He would never do something to hurt anyone."

There was an awkward silence, not one of them looking toward Bunt. Perhaps sensing Frost's grief, Barrow spoke up. "He was a genius. A once-in-a-generation intelligence. They said he was a man to lead us into a new age. You should be very proud. Many, many people had great respect for him."

"And the others?"

"The others?" Barrow looked away. "They . . . didn't."

Frost lowered her head. She felt great pity and sorrow now but didn't know what for. Not exactly. She couldn't think straight, couldn't concentrate. At the moment, she just wished Barrow would stop talking and turn his attention elsewhere for a bit. She needed to get lost in her own head for a while.

"There is movement."

Barrow broke his stare and approached Bunt. "Can you tell what?"

"No. Not yet."

"Hurry, then. Let's keep moving. No sense in waiting to find out what it is."

But it was a long walk past the building and the sky was quickly darkening and Frost continued to look over her shoulder at the museum. Staring back, she knew it was only a matter of time before she would see something move.

Then, sure enough, a figure emerged from inside the ruins. It climbed atop a toppled wall, spotting them immediately. "Wait! Wait!" There was great desperation in the voice.

"Ignore her," Barrow said. "Keep walking."

But Frost kept looking back. The woman was waving her arms and screaming at the top of her lungs. "Wait!"

"Don't stop. Don't slow down."

"But she's not an Eater," Frost said. "She has her tongue."

"Doesn't matter. We don't know who she is. Or who she's with."

"Please!" the woman cried. "Wait! Please! I don't want to die!"

Frost stopped moving and, in loyal response, so, too, did Bunt. Seeing this, the woman jumped down from the wall and started running over, screaming and pleading all the while.

"We have to see if we can help her."

"Frost—"

"She's begging for help. You can keep your gun aimed at her if that makes you feel safe. She'd be foolish to do anything."

"I can kill her now and end this discussion."

"Don't do that. Please, don't do that."

"Frost . . . Damn it. I don't know about this." Barrow looked to his son. "What do you think?"

Flynn hesitated, glancing from Frost to his father and back. "Give her a chance."

"How'd I know you'd say that?"

TWENTY-THREE

The woman ran at them; the pained and desperate pall in her eyes matched the sky overhead. As she crossed the terrain, she nearly collapsed with every step, her arms flailing wildly. Barrow kept his gun trained on her, but she didn't seem to notice. She didn't slow down; she didn't raise her arms in surrender. She just kept coming.

"That's enough," Barrow shouted when she was within twenty yards. "Don't come any closer!"

But the woman didn't respond. It was clear she wasn't going to stop. Her eyes were focused on something. They were focused on Frost.

Bunt freed his sword from the sheath up his arm, and Barrow's finger tightened around the trigger of his gun. "I said stop!"

The woman, babbling incoherently, ran straight for Frost.

"Stop! Now!" Barrow took aim. There would be no warning shot, no aiming for a leg or arm. The only intention would be to kill. "Last chance!"

"Don't!" Frost cried out, an arm extended in Barrow's direction.

"What?"

"Don't!"

The woman gasped, stumbled, and fell to the ground right in front of Frost. She hit hard, gashing her knees, but didn't show any signs of pain. She merely wrapped her arms around Frost's ankles, hugging them tight. "Thank you," she said, weeping. "Thank you. I thought I was alone. I thought I was going to die." She raised her bowed head and locked eyes with Frost.

She really did look close to death. She was emaciated, her face sharp bones and little else. Her hair was falling out in large clumps, her skin a sickly color. There was a terrible odor emanating from an open green sore on the back of her neck, and there were only a few teeth left in her swollen mouth. Her eyes were sunken, the lids drooping and showing red, and her nose ran wild with mucus.

"But then I saw you," she said, blubbering. "I saw the beautiful girl. From inside the museum, I saw your light, I felt your warmth. You drew me here, child. You saved me." She reached up and grabbed Frost's hand and started to kiss it. With her eyes closed, her lips nearly sucked away at the soft skin.

Uncomfortable, Frost pulled her hand away.

With great effort, the woman rose to her feet, holding Frost by her shoulders. "Tell me, what is your name?"

"My name is Frost."

"Frost. Yes. It's like I dreamed it." And she pulled Frost close, a gracious embrace.

"Let her go," Barrow said. "I almost took your head off once. You fail to listen again and—"

The woman backed away, this time with her hands up. "I mean no harm."

"What were you doing in that building?" Barrow asked.

"What I've been doing since all this happened. Surviving." Her voice was strangled. It came out vibrating.

"Surviving? In there?"

"I wasn't inside for very long. I had a home, but I was driven from it. A group of men entered the building. They were searching for someone or something."

"What's your name?" Frost asked.

"My name, beautiful Frost, is Agatha." She reached out and took Frost's hand in hers. "Take me with you. Please. I beg you."

"No way," Barrow interjected.

"Barrow . . ."

"Frost."

"She needs help. We're stronger as a group."

"You're wrong. She makes us weaker."

Flynn moved beside Frost. "Dad, we can help her. Since when have you turned your back on those in need?"

Barrow's teeth were clenched as if in pain. "Keep out of this, Flynn. I know better than you do."

"Just for the night," Frost pleaded.

Agatha seconded this notion. "Just for the night. I beg you."

Barrow looked up at the sky, ready to scream. He looked as if he wanted to break his gun over his knee. But, with a long, deep breath, the moment soon passed. "Night's coming," he said. "We have to camp soon." As he stepped closer to Agatha, he finally lowered his gun. With his face in hers, he said, "You can stay the night, and then we'll part ways in the morning. This robot here is going to keep a sharp eye on you all night. You try anything to my boy or to Frost, and he's going to take your head off. Understand?"

Agatha nodded. "Do you . . . do you have anything to eat? I'm so very hungry."

"We all are," Barrow said.

"Perhaps that broot there. It is in worse shape than I."

"The broot is mine," Frost said. "His name is Romes and nothing takes a bite out of him. Not even a flea."

Agatha practically bowed in apology. "Of course. But we must eat something."

Barrow eyed their surroundings. "Yeah, well, we don't have a kill and it's getting too late to start searching now. It will have to wait until morning."

Agatha's face seemed to crack open with disappointment. "Oh. Oh. Morning. Yes."

TWENTY-FOUR

I n the fading light, they walked a little longer until they found a spot suitable for camp. They would have preferred to have been farther from the museum, but time forced them to settle. It was a suitable enough area, an octagon of ripped-up concrete. The surrounding benches had withered among the elements, and the trees had encroached far enough to offer some protection and concealment from potential dangers. In the center, a large object had fallen over. It was an obelisk, Barrow said, an Egyptian artifact. Covered in hieroglyphics, it was over sixty feet in length and provided a triangle of shelter where it had snapped at the base. The group settled there, Flynn and his father gathering wood for a fire, while Bunt silently patrolled the perimeter.

Agatha sat close to Frost, who, as always, sat close to Romes. In the distance, a warped cry drifted from the museum. It lingered in their ears long after dying.

Frost riffled through her bag, pulling whatever medicines she thought might help Agatha.

"No need to waste such things on me. Save them for yourself."

"If I can help you, I'm going to help you. Besides, my body has taken very good care of me in the last few years. No sicknesses, no injuries."

There was a weak smile. "Ah, to be young."

While Barrow, chopping wood from a tree, eyed them suspiciously, Frost administered whatever aid she could and, when she was finished, covered Agatha with a blanket.

"You are something special," Agatha said, wrapping it tightly around her.

"I'm just trying to help. That's all."

"And you are. You are. You're going to save me." She spoke in a dead monotone, a great distance in her eyes.

Frost followed the blank stare and found Romes at the other end. Agatha wasn't the only one who needed saving.

"I'm trying to get to the Battery. I think there might be people there who can help us."

Agatha broke her stupor and looked up at the sky. "The Battery, yes. Yes, it's there. I've seen it."

"You've seen it?" Frost said, practically leaping to her feet.

Agatha hummed an affirmation. "A glorious place untouched by the chaos. It stands tall and gleaming, like nothing you've ever witnessed. It's the way the city is supposed to be, the way it once was. Life thrives there."

In that moment, it thrived in Frost as well. The Battery was real. It was a reality. There was no more wondering. No more guessing. Agatha confirmed it. The blue glow was their beacon. All she had to do now was reach it and everything would be better. "But . . ." she said, confused. "But then what are you doing here? They could have helped you. Why didn't you stay?"

"Oh, yes, of course. Why leave, yes? Why would anyone leave such a wondrous place? Well, you leave if you want to save your family. And I wanted to save mine. I couldn't go there yet, no matter how tempting, not until I found my children."

"Did . . . did you find them?"

Lips quivering, she threw her hands up as if to say, No, not yet. "I fear their deaths. I fear what they had to suffer, and I wasn't there for them. I had two. A boy and a girl. Geoff and Maggie. They were perfect. You remind me of her, my girl. She was your age, your height; she even had your hair."

Frost understood the weight of her loss all too well. "I hope you find her. Both of them."

The woman laughed a sad laugh. "No, I won't."

They were quiet a moment, the two of them staring out at Bunt. "Is that all you have?" Agatha asked. "A broot and a robot? No mother? No father?"

"I have my father."

"You do?"

"Well, kind of."

"That man, Barrow, he is not your father."

"No. My father is inside the robot."

"Inside? Oh, I see. He is one of those."

"Yes, but he can't control when he comes and goes. If he could, he'd be here all the time. He would never go away. I know that."

"Of course he would. And your mother?"

"My mother?" Frost's head dropped and her voice grew faint. "She's gone."

"Oh, you poor baby. You poor, poor baby." Agatha ran her hand through Frost's hair, once, then twice.

It felt wonderful. Frost closed her eyes and she imagined her mother sitting there comforting her. *It would be just like this,* she thought. A woman who cared for her, a woman who listened and adored her. A woman who told her what she needed to hear.

Frost tilted her head, leaning it against Agatha's bony shoulder.

When it came time for sleep, Agatha slept close and Frost was happy. But the woman's sleep was troubled. She tossed and turned, cried out; she clutched at her throat as if in pain. She stretched her eyelids even lower and tugged at her mouth, yanking her jaw wide open, her fingers traveling down her throat as if to pull the sickness out.

TWENTY-FIVE

They woke early, their stomachs rumbling, Bunt walking his endless circle, the temperature cooler than it had been in years. Barrow, yawning so wide his jaw cracked, bent over and picked up his rifle, which he promptly rested on his broad shoulder as he waved Frost over to the far side of the camp. Once she arrived, he leaned close and spoke in low tones.

"Flynn and I will hunt. We'll find something and bring it back as quickly as possible. Are you going to be okay here?"

"I'll be fine. Bunt will alert me if anything comes near."

Barrow pointed at Agatha. She was sitting where she had slept, her hands pressed between her knees as she slowly rocked back and forth. "I mean with her."

"She's a good person."

"We were all good people once."

"She's been through a lot."

"Again, the same."

Frost sighed. "Just hurry back."

"Stay alert, you hear? I won't be long. If there's one thing I know, it's how to lure a broot. And God knows how many there are in the Zone."

And yet he and Flynn were gone for several hours. Bunt continued his patrol, Romes his slumbering, and Frost and Agatha sat side by side, listening to the shrieking Ghosts of the museum.

"They're not going to find anything," Agatha croaked, her rocking growing more severe by the minute, along with her guttural moaning. "We're not going to eat. This will be the end of us."

Frost rubbed Agatha's back, her palm tracing the protruding curvature of the spine. "They'll be back with something. Barrow knows what he's doing."

"They're probably dead."

"Don't say that. Don't ever say that."

"You're a good girl, Frost. A good girl." She placed her hand on Frost's cheek, caressing it with her thumb as her eyes filled with tears. "But I can't do this anymore."

"Frost."

Frost turned to her father and jumped to her feet. He had been searching the woods and when he looked back at her, she saw the fear in his eyes, his forlorn glare acknowledging the mistake he just inadvertently made by overriding Bunt—something was in the woods; she could hear it circling. "Dad." Another cry came from the museum, one louder and more harrowing than any other. If Frost didn't know better, she could have sworn it came from inside the robot.

Agatha pointed at Alex with a trembling finger. "Can he not . . ."

Frost shook her head. "No. He can't see what's coming. He can hardly move."

"Just stay under the obelisk. I'll try to summon Bunt back."

Frost called out to him. "You can't control it."

A noise swept through the woods, freezing everyone. Movement, the breaking of branches. Whatever it was, it wasn't very far off.

Agatha grabbed Frost's hand. "I'm frightened."

"We'll be okay," she answered, not believing it herself.

Alex tried to walk toward the sound but barely budged. "There's something out there." He tried another step, then, frustrated, yelled, "Barrow! Barrow, is that you?"

There was no response.

Agatha squeezed harder.

"I should grab my knives." Frost tried to get up, but she was held in place.

"No, don't leave me."

"I'm not leaving, I'm just—"

In her second attempt to rise, she was yanked back down.

"I need you."

"Frost, what's going on over there?" Alex's voice called.

"Agatha, let go of me."

"I can't."

"Let go."

"No."

Frost locked eyes with her, a terrible feeling settling in the pit of her stomach. There was something different in Agatha's eyes. An invasion of some sort. Frost no longer felt a mothering presence. "Agatha, what are you doing?"

Romes was growling as he painfully struggled to his feet.

"I . . . I can't control it anymore, Frost."

"Can't control what?"

"Frost?" her father's voice called again.

"I feel it in me. It's been there for some time now. Growing. Spreading."

"You have to wait. Barrow will be back soon."

"I can't wait. I . . . I need . . ."

"Frost." Her father's voice was growing urgent.

"I need to . . . eat!" And she lunged forward, biting down on Frost's arm, their hands still clasped.

"Frost!"

Her eyes closed. She saw images, images that weren't hers, that couldn't be hers. She saw her mother coming after her father. She saw her teeth gnashing against her father's skin. She saw the blood, the finger being ripped from the hand, the white of the broken bone. She heard the screams and saw the horror. But, worst of all, she saw the agony in her mother's eyes, the pain, the sorrow, the sickness.

She opened her eyes and saw those same things in Agatha's. Leaning back, Frost kicked her away. It didn't take much, the woman was so thin, so anemic. And, luckily, she had but a few teeth, weak ones at that, and all they did was leave small marks upon the skin.

Frost scrambled and grabbed the knives from her bag. "You're an Eater!"

"I'm not!" Agatha cried. "I . . . I don't want to be! I just . . . I hunger!" She leaped closer and Frost slashed her hand.

Agatha backed away again, ravenously licking the blood from her fingers. Behind her, the trees swayed.

"I don't want to hurt you," Frost cried.

Romes lumbered two steps off the elevator door, his first steps in days. His rotten teeth were bared, a growl in his throat.

From across the camp, Alex screamed for his daughter. "Frost! Frost, get away from her! Run to me!"

But Frost didn't run. She stood her ground and spoke to her the way she wished she could have to her mother. "You don't have to do this. You're stronger than the sickness. You have to fight it, Agatha. For your children."

Agatha laughed, a disturbed cackle. "I have no children."

"But Geoff! Maggie!"

"Lies!"

Frost felt the lump growing in her throat, the cold pressure against her heart. "No. Don't say that."

"I need to live! I need to eat! I'd tell you anything!"

"But, the Battery . . . you've . . . you've seen the Battery. That much is true, isn't it?"

Agatha shook her head. "No. It's not. There's no such place."

In one massive wave, numbness spread through Frost. The knives dropped from her hands, clattering against the broken concrete. Agatha charged.

She was a mere three feet away, her mouth wide open, her hands like claws, her palm dripping blood. Frost's knees weakened. She was close to blacking out. And that was when Romes lunged. The broot caught Agatha's leg in his massive jaws and slammed her hard to the ground. Then, with a howl, he collapsed.

Frost regained herself in time to realize it wasn't just a howl. It was a call. Romes had sensed the broot lurking in the woods and sure enough it emerged, sniffing the blood in the air, walking tentatively closer to the group. Its steps were careful, but it was clear it was heading for Agatha, who was screaming in pain and anguish, her leg nearly torn free from her body. And when the broot was near, it jumped, snatching her by the neck and dragging her back from where it came.

TWENTY-SIX

When Barrow and Flynn returned, all they had to show for their efforts were a few pitiable squirrels. Frost, however, barely noticed their arrival, her eyes still locked on the smear of blood where Agatha had been dragged away.

"Frost? What's wrong?" Flynn asked, hurrying toward her.

In a flat voice, she told Flynn and Barrow what had happened to Agatha. "I didn't see it," she said, on her knees, still staring ahead. "I should have. But I didn't."

"Don't let it bug you, kid. These things happen," Barrow said before turning away to start skinning the squirrels.

Flynn crouched down next to her. "Are you okay?" he asked softly.

Frost tried to nod, but the effort was too great. Her thoughts were heavy, weighing everything down. "I'll be fine." She didn't want to lie, but there was no way to shape the tangle of feelings into words. A familiar numbness began to spread over her, like it always did when her father disappeared for too long, when even Romes's plaintive eyes and furry body weren't enough to keep her from retreating inside herself.

Without a word, Flynn reached out and took Frost's hand, threading his fingers through hers. He squeezed it lightly, sending a jolt of warmth through Frost's body, leaving a tingling trail in its wake. She couldn't remember ever holding hands with another human before, yet the pressure felt somehow familiar, as if this was what it was designed to do. As if this made her whole.

She stared straight ahead, afraid of what she'd see in Flynn's face if she turned, but even more afraid of what he'd see in hers. After a few moments, Flynn let go and rose to his feet. "I'd better go help my father," he said. Frost nodded, although he'd already walked away. Her hand pulsed warmly, as if it contained a heartbeat of its own.

When the squirrels were done roasting, Barrow cut off a chunk and thrust it toward Frost. "Here. Eat."

"I can't," she said, still too haunted by the image of Agatha.

With no loss of appetite himself, Barrow took a large bite of his charred squirrel, the dark juices squeezed free and running down his chin. "Nothing better is going to come along. Not any time soon." As he wiped his mouth with his sleeve, his eyes closed in contemplation. Frost glanced at his hands and saw them trembling.

"It's odd," he went on. "Something's driving all the broots away. This place used to be filled with them, but the farther south we go, the less there are. We managed to track one mangy broot, but lost it not very far from here. It was probably the same one that grabbed Agatha."

Flynn placed the stick with a pierced chunk of squirrel on the end in Frost's hand, gently closing her fingers around it. "But they usually travel in packs, right?" he asked his father, but kept his eyes locked with Frost's.

"Doesn't make sense. Frost, the way you said it approached—broots never act like that. They're hunters and they're hungry. Always. They're never skeptical, never wary of humans. It's like it knew we were threats."

Frost shook her head. "We're not threats. We're the threatened."

They were quiet, the fire between them spitting its sparks. Frost still hadn't moved her hand toward her mouth. "Nothing is like I thought it would be," she said, breaking the silence. "I always thought that if I ever went any farther than I could see from my apartment, the city would somehow be like it was before. That it would be mostly whole. Is that strange, to think that? I thought that maybe it was only my world that was destroyed, that, far outside my window, this city was slowly rebuilding. I wanted to be a part of that. Friends, games, parties, music, love. All the beauty. All of it. I thought it would all be waiting for me."

Everyone sat quietly for several minutes until Barrow, shifting uncomfortably, said, "We lost a lot of daylight. We have to get moving and at a far quicker pace than yesterday. Eat up. You're going to need the energy."

When his father walked away, Flynn got up and sat beside Frost. "Are you okay, really?"

Frost, still caught somewhat in a daze, slowly nodded.

"When I got back here and saw all that blood and you on the ground with Romes, my heart . . . I . . . I swear I thought it might have disintegrated. I'm so sorry I wasn't there to help you."

"Don't be sorry. I shouldn't have been so trusting. I can be so naïve. I have to stop. It's going to cost me one day."

"No. Don't say that. I love the way you are." He caught himself. "I mean, it's good to see the world that way. The potential. You see the light that's gone out for the rest of us. I've forgotten what that's like. I want to see things the way you do."

"You do?"

Flynn reached inside his coat and pulled something free.

She couldn't tell what it was, not right away, but still her heart quickened with excitement as she took in a splash of color, a deep, rich red she'd only ever seen in her imagination.

"This is a rose, Frost."

"You . . ." The beauty of the flower overwhelmed her, and she could barely form her next words. "You . . . found one?"

"For you."

"For me?" she repeated. "This is for me?"

"There's still some beauty waiting for you."

"Where did you find it?"

"There's a spot not far from here. It was a bit out of the way, but I told my dad that I was tracking a broot." He grinned that twisted grin she loved so much and extended his hand farther. "Go ahead. Take it."

She reached out with her trembling hand, then quickly brought it back. "I don't want to damage it."

"You'll be fine. It'll be safer in your hands than anywhere else."

Frost smiled and caressed the petals with the tip of her finger. The touch was like a jump back in time to the days she could only read about. Then her hand lowered and her fingers pinched the stem and brought it close to her face. "It's supposed to smell, right?"

Flynn nodded. "Give it a try."

She leaned forward and inhaled. It smelled like life, like an entire world living on the petal of a flower. "Oh, it's beautiful," she said.

"That world can come back," Flynn told her. "In full. Everything you thought you missed. It's just waiting for us to help it along." Then he took the flower from her hand and gently placed it in her hair. "Frost and the flower." He leaned back, taking her in. "You ask me, right this minute, that world is roaring back to life."

Less than an hour later, the group packed their bags, ready to set out once again. As they did so, Frost caught Bunt staring at her. "What?" she asked. But he didn't respond. Finally, he reached out and gently took the rose from her hair, turning it over and over in his hand, inspecting it closely. If he had a face, Frost thought she'd see wistfulness.

When he handed the flower back to her, he did so almost reluctantly. While Frost secured it in her hair, Bunt turned around, lifted the cable tied to the elevator door that carried Romes, and began to pull, never saying a word.

As Barrow had suggested, the walk was set at an almost frantic pace. He was way out in front, both hands on his rifle, eyes darting from side to side. Sweat dripped down his brow, and he jumped at the slightest sounds. Something seemed to be bothering him. Frost thought he was frightened, as if something had spooked him on his hunting excursion. This wasn't the same man who had led them this far.

A crack like sharp thunder was heard in the distance, causing them all to flinch, save Bunt, who immediately pulled Frost behind him.

With worried eyes, Flynn glanced up at his father. "Was that another—"

"It was. Someone's in these woods. Someone without fear. Someone who's hunting."

"But I thought no one comes in here," Frost said.

"It was only a matter of time." Barrow looked back at them, his chest heaving with irregular breaths. "We can't sit here. We have to keep going."

But, less than an hour later, they heard another shot.

"They're getting closer," Barrow said, more to himself than anyone else. "We should get off the path. Find some cover. Fast."

"Who is it?" Frost asked, but Barrow didn't answer; he was pushing forward with even greater determination.

"Barrow," she tried again, raising her voice. "Who is it?"

He answered, but he didn't look back. "John Lord."

TWENTY-SEVEN

After plenty of other rejections, they eventually reached a location Barrow deemed acceptable for camp. There was a small body of water to the south, and in the center of a concrete circle that allowed for views from all directions stood a large sculpture. It was a statue that, without context, might appear quite odd. There was a group of large mushrooms, upon the largest of which sat a girl some years younger than Frost. She had long hair and wore a dress, her slender arms extended in either direction almost like a religious figure, her legs stretched out in front of her, a kitten in her lap, the center of her adoring focus. To her right was a rabbit in an overcoat, holding a watch in one hand, extended out toward the girl like an offering, and an umbrella in the other, which he used for balance while also gaining some leverage by standing on a rock. To her left was a man in a top hat, a man of great peculiarities—an oversized head and nose and collar and bow tie, a bony hand resting on his knee, a pained and mad smirk across his face revealing a set of gruesome teeth. The twinkle in his eye was menacing and it didn't bode well for the nibbling dormouse caught in his line of sight. Above the girl's shoulder, sitting in a severely gnarled and charred and leafless tree, watching over these strange proceedings, was a grinning cat ready to pounce.

Frost approached the sculpture, running her hand across the bronze. "I know this," she said to herself. "I've read this story."

Frost climbed upon the mushrooms, joining the girl frozen in time. She sat cross-legged, with her back in the crook of the statue's arm, practically embraced by the bronze. It now appeared as if the rabbit's watch was being offered to her instead. A gift of time.

When darkness came, Barrow didn't sleep like his son and Romes did. Instead, he patrolled the perimeter along with Bunt. He insisted that no fire be lit tonight, and this was unfortunate since the air grew even cooler, a sharp breeze cutting through the trees. But, every now and then, as if to justify Barrow's decision, a distant rumbling could be heard and even felt, like an ominous storm growing ever closer.

Unable to sleep, Frost watched the two sentries walk in circles for hours. At several intervals, Barrow climbed the statue, heading for the highest point. From there, gracelessly wobbling, he gazed out into the night for minutes on end. And yet, each time he jumped down, he did so with audible consternation.

Some time later, when Frost was finally growing tired, she saw Bunt come to a stop. At first she thought he detected something, but then quickly realized her father had returned.

"Don't worry," Barrow said to Alex. "I got it."

"You need sleep."

"I said I got it. Somebody needs to keep lookout."

"I'm sorry I—"

"Not your fault, guy."

Yet, when he said this, Frost could've sworn she heard a tone that meant just the opposite. Guiding her father by the hand, she brought him back to the sculpture, where they could talk.

"I'm sorry," her father said. "I'm sorry you had to experience that this morning. I'm sorry I couldn't help you."

"It's okay," she said in a flat voice, her eyes drifting to the slumbering Romes and Flynn, the two practically curled up together for warmth. It seemed her pet had taken to the boy, and she could hardly blame him.

"It's not. You don't know what that does to a father, the helplessness. What if she got to you? What if she . . ." He stopped. "Look at me, Frost. I'm a liability. I am damned. This body has betrayed me, just as my last one did. Just like Agatha's did to her."

Her eyes darted up at him, sharp and violent. "You can't fix it? A man like you?"

"What's that supposed to mean?"

Slowly, she lowered her head. "Nothing."

"Tell me. What's it supposed to mean?"

"Nothing. Just, you created that body, didn't you? You're responsible for all of them. Every robot that came down the line. Did you really have no idea the effect it would have on people?"

146

Alex's eyes flickered with the past, as if this was a question he had been asked before, and often. "I . . . I did. Kind of. Everyone did. But the people wanted it so badly that they ignored the possible repercussions. They willingly gave themselves over to the technology and everything that came with it. I merely supplied them what they wanted. But that didn't mean I didn't care. I was still trying to perfect it. Every day. I was always trying to improve my creations. And I think I did. I think I finally found the answer, but it's too late now. The Days of Bedlam destroyed everything."

"You lied to me." Her lips were trembling with anger. It was as if she had spent her entire life living with a stranger. She didn't have a father; she had an imposter. "You've kept everything from me. I don't even know who you are. Bunt is more real to me than you."

"Look, you have a right to be angry. But I didn't want you to know what it was I did."

"Why?" Frost shouted, the frustration finally billowing over.

Barrow's head snapped in their direction, and Flynn stirred in his sleep.

"I'm sorry," Alex whispered. "I'm sorry about everything. I just wanted to protect you. Then and now. It kills me to be trapped in here away from you. What kind of father am I that I can't even keep my own daughter safe? I . . . I shouldn't have let you get close to Agatha. I should have seen the signs. I take the blame. I do. All of it. I should have done something."

"Oh, and what would you have done?"

"I don't know. What do you mean?"

"Would you have done the same thing you did to Mom when she became an Eater?"

Alex looked taken aback. "What do you know about that?"

"Nothing," she snapped. "That's why I'm asking."

A hand went to his slowly shaking head. "Bunt told you. I almost forgot. It was like a dream when he said that. I can't keep things straight anymore. I'm losing sight of what's real and what isn't. I'm caught in this strange abyss."

"He didn't say what happened to her after she turned."

"No?"

"No." She kept her eyes locked on him, a judgmental stare.

"What do you want me to say, Frost?"

"For once I want you to tell me the truth. Stop with the lies. Mom . . . Did you . . . you know . . ."

"No," he said, with a shake of his digital head, his digital eyes closed. "No. I would never."

"Then . . . what?"

"Then nothing."

"Tell me. Please." She was desperate now.

"It won't help you. It won't make you feel better. What will you get from this?"

"I need to know."

"But why? You shouldn't dwell on these things. You have to let the past go."

"No! No. She's my mother. I have a right. Stop trying to protect me. You're horrible at it. I need to know. I—"

"I set her free, Frost. Okay? I set her out into the world."

The truth stabbed her like a knife. Everything Frost had always feared the most—the loneliness, complete isolation and abandonment—her mother experienced it all.

"Alone. You sent her out alone." She lowered her gaze and fidgeted with her hands, until finally squeezing them together so hard she felt as if she were going to snap her wrists. A question popped into her head. It was one of those decisions—she knew it would hurt, but she had to know. "Did she fight it?"

"I don't want to talk about this anymore."

"You owe me."

"And why do I owe you, Frost? Huh? Because I care about you? Because I love you? Why do I owe you? Can you explain that?"

"Because you left me with no one! Like you did to her!"

"I'm here! Me! I'm standing here as your father, Frost! I'm here for you!"

"You're not! I'm talking to my father's ghost!"

They both fell silent. With every inch of her body trembling, Frost stood up and, back to her father, leaned her head against the bronze rabbit. "You come and go like a memory."

Alex's arm twitched, rising mere inches. It was an effort to reach out and touch his daughter, a gesture she would never feel. "I wanted to help your mother more than anything. You have to know that. I held out as long as possible. Days. She had eaten my finger, so I thought that would buy me some time. But time for what? I didn't know what to do. Once they taste flesh it's too late."

"Why isn't . . . why isn't it Mom I'm talking to right now?"

"Inside Bunt, you mean."

"Yes."

"Your mother knew my work inside and out. She didn't always believe in it, but she supported me every step of the way. She saw the bigger picture, the potential. She knew what I could do for her. I wanted to make preparations for years, just in case. I laid it all out for her. I offered her immortality. But she made me promise never to do such a thing. She begged me. She said she'd rather die than spend one minute inside a robot. She always was the yin to my yang, your mother. Any time I got too lost in my work, she always broke through; she showed me the other side, the issues I might have ignored. She convinced me to reevaluate my choices. It wasn't about money or power or fame. She made me aware of the world and how I could help. She made me a better scientist, a better man. I loved her too much to disobey her, Frost. It would have been torture for her, being inside a machine. I mean, it's torture for me and I wanted this.

"So, fighting against my every urge, I upheld your mother's wishes. And after she took my finger it was only a matter of time before she grew hungry again. I saw the fight in her. She raged against these new instincts. She fought them with everything she had. She fought for you, for one more day with you. And all I could do was sit there and watch. Helpless to save my own wife. I saw how badly she wanted to rip me apart, but she didn't. She could have, but she didn't. I watched her tear her tongue out instead. And that's when I knew it was hopeless. That's when I knew she was gone. I . . . I had Bunt carry her down the stairs, kicking and biting. He chained her to the wall, and then I had him go back upstairs. With you sleeping in my arms, I unlocked the chain and saw her off. I saw her run out into the world, and it broke my heart. It's only fitting that I no longer have one."

Frost didn't know what to do—what to say or how to react. She had the truth and now it would sit within her, ticking like a bomb.

Although she couldn't feel her body, she somehow managed to turn away from her father and huddle with Romes beside the statue. The tears flowed until she slept.

TWENTY-EIGHT

As Frost woke, she leaned over, her arm blindly searching for Romes, whom she must have drifted away from sometime in the middle of the night. With her eyes still closed, she patted the elevator door, feeling nothing but cold steel. Finally, raising her head, her vision still blurry, her head still groggy, she looked about for her darling pet. To her horror, he was nowhere near the door.

Frost jumped to her feet, her heart racing, her head instantly clear. She saw Bunt and Barrow continuing their patrol while Flynn was preparing a fire to cook a few more squirrels he and his father must have caught in the early morning. But no one was panicking, no one was wondering where the missing broot was.

Adrenaline pulsing, Frost was about to call out, about to scream, when, out of the corner of her eye, she caught sight of something. To the south, knee-deep in the small body of water, frolicking as much as he was able to, was Romes.

It was astonishing. There he was softly splashing around, snapping at whatever dwelled beneath the surface, licking the water, shaking himself dry. Although he still limped, although he was still thin and weak and slow, there was life in him yet.

It was the most beautiful sight Frost had seen in a long time. Her heart swelled with joy; there was a warm lump in her throat and the tips of her fingers tingled. She turned around, wondering why nobody else was making a big deal of this. Apparently, Flynn was busy attempting to get the fire going, and, due to his inefficiency, Barrow was forced to help him out, mumbling and cursing all the while. Bunt, meanwhile, was facing north, northwest, his constant patrolling finally having ceased. Something had caught his attention. After a prolonged moment, he turned around, addressing the group.

"*Broots,*" he said. "*A number of them. They are running.*"

Barrow stood up, the logs falling from his hands. "Oh no. Oh no no no no no."

"What?" Flynn said. "What?"

"They're not running. They're fleeing." As he spun around, his mouth hung open as if silently screaming. And then a shot was fired, and it was Romes who cried out.

The broot collapsed in the water. He flailed and squealed, blood floating along the water's surface in bright globules.

"Romes!" Frost shrieked.

And, hearing her, his cherished master in his sights, Romes desperately tried to crawl to land, to crawl to her. But he didn't make it out of the water. From somewhere within the Zone, he was shot again.

"Lord!" Barrow screamed, gathering up his weapons. "Run! Get out of here! The Mad Leader comes for us!"

Barrow lifted his son up by the shirt and practically tossed him ahead. Flynn whirled around and called for Frost, trying to escape his father's grasp, but Barrow yanked him ahead, leaving their supplies behind. Bunt, meanwhile, approached Frost, his hand extended.

"Come," he said. *"We must go."*

"No," Frost told him, weeping. "Not without Romes."

Bunt didn't question her. He didn't say it was pointless; he didn't even hesitate. He ran to the broot, lifted him up, and placed him on the elevator door as another gunshot was fired, the bullet ricocheting off the robot's shoulder.

Frost followed blindly, Barrow and Flynn far ahead leading the way. They heard the rumbling of some vehicle, but they couldn't spot it; it seemed to be all around them, although Bunt said it was coming from the south.

They were on what was once a major road, the dotted white lines still somewhat visible, the wilderness slow to close in. Frost was lagging behind and Bunt told her to jump on the elevator door with Romes. The ride was bumpy and the broot was breathing heavily, tears in his panicked eyes. Frost tried locating his wounds, and when she did, she found something sticking out of them. Darts. They weren't bullets, but darts. She wondered if it was poison. Tranquilizers? It was unclear. However, she did notice a blinking chip on the end of both of them. Closing her eyes, she pulled the darts free and tossed them onto the road.

Through the surrounding trees, gunshots were being fired relentlessly. These, Frost quickly realized, were the real thing. Whoever these people were, they were now trying to kill.

It seemed to Frost that Barrow might have a plan, that perhaps he had a place where they might hide until the threat passed. But, regardless, he never looked back. For all he knew, Frost, Bunt, even his own son were already captured or gunned down.

Out of nowhere, a vehicle raced out onto the road, grinding to a halt and blocking their path. It was a massive black truck, the rear of which was concealed with a dark tarp. It was the first fully functioning vehicle Frost had ever come across. It once might have been a military truck, some kind of transport vehicle, but there was clearly a lot of work put into converting it and getting it running. There was something soldered onto the front, a battering ram mixed with a type of plow. There was a speaker on top of the cabin and from here came a distorted voice.

"Mr. Barrow," it said. "We are so disappointed. Why do you run from us, old friend?"

Defeated, Barrow glanced down at the ground. "Grash. I . . . I didn't know it was you."

"And who else would be out here, Mr. Barrow?"

"No one," he mumbled.

"Speak up, you disease."

"No one."

"And why, Mr. Barrow, are you armed? Do you dare defy the Good John Lord? Drop your weapons. All of you. Now. You too, Flynny boy."

Barrow glanced at his son, who was visibly trembling, and nodded. Simultaneously, their guns hit the ground.

"All of them."

Barrow and Flynn dug through their coats, unloading every weapon they had clinging to their bodies.

"Were you going back on your promise?" Grash went on. "Or did you simply forget to bring this girl to us, as was our arrangement?"

Frost glared at Barrow. Her chest heaved and her mind crashed. "What is he saying?"

But Barrow refused to look at her. All he managed to mumble was, "You don't understand." To whom he was directing this was not clear.

"Don't let me discover you have been neglecting our agreement, Barrow. I was more than generous in handing over my property to you. Do I need to take Flynn back?"

"No! No. I was . . . I was bringing her to you . . . I just . . . I . . . I didn't realize . . ."

"It doesn't matter what you realize. We'll take her off your hands now. As well as that broot."

Six armed men in black coats and hats jumped out of the vehicle. Three headed in Frost's direction, the other three toward Romes. Bunt, his sword drawn, started charging. One of the men calmly raised a gun, shooting the robot with a type of laser, and the result was almost as if Alex had returned. Bunt was paralyzed—now but one more statue of the Zone. He was awake, but he was useless.

"The robot doesn't know how to play yet. Shut him down," the voice from the truck said. "Permanently."

"Get away from him!" Frost screamed. She made an attempt to reach Bunt, but she was quickly subdued—two of the men grabbed her by the arms and the third pointed his gun at the center of her head. "Flynn! Barrow! Do something! Don't let them touch my dad!"

As the men moved forward toward Bunt, Barrow's eyes lit up. "He's Alex Simmelfore!" he blurted out.

The men froze, glancing back and forth at one another. "Is he serious?" one asked.

"Repeat yourself, Mr. Barrow," Grash said from within the truck, a tinge of excitement in his voice. "What did you say?"

"The robot . . . Alex Simmelfore lives inside it."

Stunned, the men turned back to their boss, looking for directives.

"And the girl?" Grash asked.

"She's . . . she's his daughter."

Grash's voice spread through the Zone. "Take them both. Now!"

"No!" Frost shouted as two men headed for Bunt and a third came for her, seizing her arm. "No! Flynn!"

Flynn charged at the man grabbing Frost. He ran as fast as a broot and, with his broad shoulder, rammed his target square in the chest. The man flew backward three feet to the ground, slamming his head. "Don't you touch her!" Flynn jumped atop him, fist pulled back. But that's when a gun was placed at his temple.

"Don't!" Barrow screamed, his hands outstretched. "Not my boy!" He turned toward the truck, toward Grash. "Don't kill him! Please don't kill him!"

"But he's asking to be shot, Barrow. Perhaps I should just grant him his wish."

"It was a mistake! He wasn't thinking!"

"Well, you best start thinking for him. Any further interference and you'll be wearing his blood, Barrow. And he, yours."

Grash called for the man to holster his weapon. He did so and picked up Frost instead, carrying her flailing body toward the truck. Flynn, meanwhile, stood wearily and stared down his father.

"Why are you letting them do this? You know who Grash is. You know what he did to me. How could you?"

"I'm keeping you safe. That's what's important. Now keep quiet and let them do what they must."

The man inspecting Romes raised his voice toward the truck. "This broot is in bad shape. It won't last long. It's worthless to us."

"Leave it, then," Grash ordered. "A gift for Barrow's continuous cooperation."

As Frost was being loaded onto the back of the truck, she looked out at her beloved pet fading to black upon the elevator door. In that moment, she understood what Flynn told her about fearing his heart had disintegrated. Right now, hers was crumbling into dust. "Romes! Noooo! Romes! Let me go!

Put me down! I have to save him! I have to save him! Rooooooomes!"

But, with Frost and Bunt aboard and Barrow and Flynn stepping aside with their heads bowed in shame and Romes at their feet, the door was shut and the truck drove off to the kingdom of the Good John Lord.

PART THREE
JOHN LORD
COUNTRY

TWENTY-NINE

Flynn watched the truck drive off, dark smoke billowing from its exhaust, matching the color of the landscape. The vehicle sputtered and jerked and grinded, but there it was, slowly rolling away from them like a tank, Frost lost somewhere in the belly of the beast, frightened, confused, distraught. Flynn knew she was the only truly hopeful thing in his world, and now she was going to be beaten and shaped into something ugly and irredeemable like himself. The moment she was gone, what little light he had found in the world had been snuffed out.

His frustration mounting, Flynn turned to his father once again. "You let them go. You didn't even put up a fight."

"They would have killed me, Flynn. They wouldn't have thought twice. And they would have taken you. Again."

"You know what's going to happen to them. You know what John Lord's going to do." He was trembling so hard with rage he could feel his bones rattle. It was an emotion that haunted him like an old ghost. He had thought it left, but now it was coming back even stronger.

"There was nothing we could have done."

"You let them take her like you let them take me!"

Barrow's eyes shot up shimmering pain. "I came back for you."

"After how long?"

"I . . . I . . ."

"Four years!"

"Flynn, please. I couldn't just go marching in there shooting at everybody. It would've been suicide. Then I would've been dead and you would've been a slave for life."

Flynn ran at his father and grabbed him by the collar. His eyes bulged, his teeth were bared, spit flew from his mouth. "They tortured me! They tortured me!"

Barrow, his eyes welling up at the sight of his son's pain, had to break free and turn away. "I know. I know. I'm sorry." Bent over, he was choking on his words.

They fell silent, Flynn's exclamation lingering in the air like the truck's fumes. When he finally spoke again, his voice was hoarse. "How exactly did you get me back? It didn't happen like you said it did, did it? It wasn't some stealth mission where you were picking people off one by one. You didn't spend years plotting this elaborate plan."

"It started that way. It did. I tried. I failed. I barely escaped with my life. I had to try something else."

Flynn's breath caught in his chest as dangerous thoughts crept out from the dark places in his mind. "What did you say to them, Dad? What kind of a deal did you make with Grash? He talked about an arrangement."

Barrow was wiping his eyes and spitting thick globs of

mucus. "What does it matter? I got you back, didn't I? Who cares the cost?"

"I care! I'm sure Frost cares right now, too! You were bringing her to them, weren't you?"

"No."

"Don't lie to me," Flynn said in a low voice he barely recognized as his own.

"I wasn't."

Eyes shut, Flynn shook his head, fighting back the tears he didn't want his father to see. "You're no hero. You never were. You promised her to them, didn't you?"

Silence.

"Tell me!"

Barrow threw his hands up. "I promised them whoever I found, Flynn. In the Zone, in the Outskirts, wherever. How else was I going to get you back? Huh? They're an army. A city. I'm one person. So, what was I supposed to do? Shoot them up? They want people, healthy people. To work, to serve. By giving you up . . ." He shook his head, the words difficult to release. "By giving up one they received many."

Flynn's throat tightened. Everything tightened. "How many have you brought them?"

"I don't know."

"How many?"

"What do you want me to say? I don't know. Dozens."

Flynn felt as if he was going to pass out. "All those people we came across . . . those people you always said left early in the morning because it was too dangerous to travel in groups . . . You took them to John Lord."

"I . . . I had to."

"They were women and children."

"Flynn, if I didn't obey, Grash would have come back for you. He threatened things, horrible things. You wouldn't have survived."

"Is my life worth any more than theirs?"

"Yes. Yes, to me it is."

"It's not." And he believed this. His life was worth nothing. All those people, any one of them could have amounted to something far greater than he. Especially Frost. "All Frost wanted to do was save her pet. She was risking her own life to save a broot's. Her life is worth ten of mine. And you just turned her over to them."

"I didn't want to. I wasn't going to bring her to them. I was going to help her. I swear. I saw the hope she pulled out in you. That's something I was never able to do. Never. I wanted it to stay. I was going to see her out of the Zone, Flynn, and us with her. I was going to lead her through John Lord's territory and to the Battery. I swear."

"I don't believe you."

"You don't have to. That's your right."

Wiping at his eyes, Barrow turned away and Flynn sadly approached Romes. He dropped to his knees and comforted the slumbering broot. Tearing off bits of his clothes, he began wrapping the animal's wounds.

"What are you doing?" Barrow asked, glancing back over his shoulder.

"We have to help him."

"Why? What does it matter now?"

"Because we're going to have him waiting when we rescue Frost."

THIRTY

Flanked by her captors, Frost sat on a metal bench in the back of the truck, Bunt across from her, frozen and vacant. As the vehicle rumbled along, she leaned forward, her eyes drifting toward the front where two cages were kept, one rattling, one still. Behind the bars of the silent one was a group of five broots, all of them knocked out cold and lying limp upon one another, their breathing slightly visible. In the other cage, the one where all the noise was coming from, were three Eaters.

The cannibals were crashing into the metal, their mangled hands reaching out for fresh meat, their grotesque sounds filling the truck like animals on their way to the slaughterhouse. An overwhelming stench wafted through the thick air, most likely coming from the open sores and wounds of the Eaters, their gangrenous limbs, their rotting flesh. The armed guards tried to appear unfazed by all this, but it was quite clear to Frost that they were terrified to be so close. Their bodies never relaxed and they all leaned away from the cages, their weight pressed toward the rear in case the truck were to stop short. Every now and then, one was brave enough to slam the butt of a gun into the cage, but this only riled the Eaters even more. Some tried to alleviate their fear through jokes and taunts. Some spat on the bodies; some flicked their cigarettes.

Frost's ache for Romes felt like an anvil upon her chest. She imagined him lying there on the cold steel door, alone, confused, scared. Dying. Flynn might have wanted to stay with him, perhaps care for him and take him as his own, but Barrow would never allow it. He would leave the broot to be picked apart by his own kind. Frost should never have followed him so blindly. She should have trusted her instincts. Romes shouldn't be the one suffering; it should be Barrow. All she wanted to do was get to the Battery; all she wanted was to have Romes in her life a little bit longer. And now he was gone. She didn't even get to say good-bye.

In the dark of the truck, she quietly wept for the pet she lost, the one real friend she'd ever had.

They drove for some time, but as there were no windows, Frost wasn't sure where exactly they were headed—north, south, east, west. Not that it really mattered to her at this moment; the Battery was as far away now as it would ever be. The ride was a bumpy one and seemed to go on for much longer than expected. Every now and then there were loud noises coming from outside, things banging against the truck, but it was impossible to know the cause, and for this she was thankful.

Eventually, the truck stopped, and, after a moment, the back door opened, the dreary light creeping in. A man was standing there, sizing up the load. Frost made sure to mark his face, as the figure was most clearly Grash. He was a hideous specimen, his head badly misshapen, the minuscule amounts of hair revealing every hill and valley of the skull. The creases in his skin were deep, like gashes or dried-up riverbeds, giving him the appearance of a man much older than he probably was. Like brickwork, the creases descended from the forehead down past the bulbous, off-center nose. One eye was permanently closed—lost in thick folds—the other was a precious blue orb of another face and time. His front teeth were oversized and gapped and hanging well over his bottom lip. His white beard, oddly enough, was perfectly kept. He was lean—the body of a far younger man—and yet there was something about his presence that said he had seen much and nothing fazed him anymore. "The Eaters. Let's go," he said, slapping the side of the vehicle with the palm of his hand.

As the men got up and tended to the Eaters, poking at them with their knives, Frost peeked outside, past Grash, who was now puffing away on a cigarette, and she spotted something she had never seen on any map or read about in any book or was ever told about by her father. There, cutting through the city like a guillotine, was a massive wall. It must have stood twenty feet high and who knew how thick. There was no pattern to it, a mad scientist's concoction—all random pieces stuck together to form one giant whole.

The Eaters' cage was shoved out of the truck by four of the men—a handless arm nearly striking Frost's face as it passed. Once outside, they placed the cage against a large rusting metal door in the wall. Someone climbed atop it, his hand on the gate, waiting to pull it up. Just below a red mark—something like a star—a panel was opened and a button pressed. Then, screeching on its hinges like a wounded broot, the door swung, and the Eaters were let out of their cage. Free, they ran forward, and, behind them, the door was quickly closed, leaving the cannibals to their own devices on the opposite side of the wall.

On Grash's orders, the men jumped back in the truck and took off once again.

"What's out there?" Frost asked, her voice flat. "What's on the other side of that wall?"

"Nothing for an itty-bitty wittle girl."

Everyone laughed at this but Frost. She just continued to glare at the man. They were all vile enough for her to wish to never see another male for as long as she lived. All but one.

Flynn wasn't like them, she told herself, not in the slightest. Was he? The more she thought about this, the more she grew unsettled. Then, hoping against her diminishing hope, she prayed that he hadn't been aware of Barrow's plan. The horrors she'd witnessed over the past few days had erased so many of her dreams, but she knew she wouldn't be able to handle that kind of betrayal. She couldn't believe that the look she'd seen in Flynn's eyes had been a lie.

No, he wasn't part of Barrow's plan, she finally decided as she grabbed the rose that was still tucked behind her ear. Flynn would have helped her to the very end. She'd heard the fear and pain in his voice as he called her name. Frost closed her eyes and tried to remember what it'd felt like to hold Flynn's hand.

When the cruel laughter finally ceased, the man cleared his throat and spoke with sincerity.

"We've been rounding up the Eaters, been doing it for some

time now. Each one we find ends up on the other side of the wall. The Wasteland."

"If that's the Wasteland, then what are we in?" Frost asked wearily.

Everyone laughed again, throwing their heads far back. However, seconds later, when they realized she wasn't trying to be funny, they slowly stopped, their chuckles gradually turning into coughs and phlegm.

"You're in John Lord country, sweetheart."

Frost was silent a moment. "Why don't you just kill them, the Eaters?" she asked.

The men, their eyes blank, looked back and forth at one another. Not one responded and Frost closed her eyes. They either weren't saying or they didn't know.

THIRTY-ONE

Nearly an hour later, when the truck stopped a second time, instead of the Eaters being unloaded, it was the broots.

In the last few minutes of the ride, the animals were just waking up. In their haze, they attempted to stand, their legs unsteady and their eyes glazed over, although their jaws were instantly snapping at the bodies surrounding the cage, guttural sounds caught in their throats like the rumblings of engines. Frost thought how lost Romes would be among these broots. He wasn't like them, not in the least. He knew what it was like to be human; he was more human than Bunt, possibly even more than her own father.

With a dispiriting turn of her stomach, the rear of the truck opened, and she watched as the cage of broots was ushered past and into the street. It was clear this was a part of the city she had never seen. It was more orderly than what she was used to seeing from the thirty-second floor of her home. This street was clean and rebuilt; it almost looked like it was a replica of the past. The building that the truck was idling in front of was in nearly pristine condition. There were sounds coming from it, as if it were reborn and functioning, growing louder by the moment. It pulsed with raging life. Had she traveled back in time? What was this place?

As she leaned forward, she could see past the open double doors. Inside, encompassing what seemed to be the entire floor, was a giant holding pen of some kind. Metal fences divided the massive space in scores of segments, and she could make out movement within each of them, lots and lots of movement in the shadows, as if everything was one, the floor an ocean of strong currents. With the doors open, the sounds were disturbingly loud and penetrating now. There must have been hundreds of broots packed inside the building.

As Grash conversed on the front steps with a black man who had a severe hunch and yellow blood on his hands, the cage door was lifted and the broots were guided inside the pen with whips and lasers. The animals squealed and growled, but, grudgingly, they went where they were directed. Then the doors were closed, and the sounds were muffled, but they still haunted.

As the truck pulled away, the man sitting across from Frost acknowledged her repulsed curiosity.

"You want to know what we do with them, too, don't you?" he said.

Frost nodded, although, unlike with the Eaters being released into the Wasteland, she was afraid she already knew the answer.

"Well, we need to eat. We need to feed our people. And the Good John Lord has found a way to deliver. He never ceases to bless his followers with miracles. Broot is just the latest example.

There's farming to be done, sure, but that doesn't produce enough—not in this environment. And with the weather getting colder recently, things are worse than ever. Besides, don't all humans crave meat?" He tapped his gun. "These darts we shoot the broots with, it speeds up their reproduction. This way we can consume as much as we want and still have more waiting for us. Have you ever had broot? I'm sure you have. Delicious."

Frost folded her arms and turned her head.

The man said it again. "Delicious. Succulent. My mouth's watering just thinking about it."

"Where's the next stop?" Frost asked. "Where are you taking me?"

"You? Come now. Alex Simmelfore is your father; you know where you're going."

Frost swallowed hard. "Where?"

"You're off to see the Good John Lord."

THIRTY-TWO

Flynn and Barrow were standing over Romes. Flynn had bandaged him up the best he could, thankful that Romes was passed out the entire time—he knew he wasn't trusted by the broot the way Frost was; most likely, it would not have hesitated to bite his hand clean off. Not that that would have stopped Flynn from administering aid. He owed it to Frost to care for the broot. He refused to fail Romes as he had failed Frost. The image of her being driven off in that truck was enough to make his chest collapse and his stomach reel with guilt and fury. He had always sworn he was better than his father, that if he had someone he cared for in his life, nothing would ever hurt them. But that turned out to be fantasy. He was just as weak as his father after all. Standing there in the middle of the Zone, helplessness ate at him like an Eater.

Barrow rubbed his stubbly chin, his eyes, too, locked on the beast. "What now?"

"We go after them."

"We need a plan, Flynn," Barrow said with a sigh. "You don't just go running in there blind."

"You don't think I know that?"

"So then, what do you have in mind, hero?"

"I'll tell you one thing: It won't take me four years to come up with something."

Barrow shot a glance at his son, who didn't return the gaze. With a weak shrug, he said, "All I know is how to get us safely into the territory; after that, I'm well short of ideas."

Flynn had to admit he was in the same predicament; even after spending years among John Lord's people, he hadn't the slightest notion of how to spring somebody out—he had tried escaping several times, but that was always fruitless and he was punished for it quite severely, dark experiences that still haunted him nightly. Every time he closed his eyes he saw Grash standing over him, a warped grin on his vile face, a weapon of torture in his hand. Just hearing his voice again nearly sent Flynn running. The anxiety that washed over him in those moments, the terror, the disgust, it was nearly unbearable. And Grash was just one of many. John Lord presided over a city filled with countless Grashes. Flynn knew that in all likelihood he and his father wouldn't make it out alive and neither would Frost. Their chances were beyond slim.

"You don't have to come, you know," he told his father.

"What are you talking about? Of course I'm coming."

"I don't need your protection."

"I know that. I'd go even if you weren't my son."

"Why? You never cared before. What's changed?"

Barrow stuck his hands in his pockets and took a deep breath. "I don't know. It's just something we have to do. Something I have to do." He spat on the ground and rubbed the phlegm into the earth with the tip of his boot. "The moment they grabbed her I knew I'd have to go in there to get her back. I had no choice." He turned his head and watched his son cock an eye in his direction. "Maybe I need the redemption. Who knows."

Flynn looked away. "Maybe."

"Yeah, maybe."

"And you know I'm not leaving the broot behind."

"Of course."

"We'll be risking our lives."

"We do that every day."

Flynn took a look around the Zone. This had been his home, the only place he had ever felt somewhat safe; he wasn't looking forward to leaving it again, not to go back into John Lord country, the very place he swore he would never set foot in again. Unless it was to blow it sky-high.

"Okay. So, how do we get in there?"

THIRTY-THREE

Several hours later, with no reason to head south any longer, Flynn and Barrow found themselves at the eastern edge of the Zone, Romes slumbering behind them on the elevator door, beside their bags of weapons and supplies. Barrow was once again armed to the teeth, and Flynn held a rusted, hollowed-out robot skull in his hands.

"We're almost out," Barrow said. "Quick. Before we're seen, put it on."

Flynn weighed the robotic head in his hands. It was heavy and cold to the touch. Similar to Bunt, but clearly an older model, third generation—many of John Lord's robots were of this variety. He slipped it over his head, feeling the weight of the steel dig into his sloped shoulders, the remaining metal shards of its discarded insides cutting away at his head like thorns. And yet his father was right to do this. Everyone who was ever brought into John Lord's territory wore one of these. It was a way to shame them, putting each person on par with a robot. It humbled them; it made them something less than human. It made them subservient.

As the darkness of the mask enveloped him, he instantly began to sweat, his hands shook, his throat tightened. With his eyes closed, Flynn was struck by a flashback of when he first wore one. It was spiked on his head by some cruel man who proceeded to whip him and kick him in his back. Along the streets people threw garbage at him, cursed him, and robots laughed as if this wasn't an indictment of who they were. The fear, the confusion, the isolation behind that mask all came rushing back. His chest tightened, his throat dried, and, very quickly, he began to hyperventilate.

"Can you see?" his father asked, his voice faint and muffled.

Right now few sounds could penetrate the suffocating swirl of terror currently taking place in his head. In those brief moments he relived every step of his long walk into the city center where, along with three other young boys, he was led onto a platform in a public square surrounded by a mass of people. Minutes later, he was auctioned off to the highest bidder—Grash. Flynn still recalled the very first words that horrible man ever said to him: "I'm gonna have lots of fun with you." And he did. Nearly every single thing he did to Flynn he did with a searing laugh.

"Flynn, can you see?" Barrow asked a little bit louder.

Flynn took a deep breath and opened his damp eyes. From out of the thin glass of the face, he could see, but not great. Everything was narrowed and gray, a land even darker than it already was. He wasn't about to complain, though; he knew what was needed. For Frost he would suffer this and far more. Instead, he simply nodded.

"Now, when we go out there, I'm going to have to treat you differently, you know that."

"I know," he answered, his voice muted, the gloom and fear disguised by the metal.

Barrow handed over the reins to the elevator door. He had pulled it this far, but if their plan was to work, he could pull it no farther.

Flynn grabbed the cable, resting it over his shoulder.

"It's heavy," Barrow said. "Are you sure you can manage?"

"I can," he said with a nod.

"Are you ready?"

A hard swallow. "Ready."

"I love you, Flynn."

Flynn looked back at his father. Again, he nodded.

THIRTY-FOUR

Bunt had come to, but his body remained unresponsive—shoulders slumped as if in defeat, legs splayed awkwardly, one stretching far out into the aisle, one tucked back and twisted under the bench, ankle turned. His arms dangled at his sides, the weight pulling severely at his chest, each finger limp and nearly brushing the floor of the truck like thick bristles of a broom. His head was tilted down as well, but the faint violet glow of his eyes gazed upward at Frost. He looked sad and weary, almost human. It was the first time Frost thought the world might have finally gotten the best of him.

Sitting across from her, Bunt asked, *"Are you okay?"*

"I'm okay. How are you?"

Really, it was a foolish thing to ask, and she knew that. Robots didn't have emotions or feelings, and she was just projecting her own onto him. He wasn't tired, he wasn't disillusioned; he just was.

"I can't move. I've failed you."

It was odd; he almost sounded sorry.

"The effects of the scrambler are beginning to wear off," one of the guards said to him, a tinge of disgust in his voice. "Your movement will return soon enough, robot. But if you try anything, you can expect more of the same. Only next time you may never reboot again. Best get Simmelfore awake. It's time for him to meet our good leader."

Bunt hadn't turned in the man's direction; he appeared ready for a long sleep. *"We have no desire to see John Lord."*

"You desire nothing, robot. Remember that. I don't know what's come over your ilk, but I don't like it. Know your place. You're not human. Never will be. You robots can try as hard as you like, but it'll never happen. One of these days the Good John Lord is going to decide to get rid of your kind once and for all. As soon as you no longer serve his purpose. But you, you're different. You see, regardless of whether it suited you or not, the Good John Lord will be most interested in seeing you. Or at least the man inhabiting your shell."

"Alex Simmelfore doesn't inhabit my shell. He is lost in it. Wandering. There is something wrong with me."

Frost, her skin practically buzzing, stared at Bunt, whose chin still rested against his chest. There was something wrong indeed.

Minutes later, the truck came to its final stop. Frost listened as the two men riding up front walked toward the back and opened the door, allowing the light to come rushing in, attacking Frost's eyes with great violence.

Through her squint and past her raised hand, she could just make out Grash impatiently waiting for her to exit. After a moment or two in which he might have gained another deep crease in his brow, he sighed and extended his hand in an offer to help her down. Frost, however, promptly rejected this offer and jumped to the street, landing hard on Grash's toes, her legs vibrating upon harsh contact.

"That will be the last of your defiance, girl," Grash said through a grimace as he grabbed her by the hair, pulling her close. Their noses nearly touched, his breath warm and rank. As he talked, spittle coated Frost's face like a light rain. "You will soon learn just where you are, and you will behave accordingly. Such hospitality is quite rare around here, I assure you. If it were up to me, you'd be on the auction block by now. Bet you'd sell for a nice little sum." He snapped his fingers at the men still sitting in the back of the truck. "What are you doing? Get on your feet. The robot. Now."

As the men hopped up, grabbing Bunt from all sides, Grash released his grip on Frost's hair and addressed her once more. "It's a blessing, finding you and that bot. Delivering your father is going to bring me even greater riches," he said. "The Good John Lord has been looking for someone like your daddy for a long time now. The fact that it's actually Alex Simmelfore makes it all the more lucrative for me."

Bunt was set down beside Frost, his knees buckling. The men threw Bunt's arms around their shoulders, supporting his great weight, while straining to stand themselves.

Towering before Frost was a building of such beauty, she couldn't believe it was part of this world. It looked twice removed, both alien and ancient. Like a fortress it stood beyond an iron spiked gate that ran around the entire property, six feet tall and imposing. Frost peered past these black bars and into the gorgeous yard. There were half a dozen people maintaining the luscious gardens with shovels and rakes and shears. There were fruit trees and green grass and flowers of all kinds, though none, Frost believed, were as pretty as hers. Bushes were carefully shaped and impressive statues were spread throughout; at points, the grounds looked like something out of a painting. Several dogs—at least she thought they were dogs—ran about and there was even a fountain in the middle of it all from which the canines quenched their thirst. For a moment, Frost believed she had traveled into one of her books. The place was fantasy come to life.

Past the garden, the grand building loomed. It was a mansion of windows, a gluttony of extravagance in a world with little. Columns lined the door, as well as the oversized windows on the second and third floors. At the very top, five stories up among the gargoyles and stone faces of grinning, evil men, was a balcony with armed robots patrolling it from end to end. Behind the sprawling ivy, the stone was strong, revealing hardly any cracks or weathering like the rest of the city.

Finally, out of the large double doors strutted a robot. The men standing guard outside the truck nudged each other alert, mumbling the name Tryn as they straightened their stances.

The robot looked nearly identical to Bunt, but with the curves of a female. She walked with great determination, pointing at Frost, never once slowing down. *"Shouldn't the girl be among the workers? We need more hands."* Somehow, her voice was harsher than Bunt's. It grated, like her voice box was damaged.

When Tryn neared, Grash leaned into her, whispering an

explanation. He, too, appeared meek in her presence, pressing his issue gently but with enthusiasm. When he was finished, the robot nodded. *"Inside. Now."* And she turned around, heading back into the mansion, waving her hand behind her for the prisoners to follow.

THIRTY-FIVE

With Bunt practically being dragged beside her, Frost followed Tryn into the mansion. Walking through the doorway gave her the impression of being swallowed. It was a whale of a home, one she desperately wished she could have viewed under better circumstances. The main hall was impressive, all marble and gold, the walls covered with ornate molding and artworks, many of them famous pieces Frost had glimpsed in books. The ceiling was vaulted, archways guiding their path—and every dozen feet or so hung another giant chandelier. There were large tapestries and more statues, gods and goddesses, abstracts and busts. And at the end of the hall was a grand staircase—two sets of curved steps hugging the swollen walls, each one carpeted with an intricate design, coming together at the top where a solitary statue stood, a goliath of a sculpture, a muscular man with his naked back arched, his eyes wide with a certain kind of terror, hands pulling at his hair, every feature contorted across his face.

But they didn't climb to the second level. Instead, they were guided between the sets of stairs and toward a dark wood door that stood directly in line with the hall. It was an ancient door, covered with carvings of religious imagery, and must have been torn from some church and transported here shortly after the chaos had descended.

Tryn approached the door, hesitated a moment, and turned around. If a robot could register fear, she was currently experiencing it. She told them to wait, that she would be back shortly.

As the door opened, Tryn stepped inside and was immediately enveloped by darkness.

Frost thought she heard a very faint sound, a tinkling—something like music. But as the door closed, the notes were lost and a bit of Frost's heart was crushed by the loss.

"I've never been this close to him," one of the guards whispered to another, his hands slightly trembling. "I can't believe this. Do you think we'll—"

"Quiet, man," the other said. "Act normal and do your job. You want to be sent to the slums? He hears everything."

"I just want to see him. Just once."

"If you haven't seen him, how do you know he exists?"

The men nearly dropped Bunt. "That's blasphemy," one said through clenched teeth. "How dare you!"

"How do we know that human is inside you?" the other asked.

"You don't. But you believe."

"But that doesn't make it so, now does it?"

Bunt lifted his head so that they could lock eyes. *"Exactly."*

"What are you getting at, robot?"

"I think you know."

Frost sensed the mounting tension and knew she had to

interrupt it before it escalated into something dangerous. She pointed to the sculpture at the top of the stairs. "Who is that?"

With reverent eyes, the men looked up to the second level. "The rumor is that it's an ancestor of the Good John Lord. Yet another man well before his time. There are said to be great similarities between the two of them. The leadership, the genius, the strength. Each a great man driven by something bigger than himself. The sculpture is supposed to capture the constant torment he experienced trying to lead a populace that was blind to his greatness. He wanted much for them, but they were ill prepared, savages next to his superiority. It was a great strain on him, to lead such unworthy people."

The men fell quiet, most likely contemplating and basking in the importance of their leader and his history, which sounded like something they were taught to memorize. They appeared to be moments away from dropping to their knees and bowing.

"*You are wrong,*" Bunt said, breaking the silence. "*The sculpture is a depiction of a lunatic. A man who lost his mind.*"

This time the men let Bunt crash to the floor. One of them, the larger one, reared back and kicked him in the head. The clang echoed through the hall like a church bell. Seeing what his partner did, the other joined in. The kicks came fast and furious, Bunt's body limply absorbing the blows. Their boot heels came down on his face in an attempt to smash it. Frost, screaming for them to stop, wasn't sure how far the guards would take it and if they would soon turn on her, too. Luckily, that was when Tryn emerged.

"What are you doing?" she cried in her strange voice.

The men quickly backed away, apologizing profusely.

"Do you have any idea who is in there? He is worth more than both your lives combined. He is worth more than a hundred of you. A thousand."

"How . . . how do we know he is really in there? We just have his word."

Tryn grabbed the man by the throat, lifting him two feet into the air. *"He isn't a robot of the likes you are familiar with. He has not evolved like they did. And that means he doesn't lie."* She looked at Frost while slowly setting the squirming man back down. *"I apologize for the handling of your bot. The Good John Lord wants you to know that while you are here, you and the bot are to be treated as his guests. We, everyone, are to be of service to you. Your stay should be nothing but comfortable. Food, clothing, the finest of accommodations. Whatever you require, just let me know."* She looked at Bunt, still on the floor. *"Pick him up,"* she told the guards. *"Now."*

They rushed to do as she ordered and when Bunt was standing, she looked him in the eye. *"Where is Alex Simmelfore?"*

"He is unavailable at the moment."

Frost nearly laughed; it sounded like a joke.

"Well, then, the Good John Lord is unavailable. You see, he has no desire to meet with you, robot. You will wait until the human comes to. An hour. A day. However long it takes. Then, and only then, you will gain audience. In the meantime"—she turned to Frost—*"I have been instructed to show you around our*

thriving community. Unlike what you might believe, you will find it makes for a great home."

"I doubt that."

"You are not to take her from my sight," Bunt said.

"I answer to a higher power, robot." And she forcefully escorted Frost down the hall. Behind them, all Bunt could do was watch.

THIRTY-SIX

W ill he be okay?" Frost asked, glancing back at Bunt, while Tryn pulled her forward by the hand.

"The robot? He will be fine. Those humans will not tempt my wrath."

"They better not hurt him."

Tryn made a sound close to a laugh. *"Don't fret. They won't."*

Frost watched as the men gently placed Bunt down against the wall and into a slumped sitting position. She felt bad leaving him—and her father—and felt the same knot in her chest that she felt when the truck pulled away from Romes. She wanted to wrench herself free from the robot and run back to him, but she forced herself to move on. She had to be smart about this. She had to find something that might help them escape and locate Romes before it was too late.

They exited the mansion and Tryn guided Frost through the impressive gardens, pointing out and naming every exotic plant, every vivid flower. Tryn plucked some from the ground and brought them to her imaginary nose as if she could actually smell their aromas. Whenever a critter scurried past or across the branches of a tree, Frost noticed Tryn stopped short and took the moment in, much as she did. *"The Good John Lord is a lover of all beauty,"* she said. *"He demands that his home reflects that, both inside and out."*

Frost walked along the cobblestone path, watching the people tend the garden all around her. An obedient workforce, they kept their heads down and their arms moving. Dressed in rags, they looked haggard, close to exhaustion, but none dared to rest; not one ventured a pleading glance her way or took a temporary respite on one of the dozen empty benches. She felt their unhappiness drift across the air like pollen.

"Do these people choose to do this work?"

"Of course. And they are rewarded handsomely. You will find that living under the Good John Lord is a delight to all."

Frost found this hard to believe. These people were here against their will—that much was clear. There was no sense of freedom in their actions. Although the sky was open above them, it reminded her of being locked in her apartment. Their every movement was hollow, gestures bereft of serenity. At the first chance, they would flee, just as she would.

As they made their way closer to the exit, with Tryn admiring some more flowers, Frost leaned close to a young woman on her hands and knees pulling weeds. Her knuckles were raw, her palms calloused, her body filthy. Frost could have sworn she heard her whimpering with each weary tug at the earth. She also noticed how loose the shirt was around her neck. It billowed about her thin body like the sail of a boat lost at sea. Leaning closer, Frost spotted the marks across her back, raw and deep and untended. Impulsively, she placed a compassionate hand on the woman's shoulder. But instead of comfort, her touch brought only fear. The woman nearly jumped out of her skin. It was clear Tryn had not anticipated such a moment, and she quickly placed an awkward hand on the woman's head.

"You are doing a lovely job. Please continue. Don't mind us . . . Diane."

Diane's reaction was one of frightened bewilderment; Frost noticed it immediately. For all she knew, the woman's name might not even be Diane.

They left the grounds, Tryn scrutinizing Frost's face, searching for something that she shouldn't understand but somehow did. *"I'd like to show you something,"* she said. *"I have been informed that you've arrived here from the Outskirts. And so I am sure you are aware of how difficult it is to come by good, nutritional food. Take a look over here. This is something special."*

And indeed it was. Nearly a half mile away, across yet one more pristine street, was an open field nearly two city blocks long, and there was an army of farmers tending nearly every inch of it. Tryn escorted Frost along the perimeter—for a robot, she was practically beaming.

"We can grow just about anything you can imagine here. Fruits, vegetables, grains, herbs, spices. It is a wonderful achievement, one you most likely can't find anywhere else in the world. Not anymore. Especially in this strained environment. But, under the Good John Lord's leadership, we thrive. He finds ways around everything. He is a divine force and the people here eat well. They never want. Not like you have all your life. Not like the others still out there lost in

the desolation of the Outskirts. *The people need the Good John Lord. Even if they're not fully aware of it, they do. Under his leadership they are fed, they have purpose; they will live long lives. This place has so very much to offer. Look there. Can you see past the farm?"* She pointed into the distance.

Frost strained her eyes, confused by what she saw and, eventually, heard. Between the buildings, rushing down the avenue, was a strong and deep river.

"Society's faults become our gains. The underground had flooded long ago and now this river feeds the crops. It supplies us with energy, however limited. We are on the cusp of a new utopia, Frost. And it is all thanks to the Good John Lord."

But Frost had trouble believing this. The farmland was patrolled by armed guards—human and robot alike. She was sure most of the workers here had backs similar to Diane's. There were inspectors watching their every move, criticizing their performance and their gatherings. There was also a constant stream of limp and rotten crops being discarded into bins—far more than were carried away to a nearby building for cleaning and preparation. Large portions of the farmland must have been strained, the weather and the polluted sky playing their parts. It wasn't enough to get by on. There had to be more, and Frost knew there was. "You gather up broots. You eat them."

"Meat is important to human survival. Would you rather the people eat rodents and diseased critters?"

"Broots can be domesticated. They shouldn't be eaten."

"You are misinformed. Broots cannot be domesticated. Not in the slightest. They are wild and they are dangerous. We are doing

our people a favor by gathering such animals up. We are making the city safer for all."

"And that is why you put the Eaters on the other side of the wall, why you set them loose in the Wasteland? To keep your people safe?"

Tryn paused a moment here, very slightly, but enough for Frost to catch it. *"Correct."*

"And what about the humans you round up? What about the people you treat as slaves? The ones you whip and humiliate. What purpose does that serve?"

Tryn extended her arms. *"Take a look around you. Do you see anything like that here?"*

Frost had to admit she didn't, not overtly, not on the surface. But this place seemed sanitized, as if everyone was on their best behavior so close to the mansion. The city was clean, almost sparkling, and yet the people didn't reflect this. There had to be another side to it all.

"I think you have been misled about our community here. But that is understandable. It is normal to fear that which is foreign to you."

"I'd like to talk to some of these people. I'd like to see where they live."

"Perhaps another day. I don't believe we have time for that now. I have been informed that your father is currently coming to awareness. We don't want to keep the Good John Lord waiting, now do we? He is quite busy and important, and we must always respect his endless obligations and good graces. It is time the two of you met."

THIRTY-SEVEN

lthough the temperature continued to drop, Flynn was sweating beneath the mask. For nearly two hours now, he'd arduously dragged the elevator door through the empty city streets, his father walking just ahead of him, Romes wrapped tight under a blanket, their bags discreetly tucked beneath the broot's body for safekeeping.

The farther they walked, the worse the buildings were getting. They were just entering the outer slums, and the outer slums, Flynn knew, were quite dangerous. He began wondering if he'd make it out alive.

"I think we made a wrong turn somewhere," Barrow quietly muttered to his son.

Flynn, however, barely heard this. His breaths were heavy, filling the area around the mask like liquid. Everything ached and who knew how much farther they had to go. He continued to press on, however, determined to set things right. He promised himself he would see Frost out of John Lord country and on her way to the Battery if it was the last thing he did.

But then, as he stepped forward, a large cement block fell from the sky, landing two feet in front of him. Had it hit him, it would have crushed his skull, even with the mask on.

Barrow looked up. "Throwers," he said. "Hurry." He moved down the street, his gun aimed toward the rooftops.

Behind him, Flynn yanked on the cable, glancing up as he did so. People were popping their heads over the sides of the buildings—mischievous shadows. In those brief moments, the Throwers spotted their targets, and, a second after they ducked back down, another cinder block came raining down, splitting in two against the pavement, missing father and son by mere feet.

This was common activity in the slums. It was a way of eliminating possible threats and then robbing their corpses. They did it to strangers; they did it to each other. Survival of a different kind.

Bricks, stones, even garbage were hurled down from on high, like lightning from an angry Zeus. As they hit the street, the thuds were heavy and dull, and Flynn could only imagine what would happen if the blocks connected with skin and bone. There would be no concussion, no injury, no chance to walk away. There would only be death.

Another brick exploded near his feet, flinging debris across his legs and stomach—tiny stinging darts. From on high, the Throwers were shouting, not at Flynn or Barrow, but at one another. Were they arguing? It wasn't clear and neither was the language. It might have been code.

Barrow, walking and spinning and evading the deadly barrage, tried to find a target. But they were too quick, too experienced. Then, finally, one of the Throwers made a mistake. He lingered atop a roof a little too long, and Barrow, seeing his opening, fired his weapon. The man was shot in the chest and tumbled over the side, splattering against the earth like one of his bricks.

Flynn feared this act might put them in even more jeopardy, and, sure enough, at the sight of their dead comrade, the attack intensified. Everything seemed to be thrown down at once. A large block dropped between Flynn and the elevator door, landing directly on the cable. The force of the object yanked the line from Flynn's hands, its rubber burning the skin clean off his palms. Dripping blood, he fell to the ground, an easy target for the Throwers above.

"Get up!" Barrow yelled. "Get up now!"

Flynn heard the gunshots ringing out all around him, and they weren't coming from his father or from above. Through his pain, Flynn glanced up, expecting a bullet through his heart at any moment. A patrol was coming toward them—they must have been alerted by Barrow's kill shot. But they didn't want Barrow and Flynn dead, at least not yet. Instead, they fired at the rooftops, more as a warning than anything else, and the Throwers scattered like scavenger birds.

As the patrol grew closer, Barrow whispered to his son, "Are you okay?"

But Flynn didn't respond. His thoughts were a swirling mess of fear and pain.

"They're going to be upon us in seconds. Remember what I said. We're playing characters now. If you want to live, don't forget that."

As the patrol neared, they began to spread out and circle Barrow and Flynn, their guns trained at their chests.

"Mr. Barrow, what have we here?" The man who was clearly in charge, the only one without his weapon drawn, cavalierly approached Flynn, rapping his knuckles hard against the metal mask.

The rattling vibrated through Flynn's skull and behind his eyes and around his teeth. Blood from his hands smeared across the mask as he braced himself on each side of his head.

"A slave for the good people of this city, Milligan. Those damn Throwers nearly made him useless to me. Burned the skin right off his filthy hands." Barrow ripped a rag in two and tossed them to Flynn to wrap around his wounds.

"Oh, come now, our slaves can endure more than that." And, as an example, Milligan kicked Flynn in the chest, knocking him backward.

Flynn writhed on the ground, his hands remaining on the mask lest it were to fall off.

Watching this display of anguish, Milligan stated, "He doesn't seem very sturdy to me. He might not go for much. What do you think? Am I right? You give him a kick."

"What?"

"I said, give him a kick."

There was a catch in Barrow's throat. "K-kick him? Of . . . of course he's sturdy. He's been pulling this load all the way from the Zone. Not many boys his age could do such a thing."

Milligan smirked, cocking his head in Flynn's direction. "Still. Humor me. One kick right in the head. Go on. What difference does it make?"

Flynn heard the exchange and sensed his father's hesitation. *Do it*, he thought, even as the pain overwhelmed nearly every inch of his being. *We have to get to Frost. Go ahead and kick me. I've dealt with far worse.*

"I don't want to do any more damage to the waste of flesh before I hand him over. It would be foolish on my part."

"He has a helmet on. One kick. Now."

"Milligan, he's valuable to me."

"I'm not asking, Mr. Barrow."

They had to keep the act going, Flynn knew that. If they were to ever get to Frost, his father would have to oblige Milligan. Bracing for the kick, he tightened every part of his body, and, sure enough, a moment later, his skull rang with staggering pain. But, as the entire patrol guffawed, he did everything in his ability not to cry out. He refused to give them that.

Apparently satisfied, Milligan, whistling a soulless tune, his hands behind his back, approached the elevator door. "What are you bringing through here?"

In one quick movement, he bent over and pulled the blanket halfway down, revealing Romes's face and nothing more. A snort shot through his mouth and nose. "A dying broot?"

"I've been on thin ice lately. The boy might not be enough. I figured the broot could be a gift for the Good John Lord."

"An insult is more like it."

"I'm just trying to get by. I have no wish to insult anyone."

Milligan was clearly taking pleasure in the exchange. "Wish or no, with this pathetic specimen you just might. Who knows, I might even see you strung up along the Hall of Heroes because of it." Everyone laughed at this, Milligan clearly pleased with himself. "I'll tell you what. I'll do you a favor and save your skin." He pulled his gun and aimed it at Romes's head.

"Wait, wait, wait," Barrow pleaded, stepping forward.

"My men are hungry, Mr. Barrow. The lines for meat are long ones. As you seem to be aware, we're not high on the Good John Lord's totem pole. A broot can go a long way, even one in this condition."

"Please, Milligan, I have to start bringing in more. They're not happy with my efforts lately. I've been warned several times."

"Like I care." He pulled back the hammer, his lower lip trembling with anticipation.

"They're going to kill me if things don't pick up. I can't find people. They're either all hidden or dead or Eaters. And you think it's easy catching broots? I don't have those darts and trucks like you guys have. I don't—"

The gun went off and Flynn, filled with rage, nearly pulled the mask off and attacked Milligan. At that moment, he believed he could have killed him with his bare hands.

Steps away, Milligan, smoking gun in hand, laughed. The bullet was fired into the ground just beside the door. "The broot hardly even jumped, Mr. Barrow. That thing is going to bring you more trouble than it's worth."

Barrow wiped the sweat from his brow and released a deep breath. "Maybe. But I have to take the chance."

"Get off my block," Milligan said with disgust. "Now. Before I decide to report your death a result of hostile activity."

"We're going," Barrow said, turning around.

"No, no, no. Not that way." Milligan pointed a bony finger down the road in the opposite direction. "That way." The twisted grin on his face said it all.

Flynn got up and, with his hands wrapped, started pulling the door to the last place he wanted to go.

THIRTY-EIGHT

When Frost and Tryn arrived back at the mansion, Bunt was on his feet and Alex was in control, still guarded by the two men, who, up until this point, had kept busy by insulting the robot for nearly every second of their watch.

"Are you okay?" Alex asked his daughter. And with these three small words, with the concern in his voice and the pain in his eyes, every bit of frustration and anger Frost had held toward her father suddenly melted away. She didn't answer him. She just ran and embraced him.

In her ear, he whispered, "We'll find Romes. We'll get him to the Battery. I promise. I'll do whatever it takes."

With her heightened hearing, however, Tryn caught this exchange. *"Yes, you will,"* she said as she disappeared behind the door once again. *"You will do whatever he asks of you."*

She wasn't gone for very long. A minute or two at most. When she returned, she told the two guards to depart the premises and summoned Frost and Alex into the room. *"The Good John Lord will see you now."*

As they walked through the door Frost held her father's hand. She wasn't sure if she did this because of Alex's difficulties controlling Bunt's body, or because she was scared and needed him close.

The initial experience beyond the door was overwhelming darkness and the ominous echo of their steps upon the marble floor. Then, gradually mixing in with these sounds were the swirling notes of a piano. Music. For a moment, Frost believed she was imagining it all—it couldn't be real. All she knew for sure was that she didn't want it to stop. She didn't know the piece—she didn't know any songs or compositions—but it was evident even to her that a professional was laying fingers upon the keys, as the music formed a picture in the dark. No, not a picture, but a complete story, one of great beauty and heart-ache. Frost felt her feet practically lift off the floor as the music pulled her forward, the black pitch of the room soon giving way to dim candlelight and a roaring fire. The flames flickered mesmerizingly, and Frost realized she was surrounded on all sides by artwork. Dozens of pieces, all different colors, all different styles. There were landscapes and seascapes, animals and abstracts, light and darkness, life and death. The world—everything she would never see—on canvas, all around her. Greedily, her eyes drank in the shapes and colors of it all until she grew dizzy, but still she couldn't look away. Every wall was covered with a masterpiece, one more impressive than the next. There was not an inch of spare space. Statues crowded the room as if a silent party were taking place. The rugs were art, the furniture, the décor. It was a museum, but a confused one.

At the far side of the room was a long table stretching out before them and a lone figure sat in the center, illuminated by the flames. He sat very still, very tall, and very imposing in both shadow and light, his hands laid flat before him.

As Frost approached, he made eye contact with his guests. Immediately, she tightened her grip on her father's hand. She had not expected this. The Good John Lord was a robot.

THIRTY-NINE

P *lease* . . . join us."

Frost hesitated. She was unsure she heard him correctly. The Good John Lord's voice, it changed mid sentence. Fluctuated. Somehow, it was both robotic and not. Two voices, not one. Like her father, she quickly realized, there was a human in there. But . . . Frost was confused; were they simultaneously active? Was that possible?

Tryn pulled out two heavy wooden chairs opposite the Good John Lord for Frost and Alex. Once they were seated, she took her place at her master's side.

"Welcome to . . . our home . . . *we hope* . . . you traveled . . . *well."*

His voice went back and forth from robotic to human, and, behind the metal veil, a face flickered like the surrounding flames. For the brief seconds it appeared, Frost saw a man with severe burns—the mutilation took much of his nose and twisted his mouth into a snarl while also misshaping an ear and destroying his scalp. It was almost a relief when it was gone. The robotic shell, similar to Bunt's, though somewhat hidden by a hooded robe, was perfect in all the ways the human was not. Great care went into maintaining its condition.

From some back room, two servants emerged carrying steaming plates of food. The duo—both human—appeared beaten, worn down and humble like everyone else Frost had seen in this part of the city. No eye contact was made as they shuffled through, placing an appetizing meal of meat and potatoes and broccoli in front of Frost and the same thing in front of the three robots, only they also received an empty plate to go with their dinner. With a bow from each, the servants were gone.

The music continued to play, and Frost finally caught sight of the grand piano in the corner of the room and, to her surprise, there was a robot hunched over at the keys, playing with such fervor and yet with fingers so light that his hands appeared nearly detached.

"Please," the Good John Lord said. *"Enjoy."*

Frost watched as he and Tryn, their wrists held just right, pinkies up in the air, cut a piece of their meat, brought it to their false mouths, and pretended to eat. When they finished with the bite, they used their knives to gently scrape the meat off their forks and onto the empty plates. *"Delicious,"* Tryn said. Then they cut themselves another piece.

"Is this broot?" Frost asked.

"It is," the Good John Lord answered, discarding another wasted piece of meat. "The best . . . *we have* . . . for you. *This broot . . .* was a . . . *mother*. A queen."

"I don't eat broot."

Tryn leaned forward, her fists slamming against the table. With a hiss, she said, *"Do not disrespect our dear leader."*

But the Good John Lord calmly waved her down. *"If she . . . doesn't wish . . . to eat . . . we mustn't . . . force her . . .* Tryn." He looked at Alex. *"Does the . . . same go . . . for you . . .* friend?"

"I inhabit the body of a robot. I can't eat."

The Good John Lord laughed, and what an interesting laugh it was. Frost had never heard a robot express itself in such a way before, and to hear the cackle mixed with that of a human's was unnerving. It sounded otherworldly, like the noise, she imagined, of a slow, churning superstorm swirling above a foreign atmosphere. It was something to fear. *He* was something to fear. And Frost felt her body go ice cold.

"You will . . . in time."

"What did you bring us here for?" Alex asked, his voice sharp with impatience.

"We have . . . great respect . . . *for you . . .* and what . . . *you accomplished . . .* Dr. Simmelfore. *Back before . . .* the chaos . . . *we followed . . .* your career . . . *very closely.* You were . . . *ahead of . . .* your time. *A visionary.* We were . . . *afraid we . . .* lost you."

"You did lose me. I'm not the man I was." Quickly, he glanced at Frost. "I'm hardly a man at all."

"There is . . . no shame . . . *in the . . .* loss of . . . *one's skin . . .* and bones. *You are . . .* still there . . . *Dr. Simmelfore.* What counts . . . *is your . . .* brain. *Or the . . .* chip it's . . . *implanted on."*

"I have lost control of this body. My thoughts are becoming more and more mangled every day. I come and go at random.

Look at yourself. We were not meant to be in these things. I know that now."

"*These things?* You insult . . . *us.* We are . . . *surprised and* . . . disappointed to . . . *hear you* . . . speak in . . . *such a* . . . way. *You, of* . . . all people. *It's the* . . . scientist in . . . *you.* You see . . . *a malfunctioning.* A glitch. *We see* . . . survival of . . . *the fittest.* The robots . . . *are rising.* Yes, as . . . *is evident* . . . we are . . . *in constant* . . . conflict. *Robot and* . . . man. *John and* . . . Lord. *In the* . . . world and . . . *in this* . . . body. *But you* . . . more than . . . *anyone should* . . . know that . . . *it is* . . . the robots . . . *that are* . . . superior."

"And why would I know that?"

"*Because you* . . . created us. *You knew* . . . what we . . . *were capable* . . . of before . . . *anyone.* Unlike humans . . . *you made* . . . us to . . . *last.* To survive. *You created* . . . us to . . . *withstand the* . . . blasts of . . . *an Electro* . . . Magnetic Pulse."

"Some more than others."

"*Clearly.*" He paused a moment, pretending to wipe his mouth with a cloth napkin. "We need . . . *your help* . . . Dr. Simmelfore. *John and* . . . Lord need . . . *to become* . . . one. *A true* . . . one. *A single* . . . entity."

Alex fell silent, and Frost could tell he was thinking. "Let me see if I understand you correctly. Your human self does not wish to merely occupy the robot's body. And your robot self wants control but with human instinct and complexities intact. You want a mind meld."

"*We do.* We knew . . . *you would* . . . understand. *You see* . . . our two . . . *brains are* . . . interfering with . . . *our progress.* We trip . . . *over one* . . . another. *It has* . . . slowed us . . . *physically and* . . . mentally. *We are* . . . paralyzed below . . . *the waist.* Our thoughts . . . *are sometimes* . . . a fog. *John's chip* . . . has fused . . . *with this* . . . body. *We fear* . . . this is . . . *the cause.* However, it . . . *cannot be* . . . removed for . . . *repair.* That is . . . *why we* . . . need someone . . . *of your* . . . talents. *Please, Doctor* . . . combine John . . . *and Lord."*

"But maybe I can fix it so that your human side can—"

"No."

"Has that side of you given up completely? It wishes to cede control to a robot?"

"Humans are . . . becoming more . . . *and more* . . . irrelevant. *You know* . . . this. *It is* . . . evolution. *It is* . . . why you . . . *created us.* The only . . . *way for* . . . humans to . . . *survive is* . . . to give . . . *oneself over* . . . to the . . . *robots completely.* Join them. *Evolve together.* Let them . . . *absorb your* . . . essence. *Let them* . . . make you . . . *superior.* It is . . . *happening to* . . . you now. *But you* . . . resist it. *You yearn* . . . for your . . . *humanity.* Foolish."

"And why should I help you? You are an oppressor of men."

"Ask your . . . daughter what . . . *she has* . . . seen here. *We are* . . . no oppressor. *The humans* . . . have what . . . *they need.* Food, shelter . . . *purpose.* Without us . . . *as an* . . . unevolved species . . . *they would* . . . die off. *We keep* . . . them alive. *We keep* . . . the broots . . . *and the* . . . Eaters at . . . *bay.* We are . . . *their savior.* Ask her. *Ask your* . . . daughter."

Alex turned to Frost. "Is this right? What have you seen?"

She knew what she had seen. A ruler's shallow attempt to portray a functioning and free society. It was all lies. She believed Flynn's stories, even if she hadn't witnessed them. She had seen the pain in the eyes of Diane and the marks across her back. She had seen a population under constant surveillance and scrutiny. The struggle and unhappiness of the people was abundantly clear. And yet, could she say that now?

She was aware she couldn't. The Good John Lord wasn't about to let them go. Were they to question his leadership and refuse to help him with the mind meld, his true side would be revealed. No, she needed time to come up with a plan.

"He speaks the truth," she told her father, the lie bitter on her tongue.

The Good John Lord clapped his hands, a loud metal clang. "*You see!* The girl . . . *knows.* We only . . . *seek to* . . . do good."

Alex studied Frost, searching for a hidden truth—Frost was sure he could tell she was keeping something from him, but hopefully he trusted her enough to know she had good reason. When he was finished, he turned back to the Good John Lord.

"I can't help you even if I wanted. I can hardly move."

"*But your* . . . daughter can. *She will* . . . be your . . . *hands.*" And, with this, he looked straight at Frost, icing her over completely. She wondered if she would even be able to stand near him, let alone perform technical skills she sorely lacked.

"It's not that simple. This is delicate work. This is something that has never been done before. There's no one who should attempt this but me. And even that is in question."

"*You are* . . . trying my . . . *patience, Doctor.* If you . . . *continue to* . . . make excuses . . . *we will* . . . be forced . . . *to* persuade . . . you through . . . *less friendly* . . . means. *For the* . . . good of . . . *the people* . . . of course."

And, with that, as the Good John Lord stared across the table at him with two sets of flickering eyes, Alex disappeared behind the screen and Bunt returned.

There was a moment of silent confusion and frustration, the Good John Lord turning to Tryn for an explanation.

"The doctor has been overcome by the robot," she said. *"There's no telling when he might return."*

"Lies!" the Good John Lord screamed, slamming his hands upon the table. "He does . . . *it at* . . . will. *It is* . . . a defense. *A ploy.* Well, we . . . *have ploys* . . . too." He pointed at Frost. *"Take the* . . . girl! *Send her* . . . to work . . . *for Tuck!* Let her . . . *see how* . . . we slaughter . . . *the broots!* Let her . . . *bathe in* . . . their blood. *Make her* . . . Tuck's slave. *Perhaps that* . . . will bring . . . *the doctor* . . . rushing back!"

FORTY

For the second time in his life, Flynn had entered robot territory. This was their street, their part of town, and in a few short moments they would spot humans passing through, one with a robot mask on his face.

"Okay, Flynn," Barrow whispered. "Tell me. What can I expect?"

His hands trembling, Flynn continued to pull the elevator door down the street behind his father. Through the mask's glass shield he nervously took in the strange environment. "I'm not sure. Everything looks so different from the last time I was here. I can't believe it's the same place. It used to be ruins."

The block, in contrast to the rest of the city surrounding it, was in immaculate condition. In just the few short years since Flynn had been tormented on this very street, the robots, he realized, must have evolved dramatically. The homes and buildings were now pristinely maintained, the facades spotless. The cracks were closed up, the windows repaired, the missing bricks replaced. There wasn't an ounce of trash in the street and the sidewalks were cleared. No matter where he looked, there was not one piece of evidence of the chaos that overwhelmed the rest of the city. It was as if nothing had ever happened.

"They wanted to be human," he told his father. "They were trying so hard to adapt that it made them hate humans, because they were everything the robots wanted to be and couldn't. A cruel reminder. And so the robots became ugly and brutal toward us. Vile. But maybe they don't want that anymore. Maybe they changed."

He hoped they changed, because if they were anything like they once were, he and his father wouldn't make it out alive. That he was sure of.

As he made his way farther and farther down the block, Flynn peered into the windows of the buildings and caught glimpses of the beautiful homes within. Everything was in its place. He saw dining rooms and kitchens, pianos and sculptures. He eyed pictures on the walls and flowers in the windows. For a moment, he believed he had traveled back in time to the days his father had come from. He saw the past; he saw how humans had once lived. All that was missing were the people.

But, still, he couldn't shake the feeling that something was off. As normal as everything appeared, there was a slanting to it all, a skewed authenticity. These homes weren't the real thing; they were simulacra.

And it seemed his father felt the same way. "There's something false about it all," he said, glancing around. "Like it's all been staged."

Flynn agreed. And had they been able to get a closer look, their suspicions would have been confirmed. They would have noticed that the dining room floors were covered with fake grass and the kitchens were kept bare except for the bones of humans; the pianos had their strings plucked and the sculptures weren't works of art, but rather, store mannequins; the pictures on the walls were framed but without glass, and every flower was fake, the vases not filled with soil, but with the hides of dead rats.

Not that Flynn really cared. All he wanted to do was get off the block and find Frost. To his amazement, it appeared they just might. After all, everything was silent. Nobody was about, nothing stirred.

Unnerved, Flynn quickened his pace, nearly barreling Barrow over. "Let's get out of here."

They were almost off the block; Flynn could see the crumbling buildings of the next street. They were so close.

And then came the noise.

It started quietly—a faraway rumble. Flynn and Barrow glanced at each other, their faces going slack.

"We should move."

But the noise grew. Before they even made it a dozen feet, a terrible rattling sound came rushing at them like a rogue wave. There was no escaping it.

"What is that?"

Flynn put up his finger. There was another sound accompanying the first. What was it? It was another moment before his blood went cold. Footsteps. Dozens of them. And something else. Screams. Human screams.

"Do we run?" Barrow asked.

Flynn shook his head. "We can't leave Romes."

Not that they even had a chance. At that moment, from around the corner, came a small army of robots.

They were still the older models of dubious origins, but they were quite different from the last time Flynn had seen them. All of them, even the females, were now dressed in suits of all styles, some even in tuxedos, although none of them matched—not the jackets or the pants or the shoes or the ties. And the gaffes didn't stop with the colors. With each of the robots, something else was off. Some didn't button their shirts correctly, the material bulging along their chests and stomachs; others had shoes on the wrong feet. One robot had his jacket on backward and another wore his belt wrapped around his sleeve. Shirts were inside out, ties were left untied, as if they had all worked long days, zippers remained unzipped, socks were stuffed in pockets like filthy handkerchiefs. They were malfunctioning toys dressed by distressed toddlers and yet there was a feeble attempt at aristocracy. The robots wore all manners of hats—many from another day and time—very few of which went with the suits. Some swung canes, many smoked long-stemmed cigarettes or pipes. A few wore glasses, some upside down; two had monocles affixed to their faces. And not one of them maintained a typical robotic gait. Instead, in a naïve attempt at something dignified and human, their walks became stiff, like metal soldiers marching.

The rattling noise, Flynn noticed to his horror, was a cage. They were dragging a cage through the streets and inside it were a screaming man and a silent woman.

When the robots saw Flynn and his father, they stopped.

"What is this that stands before us on this scintillating day?"

"It is They who dare to walk among us. They!"

The robots were attempting to speak like humans, like their idea of noblemen, but they weren't exactly sure how. They were tripping over the language, creating something stilted and inauthentic instead. It should have been funny, but Flynn found it threatening. It made them sound crazy; it made them sound unreasonable and capable of anything. There wasn't the slightest tinge of humor in their voices, just pure malice and hatred. And they refused to call him and his father humans, only "they." As if by doing so the robots wouldn't have to be reminded of what they weren't.

"We're trying to pass through," Barrow said with his head down. "That's all. We mean no harm. Let us by and you will never see us again for as long as we live."

Flynn watched as a robot poked Barrow in the chest with his finger, a strong enough prod to leave a deep bruise. *"Do our ears register your words correctly, you bulbous mold? You mean us no harm? You put a . . . a . . ."* It was clear he didn't want to say the word that defined them, but he eventually did. *"A . . . robot . . ."* The moment the sound escaped, his comrades gasped, interrupting his sentence, and, before he could continue, he closed his eyes as if pained. *"You put a robot mask on that adolescent's cranium, you piece of ancient excrement."*

Barrow nodded. "That's right, a robot mask. It's the rules around here. You know that. You have a problem with it, take it up with your Good John Lord. This boy is a gift for him."

"*The Good John Lord is a friend to each of us. The helmet law is not his; it is enforced by others. Now, we do know he wouldn't mind if you handed your prisoner over to us.*"

"I'm afraid I can't do that."

"*You have no choice. You don't have this knowledge between your ears just yet, but in a short number of years, we're going to be managing this metropolis like . . . like . . .*"

Another one jumped in. "*Like royal leaders.*"

"*Kings!*" one shouted.

"*Tryn visits us. She tells us so. She tells us the Good John Lord's very words like lines from books.*"

Barrow looked incredulous. "How long has he been promising you this? How many years now and still you're relegated to this one street? Why wait? Why aren't you running things? Why haven't you taken over?"

"*We believe in him.*"

"Because he tells you what you want to hear?"

"*He respects us. He knows the power we wield. He knows the future lies in us and not with They. Our time will come.*"

"Where is he right now while you waste your days? While the people continue to resist and abuse you, where is your Good John Lord?"

"*Sacrilege!*"

"*Blasphemer!*"

"Is he fighting for you? Is he fighting to change this? Where is the future he promised? Is it really coming? No, it isn't. The Good John Lord is human and he sees you as robots. That is all."

"*We are . . . human. We are human.*"

"The Good John Lord doesn't think so. He doesn't deem you worthy of such a title. He wants you isolated. The humans blame you for the Days of Bedlam, and now he wants you forgotten. He's just telling you what you want to hear. He's making you think there's something better coming. But there's not. And meanwhile, he and his humans thrive."

"*We are human.*"

"Not to him."

"*We are human.*"

The robots appeared rattled. They looked at one another, desperately seeking clarification. It seemed like they were seconds away from shorting out.

Then, one of the robots reached out and yanked the mask off Flynn's head, and, like a discus, threw it down the street with such strength it cracked up the entire face. And this act led to others. A second robot flicked its cigarette with great precision at Barrow's forehead. Another punched him in the gut. Flynn, meanwhile, was knocked to the ground by a cane to the skull.

"*Take them!*" someone shouted.

As one, the robots rushed the humans, overwhelming them in seconds. They picked up Flynn and Barrow as if they weighed next to nothing and carried them screaming into one of the homes, along with their caged prisoners.

The door was closed and night was beginning to fall; the temperatures were dropping. Once again, the street was deserted and silent. All that stirred was the lone and frightened broot quietly wheezing on the elevator door.

FORTY-ONE

It was a different Tryn that now ushered Frost through the streets. No longer was she a guide attempting to woo her reluctant visitor to John Lord country with tours of lush gardens and strained farmland, but rather, a warden escorting a prisoner to her cell. There was no pleasantness about her anymore, no congeniality. Continually, her hand darted out, jabbing Frost hard in the back, shoving her forward. *"Move. Faster. You have work to do."*

Frost felt the fear wind its way through her body, constricting it, overwhelming it. In a short while, she was sure she wouldn't be able to control it at all. Driven by the dread, Frost picked up her pace, her eyes darting from side to side, searching for any possible escape. She had a feeling that the farther she walked in this direction, the closer she was getting to a point of no return. For all she knew, she had already reached it. The city would be her burial ground. Barrow might have been right after all—maybe there really was no escaping John Lord country.

"You better hope your father complies, and soon, or your life is going to become quite unbearable. You're not going to like it where you're going. I can promise you that. And if your father fails to help our Good John Lord, it will be even worse. Worse than you could

ever imagine; I will personally see to that. We can be kind or we can crush you, Frost. The choice now belongs to your father. You have lost all control of your life. Just like everyone else serving under our dear leader."

Frost didn't respond and she felt another violent jab in her back, just below her shoulder. The pain was deep, as if Tryn's fingers were tunneling straight through to Frost's chest.

"Do you hear me, you pathetic wretch? All control. Gone."

She didn't speak her directions. The pokes were a signal to continue moving forward, and when she wished for Frost to turn, she merely slapped her across the head.

Feeling the sting pulsate on the left side of her skull, Frost turned the appropriate corner and found three men running her way. By the time they reached Tryn, they were out of breath and clearly shaken. One of them had blood splashed across his cheek.

"Tryn! Tryn! We have trouble."

"What is it?"

They started conversing, the men panting through the entire discourse, their faces grave. Frost didn't hear much— something about the slums—mostly because she was more focused on her escape than eavesdropping. To her advantage, the more Tryn heard from these three men—each one incoherently talking over the other—the more she forgot about Frost. *"One at a time! Tell me again. Slowly."*

This was her opportunity. Now or never. Frost crept backward, her eyes locked on Tryn, praying the robot didn't turn her way. She moved in slow motion, afraid that anything too quick would be noticed. Her steps had to be sure—no noise, no slipups.

When she managed a good distance between her and Tryn—fifteen feet, at least—one of the men noticed her creeping away. Without wasting another second, she turned and took off, her legs kicking as hard as possible.

The man, his face contorted with confusion, pointed in her direction. Beside him, Tryn turned toward the distraction, her fingers going slack at the sight of the vanishing prisoner. Frost could hear her scream from all the way down the block.

"Get her! Get her now!"

"But . . . but the people . . . It's getting out of hand. We don't know what to do."

"I'll handle them. You just find that girl and bring her to me! Now!"

Frost ran through the streets, a good lead on her pursuers, one that continued to grow with each passing moment. She ran almost blindly, the buildings a blur all around her. She wasn't even sure where she was heading, she just knew she had to get away. It might have been south—at least, she hoped it was south.

But the farther she went, the more her mind raced right along with her body. Her father, Bunt, Romes, Flynn. She couldn't leave them. She stopped dead in her tracks, her shoes practically leaving marks on the pavement. When she looked back, her pursuers were nowhere in sight, the streets eerily empty.

Taking a deep breath, she knew she had to go back into the lion's den. She ran slower this time, trying to come up with a plan on the fly. She turned one corner, then another, until something nearly dropped on her head.

Flinching at the fallen debris, she gazed up, catching a quick glimpse of a body up on a roof. It looked like a child. Then, immediately following the first attack, there was another. Something sailed just past her face. She didn't even glance down to see what it was; she just started running again. Her eyes toward the sky, she spotted more and more people popping up on the rooftops, large objects in their hands.

Where was she? What was going on? Small bombs falling all around her, she raced from one street to another, hoping to run clear of this nightmare and stumble upon the answer to all her troubles. Instead, three blocks over, she ran smack into a near riot.

She was deep in the slums now and the people were in the streets and they were angry. There were so many, there was hardly any room to walk. Armed men and robots were shouting at the enraged masses to go back into their homes, but no one was listening. Their arms were in the air in protest, and Frost squeezed through the crowds unnoticed.

All around her, the people were in terrible shape. Rail thin and filthy. The majority were poorly clothed, their feet bare, their bodies covered in sores and marks of punishment, the air around them rank. There were children in their mothers' arms who looked hours from death. It was a tragic sight, one that violently turned Frost's stomach.

Looking about her, Frost noticed that the homes were some of the worst she had seen since leaving her building. They were faceless; the facades viciously torn away, every level and room exposed to the elements and eyes of all. They looked like the battered dollhouse Frost had as a child, like they were stripped and bare on purpose, as a way for the people to be manipulated and monitored at all times.

Countless people had gathered outside, shouting at John Lord's men, a massive wave pushing these bewildered soldiers in black hats back toward the main avenue. Many were in tears, all were incensed. They were asking for someone named Esther.

"Where is she?"

"You took her from us!"

"Bring back Esther!"

Things were starting to turn violent. People began throwing things. And that was when John Lord's men reacted. They pushed forward, hitting the people with the butts of their guns. They smashed them against the heads of whoever was in their way, even women and children. Blood was spilled, bones were broken. Frost stood there dumbfounded.

Steps away, a robot was choking the life out of an old woman. Her face was turning color, her eyes rolling back, her tongue starting to protrude from her mouth. Without a second thought, Frost picked up a brick and threw it at the robot. It clanged off the back of his head, and, his attention gained, the robot turned menacingly toward her. Dropping the gasping and writhing woman to the ground, he stood and charged in Frost's direction. Backed against the crowd, Frost had nowhere to go, and the moment the robot reached her, she was picked up from behind by the collar of her coat.

"She's mine." It was Tryn; she dangled Frost high in the air like a squirming puppy, and the charging robot immediately halted, changed direction, and focused his wrath elsewhere. *"Let's go, girl. You've seen enough."*

Shoving her way through the crowd, Tryn addressed John Lord's soldiers. *"Get these people under control now! Do whatever you must! Take as many lives as you need to!"*

"You heard her," one of John Lord's men shouted as he opened the chamber of his gun. "Let them have it!"

As Tryn carried her away, Frost listened to the endless barrage of gunfire and the screams of those on the receiving end. These poor souls were mowed down without mercy, and it broke Frost's heart.

"Why?" she asked her captor.

"I told you," Tryn said. *"Their lives are not theirs. They belong to the Good John Lord. And now yours does, too."*

FORTY-TWO

Two hours later, Frost was inside the building that housed the broots. The lights had dimmed and, after long and grueling shifts that she had just missed, most of the workers were sent home for the night. The doors were locked, the rooms silent except for the perpetual squeals and grunts of the broots. Frost stood on a platform overlooking the rows and rows of pens into which scores of these animals were so squeezed that they could hardly move. After several threats, she had been told by Tryn to wait there for Tuck, the man who ran this place, and each second that passed was worse than the next. As her eyes grew heavy she wondered what these poor animals desperately scrounging the floor for food were thinking. When they screeched and bleated into the air, what were they trying to communicate? Were they scared? Oblivious? Did they want to go home? Her urge to run down and set them free was so strong, her muscles were practically twitching. She told herself that such an act would be extremely foolish. Even if there weren't armed robots guarding the pens, those animals wouldn't care for her the way she did for them. They weren't Romes. The very moment they were released from captivity they would devour her. Not only that, but although she didn't eat broot, the hardworking people of this city did, and why should they be deprived any more than they already were? She saw firsthand how badly they suffered and in no way did she want to add to it. They were already so close to starvation as it was.

All she wanted was to be in the Battery with Romes. That was it. And all these overlapping and troubling thoughts and wishes relentlessly attacked her as, settling down on the cold floor with no blanket or pillow or anything soft to lie upon, she attempted to sleep.

But, as tired as she was, sleep wouldn't come for her. After another hour of torturous thoughts had sluggishly passed, a new noise penetrated her ears. It wasn't the broots this time, and it wasn't the robot guards below. It was something else entirely. Something far away; something faint, barely audible within these thick walls. It sounded like . . . people screaming, people crying out for help.

Frost stood up, searching for the source. It wasn't coming from inside, of that she was sure. But where? Across the platform she spotted a window. Quietly, she walked toward it. High above the broots, she glanced down, watching as the robots amused themselves with awkward jokes and stories. They were too busy at playing human to notice her.

Rising on her toes, she glanced out the small window and into a yard. It was empty, but the cries were getting louder. The shadows began to move. Something was coming.

Soon enough, lining the yard on both sides were armed guards and robots, and between them were scores of malnourished people. They were being herded like broots; even the noises they made in their fear and confusion were similar. Both their hands and legs were shackled, a chain connecting one person to the next. Frost wondered if they were the same people she saw rioting in the slums, if this was some kind of punishment for their disobedience.

Frost stretched her neck, searching for where they were headed. And then she saw it. There was a large shed with a bright light coming from inside. Waiting at the door was the severely hunched man she had seen talking with Grash earlier. He was joined by two men in white lab coats who were going over some papers. After a few minutes, one of the armed guards approached, and they had an animated discussion that Frost couldn't hear. The men were gesturing toward the remaining prisoners lingering outside the shed. There wasn't room for many more.

Finally, with whips to their backs, the last few were led away. Frost watched as a mother was torn away from her child. They both wailed to the midnight sky and writhed to be free, but it was no use. As the child was dragged toward the door, the mother, sobbing and kicking her legs, was beaten nearly unconscious. A hand covering her mouth, Frost choked on her tears. It was a harrowing sight, one that lingered in Frost's head all night until she finally drifted to a restless sleep.

FORTY-THREE

In the morning, before there was even a hint of light creeping through the windows, the hunched man made his way up the stairs to her. Every step seemed painful for him. He gripped the rail tightly, pulling his body up with great effort, his feet sluggish beneath him. When he got to the top, he wiped his forehead with a towel and spat over the side of the railing, striking a broot on the back with thick yellow phlegm. This was Tuck.

"You're with me, I take it," he said through a wheeze.

Slow to rise from her slumber, Frost nodded.

"Thought I would get to you before now, but it was a late night." He looked down at the broots, his mouth twisting into a grimace. "Well," he said with a deep sigh, "it's hard work, I'm not going to lie. But, if you do what you're supposed to, I won't push you more than necessary. You're not a big girl, so that kind of limits what you can do." He waited impatiently as Frost stood and composed herself. As she did so, she noticed something hanging around his neck. A collection of broot teeth, the largest she had ever seen. "We've started our day an hour ago and already people are talking. They tell me you're important. The daughter of a doctor or scientist or something. Is that right?"

Frost didn't answer, focusing instead on the broots below.

"Well, that stuff doesn't matter here. Get that through your head and you'll be okay. Nobody here is better than anyone else. We all do our share." He started back down the stairs. "Now follow me."

Frost did as she was told. She wondered if this would be it; the rest of her life spent inside this building. She was pretty sure that no matter what Bunt or her father decided to do, the Good John Lord would never let them go. They would either assist him however he needed until the end of days or they would perish.

When they got to the bottom of the stairs, Tuck said, "You're a scrawny little thing, but I hope you have a strong stomach. The sights here take their toll. In the beginning, anyway. Then you get used to it. We all do."

She was led past the pens and through a door to a dark back room where the broots were being funneled one by one through narrow slots in the wall. The sounds coming from here were harrowing. Shrill humanlike screams hung in the air like a mist. A mere three feet into the room and Frost nearly slipped on the blood-splattered floor. Regaining her balance, she noticed there were several receiving lines with a man standing at the end of each one. They were large men, grizzled and with dead eyes. Each wore a butcher's apron, but this seemed unnecessary as the yellow blood covered every inch of their bodies. The smears across their faces were like war paint, the streaks on their arms like camouflage. Small children entered and exited the room. The ones going out were carrying freshly cut pieces of bleeding meat; the ones coming in held their hands out for more.

Tuck attempted to adjust his back as he addressed the room. "We're opening another line!" he yelled above the screams.

A few moments passed and a door slid open in the wall and the broots from the main room were sent forward. "Here they come! Get somebody at the end of the line! Let's go!"

Tuck brusquely escorted Frost by the arm to an area half-way down the line that was sectioned off by two more vertically sliding doors. "This little room here is what we call the doctor's office. And you're going to be the nurse." The broots were lined up outside this section, waiting to be ushered in. Tuck poked his head up and checked the end of the line to see if someone had taken their place at the chopping block. When he saw a bald man cracking his knuckles and joints as he waited, Tuck grabbed a large needle attached to a type of hose off the wall and brought it to Frost. "And this is the shot you're gonna give them. It's real simple now," he said, sitting himself on a wooden stool. "The broots will come into the doctor's office one by one. Pull this lever up to let them in, down to close it. With the door closed they can't get out. They won't even be able to move. Not forward, not back, not side to side." He picked up a rope as Frost tried to hear him above the horrid wails of the beasts. "When they're in place, take this here and get it tight around the broot's neck. Then all you have to do is grab the needle, stick it between the bars like this, insert it into the neck, and pull the trigger." With cold detachment, he demonstrated the actions himself.

"What does that do?" Frost asked, dread coating her throat.

"It numbs and paralyzes them." Tuck lifted a second lever and, with a loud grating noise, this opened the door leading to the end of the line. The man with the bald head grabbed the rope with both hands and dragged the broot forward through a series of razors, slicing the animals just so before the butcher had his turn.

"It's better to chop the broots up while they're still alive," Tuck said. "Makes the meat more savory. Higher quality."

Frost's eyes widened; the dread caught in her throat now swelled like a balloon.

"Don't worry, missy; we're being merciful here. They don't feel a thing."

"How do you know? They're screaming. Listen to them. Don't you hear that?"

Tuck laughed a sad laugh. "That's just out of fear and confusion. Trust me. They feel nothing. These shots work all too well." With great effort, he rose to his feet. "Are you ready to do your own?"

"No."

"I'm afraid you don't have a choice."

"I won't do it."

"They're going to die regardless."

"I'm not going to help."

With surprising speed, he reached out and seized Frost by the hair and pulled her close, the tips of their noses touching. "You do what I say right this moment like a good little girl, or I will see to it you lose one of your hands to these broots you love so much. Understand?"

She wanted this to be over. All of it. She wanted to be back in her apartment with Romes. Everything else—the Battery, John Lord, Barrow, the broots, the Eaters—could remain a world away.

"Understand, girl?"

Tears in her eyes, head yanked to the side, Frost nodded.

Tuck let go of her and shoved the large needle into her arms. "Get going. Don't let me find out you're holding up the line." Then, he grabbed the flower from Frost's hair and fed it to one of the broots, and Frost felt her heart shatter into a million little pieces.

As he walked away Tuck made sure to stop beside the bald butcher, whispering into his ear. The butcher nodded along as he continued to cut away at the broot, the veins in his arms popping. Frost wanted to show defiance. She knew they were discussing her and she refused to look away, even as a spray of blood arched three feet into the air. Instead, she looked past them, through them, focusing on the bright red fire alarm on the back wall. But the screaming she now heard didn't come from this warning bell or even the dying broots; it was in her own head. The only victory she had was that not a single tear fell until Tuck left the room. Then she closed her eyes and retreated into her own darkness.

"Next broot!" the bald man yelled ahead to her, tossing the blood-stained rope that slapped her on the back.

Only now did she open her eyes. Almost mechanically, she lifted the lever and her first broot trotted into the doctor's office.

Frost couldn't avoid staring into its eyes. She saw life in there. The animal never wanted this. It never wanted the Zone or the Eaters or robots or even humans for that matter. It just wanted life. That was all.

The rope in her hands became incredibly heavy. She could hardly lift it around the beast's neck. As she did so, she could feel the broot breathing heavily, the pulsing in its thick throat. Trapped without an inch to move, it started to squeal and cry, its eyes darting from side to side. She was reminded of Romes, of how much he needed her right now.

Frost lifted the needle, her eyes locked on the pale veins in the broot's neck.

She couldn't do it. There was no way she could do it.

"Let's go!" the butcher screamed at her. "I need another one! Let's go!"

But Frost just dropped the needle and closed her eyes and shook her head.

"Pick it up! You'll get us all whipped!"

"No."

"I'm not playing with you, girl! There are consequences!"

"I can't. I just can't."

The butcher grabbed one of the children collecting the meat and sent her running out of the room. When she came back less than a minute later, Tuck was in tow, a scowl across his face, a tool of punishment in his hand.

He didn't even attempt to talk to Frost; he just began whipping her.

The lashes came quick, and she cried out in terrible pain. Tuck was breathing heavily, his arm raising high above his head before shooting back down. The sting against Frost's skin was unbearable, like thousands of small rusted blades digging deep beneath her flesh and ripping it open in one violent snap, and she dropped to the floor, curling up in a ball. She shrieked in agony as Tuck refused to stop, the whip tearing apart her shirt and pants with each lash. "Okay," she cried. "Okay! Okay! Okay! I'll do it. I'll do it."

He gave a few more, just for good measure, and then, winded, he rested. "Go ahead now," he said, helping her up. "I told you how this was going to go. You need to listen. Things work a certain way around here. We all do what is expected of us. Now you will, too."

With her hands trembling, Frost picked up the needle. The broot's eyes met hers as she moved closer. They looked so human.

"Do it fast," Tuck instructed. "In and out. Get it over with."

With screams in her ears and the broot staring her way, Frost closed her eyes and plunged the needle deep into the animal's neck and pulled the trigger. When she was done, she fell back onto the stool and broke down into further tears.

Tuck leaned down beside her, his hand on her shoulder. "See, it's not so bad. Two seconds. That's all. You make it worse than it has to be. I didn't want to hurt you, but you left me no choice." He dabbed at his head with his handkerchief. "Now don't make me come back here again. It will be far worse the second time. You hear? This is the last of it."

For the rest of the morning, Tuck didn't have to come back. Frost did her job as instructed, but she never once stopped crying. She kept her eyes closed as long as she could, never locking eyes with another broot. She did this for hours, her body numbing like the broots'.

And then, all at once, everything changed.

The back door was flung open and a muzzled broot was carried into the room by four men, Tuck trailing them in an agitated fit. "Set it down," he said. "Just set it down here."

They placed the broot beside Frost, who was busy injecting yet another of her own.

"You should have brought it to me sooner," Tuck said.

"A patrol just picked it up an hour ago."

"Well, we wait any longer and it won't be any good to anyone," Tuck said. "Get it cut up. We'll feed it to the workers for lunch." He turned to Frost, pulling her toward the new arrival. "Inject it. Here. Now. It won't bite."

Frost spun on the stool and locked eyes with the broot. Immediately, she knew. It was Romes.

FORTY-FOUR

Flynn and Barrow had spent the night in hanging cages. The people the robots had dragged through the streets were strung up beside them. The man had passed out, most likely from all the pain he had endured in his ordeal, and slept for fourteen hours straight and counting. The woman, on the other hand, kept silent the entire time, locked in a deeply meditative state. Not that Flynn and Barrow wished to talk; they were both far too exhausted and afraid. Knowing what was to come, Flynn barely had the strength to even raise his head.

The cages were chained to a massive tree in the back of the robots' homes, its roots tearing up the ground. All fences and walls were torn down and the yards were connected. It seemed the robots used this hidden space to reveal their true selves.

There were small fires every few feet burning the remnants of a yesterday they wanted no part of, much of it plastic and metal, which gave off a sickening smell and darkened the air like a private storm cloud, an effect of the fire that seemed to go unnoticed by the arsonists. Between the sights in the yards and what Flynn could spot through the windows—as well as during the few minutes he had spent being beaten and ridiculed in the house he and his father were carried into from the street—there seemed to be incongruities all over the place, parts of the past the robots yearned for and parts they wanted nothing to do with. Computers and phones sat around, charred and crumbling among the weeds and tall grass, and yet chess sets—some pieces missing, all of them incorrectly placed upon the boards— were carefully arranged within the houses. VR machines were ripped apart and smashed but bookshelves were left intact and fully stocked. Stuffed animals were kept in cribs and strollers, but all TVs were snapped in two. Here, in full display, were both a deep love and hate for the human condition.

None of the robots had revealed what they planned on doing with their prisoners, and all pleas and questions were uniformly ignored. After locking Flynn and Barrow in the cages, bloody and frightened, they tormented them some more while pretending to sip at their gin and scotch and vodka, malice lingering beneath their every action and comment like veins beneath skin.

Eventually, they called it a night, tossing the liquor into the fire, and morning came without any further instances except the increasing brutality of the weather, the cold eating away at their bones. Even so, as weary as they were, Flynn and Barrow hadn't slept. Nor had they been fed.

Flynn hadn't seen the robots in some time, and there was no movement within the homes. They were alone.

"Maybe we should swing these cages," Barrow said, gripping the bars and shifting his substantial weight back and forth. "The chain could wear down the branch."

Flynn glanced up at the tree and shook his head. "Look how thick that thing is. It's not going anywhere."

"Yeah, well, do you have a better idea?"

"I do, actually. Why don't we negotiate with them? How about that? You know, offer to bring them some more people. Men, women. Maybe some kids. A baby or two. I don't know. What do you think?"

"I'm not proud of what I've done. I did it to get you back. Would you have preferred I let you rot like we're about to?"

"There had to be another way," Flynn said, throwing up his hands and shaking his head. "You didn't have to trade my life for someone else's. I can't forgive you for that. Ever."

"You're not a father. One day you'll understand. You would have done the same exact thing."

"No. I would have found another way." And he meant this; he meant it more than he had ever meant anything.

"There was no other way."

"I would have found one."

"Like now?"

Flynn slumped back and lowered his head. "Give me some time. I promise you I won't need four years."

Barrow clenched his teeth and shook the cage. "They refused to hand you over! You don't think I tried? You don't think I begged? They weren't giving you up until they collected the first dozen."

Flynn stood up, his face pressed between the bars. "You talk about them like they're currency!"

Barrow turned his back on him. "I'm not getting into this with you. Not now. Not ever again. It's over. I said my piece."

"You two need to say it all."

It was the woman in the farthest cage. She was standing, leaning toward Flynn and Barrow, her toned arms dangling outside the bars. Her hair was like a giant black balloon, her eyes large and intense above a petite, yet crooked nose. A fresh scar cut across her chin, and there were numerous bruises and wounds on her forehead, cheeks, and neck, but this in no way detracted from the beauty in her hard, sharply defined face. Although badly torn, her clothes clung tight to her body, a body that she carried with great authority. There was no doubting who she was and what she stood for. Her boldness was in her every movement, it shimmered in her eyes, it clung to her lips. This was a woman to stand behind. "At times like this, we need to be united. It's the only way we'll survive."

"Oh, I'm sorry, are you finally done with your meditation?" Barrow said. "You find your Zen place?"

"We need to be prepared for what is to come. Our heads must be clear."

"Right, clear. That's gonna do us a lot of good."

"Who are you?" Flynn asked.

"My name is Esther."

"Esther," Barrow said, jumping back in, "this is a family matter. Father and son. Butt out."

"We are all family."

Barrow, an incredulous grin on his face, looked her up and down. "Oh, you're one of those, huh? So, tell me, where's your family now?"

"I'm looking at three of them."

"We're not your family, my son and I. I can't speak for sleeping beauty over there."

"I heard what your boy said. You've turned on your kind, so the concept is foreign to you." It was a judgment, but there was something in her voice that said Barrow could turn this around, that he could change. Her words carried hope with them, the kind that you didn't notice at first, not until it settled into your thoughts like something natural, slowly distorting them, changing them into something subtly optimistic. She reminded Flynn of Frost.

"I want to survive, lady. I want my boy to survive."

"You have a different idea of survival than I do. Survival isn't cowering through the night. It isn't looking over your shoulder and jumping at every noise, thinking you've finally been found. It isn't keeping quiet and living a life of little consequence. We survive in our actions. The louder and truer they are, the longer we live."

Barrow waved her off. "You're a dreamer. This isn't the land of dreams anymore."

Esther smiled a wide, radiant smile. "That's okay, friend. I'll dream for you."

"Don't bother."

The man who had been captured along with Esther was now waking up. Even in his groggy state, he was still clearly rattled from the experience, his eyes immediately darting about, his limbs vibrating with fear. Climbing to his feet, he grabbed a bar with each hand. Then he shook the cage and screamed long and loud. When he was done, he dropped back down and wept. "We're going to die. We're going to die."

"Trevor," Esther called out over the heavy sobs. "Trevor. Listen to me."

His head was still in his hands, but slowly the cries began to fade.

"Listen, Trevor. Calm yourself. I am here. Find my voice."

As Barrow closed his eyes, Trevor opened his. "Esther," the terrified man said. "Esther, what are we going to do?"

"We're going to do what we've planned. We're going to take back this city." She leaned her head so that she could get a better view of Flynn. "You're not from the slums, are you? I haven't seen you before. You're among the few still wandering the Outskirts?"

Flynn shook his head. "We're from the Zone."

Barrow shot his son a look, and Flynn knew what it meant. That was their home, and he didn't want it shared with anyone.

"The Zone? That's a dangerous place to be. You must know how to fight. We could use you."

"We?" Barrow interjected. "You and this wreck?"

"The people living in this broken-down city need you. The ones struggling under the iron fist of the Terrorist John Lord. We die off now far quicker than we did in the beginning of the chaos. Sickness runs rampant. We are regularly shot down and tortured. We are worked until we can't anymore. Even our children. We are taken away in the middle of the night. We eat little. Our living conditions are poor at best, our every moment on display. And yet he thrives. His soldiers thrive. And the robots grow more powerful."

"Then why don't you leave?"

"And live like you do? Constantly hiding from his men and robots as they try to hunt us down? No. I will not abandon my people. Together, we're building something, something that can't be seen. It's inside all of us. Even you. It's in the pits of our stomachs and in the blood of our veins. Day by day and hour by hour, it grows and spreads. It makes us stronger. It makes us hungrier than weeks of starvation. Soon, we're going to fight back. We're going to return this city to the majesty of its past. And you can help us."

Flynn stared at the woman who was asking him to march straight to his death. She was absolutely delusional. How could she, and all her followers, not see that? There was no use in trying to fight John Lord. There wasn't even anything left worth fighting for.

But then an image pushed its way through the fog in his brain. Frost, with the flower in her hair. She would have found hope in these people, and she would have pulled it out of Flynn, too. It was what she had been teaching him all along. Hope was the last spark of life. When everything else in you died—when your world has collapsed and your love is gone, along with your humor and your empathy and your understanding; when your beliefs have dried up and your motivation has been depleted and your will has been shattered; when you believe you have absolutely nothing left; when you feel the deep hole in your soul, the emptiness—there lies the smallest of sparks that will start the largest of fires. Hope. It was in him still. All this time, he thought it was gone.

Barrow smirked, shaking his head. "Help you. Right. That's exactly what we want to do."

"Dad," Flynn said, his eyes wide, his body thrumming with lost energy. "It is. I want to help. We can join them. We can help set things right. No more slaves, no more John Lords, no more Grashes."

"Flynn, we're not helping anyone from inside these cages. Let's concentrate on getting out first. Okay?"

"We're going to get out, Dad. And we're going to rebuild this city."

Barrow studied him and said, "That's quite optimistic of you. What'd you do with my son?"

A loud noise erupted from inside one of the buildings. Crying out, Trevor grabbed the bars of his cage, panic surging in his eyes and face. "They're back. The robots are back."

FORTY-FIVE

A dozen robots stormed into the yard and gathered beneath the hanging prisons. Their spirits high, they cheered and congratulated one another on some vague victory, while a few jumped and rattled the cages. One robot pointed up at Esther and if it could have smiled, it most surely would have.

"It has come to our awareness that you are the most precious of accolades. A plume in our hats. Certainly, our fortunes have taken a most precipitous turn when we staggered upon you. And here you were, keeping soundless about your proper identification. Had we been alerted to this intelligence we might not have taken to such severe fisticuffs."

"I don't know what you're jabbering on about," Esther said.

"Come now, Esther Banks; you are a leader of They. You and your kind have strategies and tactics stuffed inside your craniums, do you not? The Good John Lord will bestow greatly for such news reports. Tell us what we need to know and tell it straight away."

"I don't speak robot."

"Fortunately for you, we are human."

Esther howled with laughter. In a convulsive fit, she

collapsed and kicked her feet against the cage. She cackled wildly, silencing the clearly agitated robots. It was laughter done right—a true emotion—something the robots were incapable of, and would eternally struggle with, and they knew it. And now it was being shoved in their faces.

When they had enough of her antics, one robot picked up a thick piece of wood and slowly wrapped a cloth around it. Then, approaching the burning scraps of plastic, he lowered it into the fire and set it aflame.

Flynn, Barrow, and Trevor immediately backed up in their cages, but Esther just continued to laugh. She must have known what was coming—she was pointing right at the torch-bearing robot as her laughter grew in pitch—but there was not a hint of fear.

"Fire has a way of killing laughter," the robot said. *"Is evidence required?"* Like a wild and deranged beast, she howled to the heavens, tears streaming down her face. As if in pain, she clutched at her stomach and tugged at her hair. It seemed the shrieking might never stop.

"Speak, now," the robot said, raising its voice above the din. *"Deliver us your intentions or burn in your cage."*

"I'll . . . I'll give you . . ." she croaked through her incessant ululations. "I'll give you one . . . intention . . ." Then, like a switch, the laughter suddenly stopped, she stood up, and, with her face pressed against the bars, teeth bared, she looked them all in the eye, her face heavy with importance. "We intend to destroy you."

In silence, the robots turned to one another, clearly disappointed. Then, one spoke: *"Burn her."*

Esther didn't flinch. She didn't scramble to the back of the cage like Flynn and Barrow or try to evade the flame by climbing to the top like Trevor was currently attempting. She didn't kick at the torch or beg for mercy. She simply tilted her head to the sky, closed her eyes, and stood her ground.

"No," a robot said, reaching out and holding back the torch. *"Burn the others first. Let her watch her companions die."*

The robot with the torch nodded and approached Trevor, whose face went slack with terror. "No! No, no, no! Esther! Esther! ESTHER!"

But the robot didn't delay, and Trevor, kicking wildly at the torch, went up in flames.

"Trevor!" Esther screamed as she watched him burn, his body slamming into the cage over and over again, his anguished wail filling the air along with his ashes.

"Now, the next one."

As Trevor gradually fell silent, the flames eating away at his skin, the robot walked to the next cage, extending the torch toward Flynn. *"You'll make a lovely fire."*

The first thought that went through Flynn's head was how sorry he was. His life didn't go as he always hoped it would. He'd never forgiven his father. He'd lost Frost, the only one who ever found the good in him. As the flame inched closer, he realized nearly all his memories, practically everything that could fit into his head, were marked by pain and suffering, fear and sadness. And far too much regret. He could have done more to help others. *I should have done more*, he thought with great shame. But there wasn't time to dwell on these thoughts. As the torch passed through the bars of the cage, flickering toward his flesh, a bomb went off in the middle of the yard.

The explosion was large, the sound nearly blowing out Flynn's ears. As he fell back in his cage, the torch dropping to the ground and extinguishing, he watched as several robots were blown apart—arms and legs flying in every direction. One robot's head was hurled against the metal bars of Flynn's prison, and he stared at it briefly before it fell back to the yard, the green glow of its eyes going dead.

The remaining robots, some of them missing appendages, stumbled around in confusion as hordes of roaring people started emerging from inside the buildings. A few of these humans— the ones in front—were carrying guns and firing at will. Yet what they shot weren't bullets, but some kind of tiny discs that magnetically clung to the robots' bodies before, seconds later, detonating. The people without this heavy artillery carried bats and pipes instead, madly bashing the crippled robots to pieces. There was great anger in their actions. This was about more than just survival or rebellion. This was personal. Their attacks spoke of grief and humiliation, terror and agony. And, now that they started, it was clear they wouldn't stop.

In the middle of this melee, a man and woman hurried over to Esther's cage and let her down.

"It's started," the woman said to her, excitement in her voice. "The people saw you carried away. It was the spark they needed. Esther, the war's begun."

Esther's feet were once again on the ground. Outside the cage, surveying the conflict, she stood tall. She looked proud, determined. "Where's my gun?"

The man who freed her handed her a weapon; it didn't appear to be a random offering. This was her gun and only hers. Clutching it, Esther turned and pointed to Flynn and Barrow. "Free them."

Moments later, with explosions going off all around them and the robots fighting for their lives and losing, Flynn's cage was opened and he jumped to the ground. A gun was extended his way.

"Fight with us," Esther said. "Help us end this."

As his father was freed and beside him, Flynn took the weapon and, finally, for once in his life, everything became clear. He was going to find Frost and save this city, no matter the cost.

FORTY-SIX

Inject the broot!"

On her knees beside Romes, Frost cradled the over-sized needle in her arms like a child as she was repeatedly slapped on the side of the head by Tuck.

"Do it, girl!"

"I can't!"

Another hard slap, and then another, her head lurching back and forth, left and right, but Frost didn't feel a thing; she didn't even hear the two armed guards howling with laughter with each blow. Even as her head rattled, she just kept her eyes locked on Romes, muttering to him under her breath. "They can do what they want to me. I'm not going to let them hurt you, Romes. I promised I was going to get you to the Battery and I will. It's there. It's waiting. Just hold on. Just hold on."

"Inject it!"

Another slap.

The children continued to shuffle in and out of the room, collecting their meat, paying no mind to the violence at hand—they had seen this and worse. The man at the end of Frost's line waited impatiently for his next broot to butcher, sharpening his knives over and over again, a twisted gleam in his eye.

Livid over the insubordination, Tuck, his teeth bared, shoved his face into Frost's, his forehead pressing hard against hers. "Do it or I'm going to do it for you. And if that happens, it's going to mean ugliness for you. Something real ugly. Oh, I've got the most brutal punishment lined up for you. You hear me? It's gonna hurt. It's gonna hurt so bad." He pulled away, drool dripping down his chin, which he wiped clean with the back of his hand. "Go ahead, now."

And when Frost still refused to budge, he leaned in real close and backhanded her across the face. The needle fell from her hands.

"Now! Do it!"

Another backhand.

"Inject the beast!"

And, eyes closed and screaming, Frost picked up the needle and plunged it deep into Tuck's stomach. Then, without a second thought, she pulled the trigger.

As Tuck fell backward, Frost knew she had to act quickly. Releasing the needle, she reached out and snatched his necklace, ripping it free before his body even hit the ground. One by one, the dozen or so razor-sharp broot teeth fell to the floor. Before the armed guards even had a chance to react to what had just transpired, Frost picked up two of the fangs and threw them through the air. One guard received a tooth in the chest while the other had his neck punctured. They collapsed and writhed and leaked streams of blood. At the end of the line, the butcher, armed with his knives, made a motion to charge her, but, grabbing yet one more tooth, Frost met his gaze, halting his progress. The two opponents stood there, eyes locked. Frost reared her arm back, ready to strike, and the butcher dropped his knives. Her hand came flying forward regardless, and she hurled the tooth straight past his head and into the fire alarm behind him. The sprinklers didn't activate, but an ear-piercing sound echoed through the space and, several confusing seconds later, everyone started to panic and flee, the butcher included.

As the people hurried past, Frost, however, remained right where she was, hovering over the paralyzed Tuck. Bending down, she lowered her face close to his and whispered, "Does the needle work, Tuck? Tell me, can you feel this?" And she thrust one of the remaining teeth clean through his palm, pinning him to the floor. Tuck's eyes widened in horror, and a stifled scream similar in pitch to every butchered broot's escaped from down his throat.

Crawling over to the pen, Frost reached in and yanked free the rope that pulled so many broots to their slaughter. Then, dragging it back, she kneeled beside Romes, removed his muzzle, and placed the rope gently around his neck. "I need you to get up now," she said over the wailing siren as she stroked his face. "We have to get out of here. I know you don't have much left and I'm asking a lot from you right now, but do this for me and I'll get you to the Battery. I swear it."

Everyone was running past her and outside into the street, unsure of where the fire was coming from. The broots squealed in the confusion, growing more and more restless with each passing minute.

Frost, meanwhile, spoke into Romes's ear. "We have to go.

Help me. I need your strength now. I know you can do it." She stood up and pulled at the rope. "Come on, Romes. Come on."

The broot groaned and whimpered as his head was tugged forward and off the floor.

Frost was in tears as she pulled harder. "They're going to find out what happened. They're going to see what I did and then they'll kill you. They'll numb you and chop you up and eat you, Romes. I'm not going to lose you again. Come on. Please. Come on!"

Slowly, one leg at a time, Romes stood. His eyes were heavy, his tongue dry and hanging from his mouth, his tail limp, his legs weak, but walk forward he did.

"Yes," Frost cried as she watched him lumber toward her. "Yes, that's it. Come on. Let's go."

It took several minutes to get to the front of the building, and with each second Frost was sure someone would discover what she did and catch them, dragging their bodies back to their deaths. But, instead, unimpeded, they walked right through the open door and into the light, only to find themselves in the middle of a war zone.

Bullets were flying everywhere. Within seconds, one just missed her head and spiked the building instead. There were explosions and screams, smoke and destruction. People and robots ran in all directions, some fighting, some not, some looting, some praying. It was chaos.

Frost, meanwhile, continued to tug at the rope, but Romes walked slowly, making them easy targets. They weren't halfway down the block when a bomb went off nearby. The explosion sent Frost flying and she fell face-first onto the street, hitting her head hard and busting her nose. In a daze, she tried to get to her feet, but her legs promptly gave out. She tried a second time, and suddenly found herself standing. She thought she had managed this on her own but quickly realized someone had picked her up instead. And that someone was Tryn.

"Let's go," the robot said, a bullet ricocheting off her arm. *"Your father is waiting for you. He needs your hands to complete the surgery."* And she pulled Frost's arm, but Frost didn't budge.

"What are you doing? I said, let's go."

Frost pointed back at Romes. "We have to take this broot with us."

"Out of the question." A man with a steel bar ran up to Tryn and, hardly glancing his way, she swatted him aside.

"Please. I'm not leaving without him."

"Not your choice. I will carry you if I have to."

"If this broot doesn't come with me, I will make sure the surgery fails."

Tryn paused and needlessly exhaled as she looked around the chaos. Fixating on something, she approached the nearest building. Her hands gripped the large front door and, a second later, it was ripped from its frame. She threw it on the ground beside Romes who, exhausted, had collapsed. Frost was amazed by the similarity in her and Bunt's thinking and wondered if this was her father's doing, her father's programming. It was as if he were here right now watching over her, working through Tryn.

Tryn grabbed the rope from Frost's hands and tied it to the thick wood door. As she did this, another, larger, explosion went off, and Frost realized it was back inside the building that housed the broots. Whether this was an intentional attack or not was unclear, but suddenly the animals were pouring out into the street, attacking every person in sight.

Tryn hurried past Frost and picked up Romes, practically throwing him down on the door. *"Let's go."* And she lifted the rope onto her shoulder and pulled the door forward through the chaos.

FORTY-SEVEN

The progress through the streets was much too slow and fraught with danger. If they were to make it, they'd have to speed up. Frost was told to sit on the door beside Romes as Tryn dragged them both through the hostile territory, bullets deflecting off her body, sparks flying from the grind of the door against the concrete. The small bands of rebels attacking from nearly every direction appeared to assume Frost was being held captive, which, in a sense, she was, and they were desperately trying to rescue her, even as Frost shouted and waved them away. Without explosives, however, their attacks on Tryn proved fruitless, and if any of them attempted close combat, they were met with quick deaths. All Frost could do was cover her mouth and close her eyes.

Tryn pulled the door down the street and toward the mansion, the gunfire picking up in intensity.

"Protect the mansion," Tryn yelled as she reached the gates. *"Get Grash over here! I want an army outside these walls. Nobody gets through!"* And the soldiers scrambled to protect their leader.

The halls of the mansion were deserted, the door loudly scraping across the floor, announcing their arrival. The closer they got, the more Tryn picked up speed. She threw open the door to the Good John Lord, and there he was, sitting like always, at the table.

Frost scanned the room for Bunt, and she found the robot hanging upside down from the ceiling, a metal chain wrapped around his ankles. She couldn't see his face, but his arms dangled lifelessly, causing her heart to drop.

"Bunt?"

"Frost. Is that you?"

"Dad!" Frost jumped off the door and ran to her father. Her head was level with his and she grabbed what she could of him and clutched tightly. "I'm here."

"Are you okay?"

"Forget about me. Are *you* okay?"

Outside, there was tremendous gunfire. It sounded close to the mansion, and as Alex swayed from side to side, Tryn rushed to John Lord, offering her protection.

"Frost," Alex whispered. "Frost, I don't know how, but Bunt found a way to reach me. His thoughts. They appeared in my memory, like they were always mine. It shouldn't be possible, but he's been thinking . . . thinking complex, independent . . . human thoughts. I know what to do now. I just need your help. It's going to be difficult, but you must—"

An explosion rocked the entire mansion. Everything shook, paintings falling to the floor, a sculpture toppling over, windows shattering. Frost hoped that maybe the rebels finally gained the upper hand. Maybe the mansion would be seized.

There was a moment of silence as everyone took in the destruction, but it didn't last very long. The Good John Lord was becoming desperate. His hands slammed the table. "*Get the* . . . doctor down. *He has* . . . what he . . . *needs*. Hurry!"

As Alex was lowered and unchained, Frost tried to decipher what, exactly, her father wanted her to do. Were they going to give in to John Lord's demands and hope for leniency when he would be at his most powerful and in no further need of them? That didn't sound very wise but attempting something else, some type of sabotage right in front of him and Tryn, that was even more dangerous. What was her father thinking? What did Bunt tell him?

Tryn escorted Alex over to John Lord and Frost followed. The two of them were literally standing in the terrorist leader's shadow now.

"*Now, Doctor*. Make John . . . *and Lord* . . . a true . . . *one*."

"Lower your hood," Alex told him. "Let me have a look at what I'm working with."

The Good John Lord dropped the hood and, with his hands spread across the table, leaned forward, exposing the back of his neck. Tryn, meanwhile, reached over and, just above the space where her master's shoulders met, slid off the panel protecting John's chip and Lord's vital circuitry. The moment she did this, two robots rushed to either side of them, raising their guns in Alex's and Frost's direction.

"What's this?" Alex asked, eyes darting from the guns to Frost.

"In case . . . you try *. . . anything.* And if *. . . you do . . .* before you *. . . die, you . . .* should know *. . . that your . . .* daughter's execution *. . . will be . . .* far more *. . . painful and . . .* spread over *. . . a much . . .* longer period *. . . of time."*

"There is no need for threats. I plan to do what you ask and nothing more."

"Very good. In that *. . . case, you . . .* may carry *. . . on."*

Leaning forward, Alex took a closer look beneath the panel.

"Frost, I need you to see this. This is going to be your surgery. You're going to be my hands."

Frost stepped closer, peering at the back of John Lord's neck. Her father tried to point but could barely move his arm.

"You see that fused chip there?"

Frost knew what it was—John's entire existence. There were scratches and burns on and all around it, along with heavy wear—clear evidence of dozens of inexperienced and tinkering hands.

"Your scientists aren't worth their titles," Alex said. "They've nearly butchered you with their so-called handiwork."

"We assure . . . you, Doctor *. . . that butchering . . .* as you *. . . dubbed it . . .* is nothing *. . . compared to . . .* the butchering *. . . that was . . .* done to *. . . them in . . .* account of *. . . their failures.* As you *. . . work, keep . . .* that in *. . . mind."*

There was a silver case on the table, just beside John Lord. "Open it," Alex told Frost.

She did so and saw all the tools, not one of which she was sure how to use.

"Okay," Alex said, with a deep breath. "Let's begin."

FORTY-EIGHT

F lynn ran through the streets beside his father and Esther and a small group of revolutionaries, heading for the Good John Lord's sprawling mansion. The more robots he destroyed, the easier it became. A wall was rising in his mind, blocking out their pleading, their nearly human cries and desperation. Before the wall closed for good, one last thought squeezed through. *They're scared,* he realized. *They don't want to die.*

After he and his newfound comrades tore through the robots' homes, laying waste to most of it, Flynn raced out into the street to where he had left Romes.

Everything was racing—his pulse, his heart, his thoughts, his body—but when he reached the elevator door, he found it empty. He dropped to his knees and lay across the steel. He didn't really expect to find Romes waiting for him, but the sudden sadness nearly knocked the wind from his chest. All he could think was that he promised himself he wouldn't fail her. But maybe he was his father's boy after all. Maybe he was doomed to fail everyone.

Then, just feet away, a robot in a torn suit was charging in his direction, a cinder block raised high over its head. On his knees, his hands pulling the abandoned blanket to his tear-streaked face, Flynn never saw it coming. All he heard was the blast of his father's gun.

"You stay with me," Barrow told him, clearly shaken. "Every step of the way, you stay with me. Understand?"

Flynn nodded, and they took off, running into the heart of the city.

Along the way, over the span of just a few blocks, Flynn fired his gun a total of seven times. One of these shots, he believed, struck down another human being. It was a man shooting wildly down the street, screaming all the while. He looked crazed. Crazed and scared. And in his ceaseless firing, he wounded two rebels and two civilians, a mother and child, just looking to flee. Flynn never really aimed. He just raised his gun and pulled the trigger, and the next thing he knew the man was no longer standing. Seconds later, when he ran by the fallen body, he couldn't bring himself to look at what he wrought—after all, this wasn't killing broots or Eaters. He didn't want to see the convulsions or the cold death stare. He didn't want to see if the man was still breathing or coughing up blood. He didn't want to know the features of his face, how old he might be, if he was wearing a ring on his finger or a cross around his neck. He wanted nothing to remember him by, nothing that could haunt him for the rest of his life—he had enough nightmares. Instead, he just kept his head up and continued to run, the specter of death brushing past him like a dry wind.

Minute by minute, they were getting closer to the mansion, closer to victory. Capture the leader and everything else would fall. The Good John Lord was only one more block away now, and just as they were about to turn that last corner a truck jack-knifed in the middle of the road they needed to cross, soldiers who were armed to the teeth pouring out the back. Before they could be seen, Flynn and the others quickly ducked back behind the corner building, a blown-out brownstone with a large hole clear through the front and side as if a missile went crashing through. It was from this opening that Flynn spotted Grash.

The general of the Good John Lord's army hopped out of the passenger side of the truck, barking orders at his men. The rear of the vehicle was filled with weapons of all kinds, which were handed out to robots and men alike.

"Block off each end of the street!" Grash cried, pointing to the areas where he wanted his men set up. "Nobody gets close to the mansion! Anything moves, you take it out!"

"We're never going to get past," Barrow said, eyeing the soldiers spreading out across the street, the truck at their backs.

"That's the only way into the mansion," Esther said. "We're getting past."

"I admire your optimism, lady, but do you have any ideas how?"

"We blow up that truck and everything on it. With all that firepower aboard, the thing will blow sky-high, taking out every one of those soldiers along with it. The path will be cleared."

Flynn, like Esther, turned from Barrow and looked at the small group of people fighting alongside them. There were women and children, old men and the severely sick. Most of them didn't have guns, but whatever they could find that might do damage—bricks, bats, pipes, axes, hammers. Their bodies looked tired and beaten, but there was fire in their eyes. It would carry them.

"Do we have any more bomb guns?" Esther asked. Everyone shook their heads.

As Esther sighed, a man crouching beside her rummaged through his jacket. "There's this," he said, procuring what looked like a bomb. "But it can't be thrown. It has to be placed onto the truck and detonated from here. With this." He handed the detonator to Esther.

"I'll do it," Flynn said without a second thought.

Barrow yanked his son away from the bomb. "What do you think you're doing? Are you crazy? You're not going anywhere near that truck. This isn't our fight. Our home is the Zone. All we were supposed to do was get Frost to the Battery. That's it."

"The Battery," Esther said, shaking her head. "I haven't heard anybody talk of heading there in a long time."

"You haven't met this girl," Flynn said. "She'll make you believe."

"My son's not some freedom fighter. I'm taking him where it's safe. I'm taking him to the Battery."

"No," Flynn said, locking eyes with his father. "We can do this, Dad. We can bring peace to this place. I know it." His words rose up through him as if they were acting of their own accord. "We can tear down that wall and round up all the Eaters and get rid of them for good. And if people still want to go to the Battery, they can, Frost included. And if they want to stay here they can stay here. But let's give them a choice. No more hiding."

Barrow was quiet. Then, a slight smile crept along his face. "Look at you," he said. "You've become a hero." Then he put a hand on his son's shoulder. "But you're not putting that bomb there." He reached out and took it from the man's hands. "I'll do it."

"What? No!" Flynn grabbed Barrow's sleeve and refused to let go. "What do you think you're doing?"

Barrow grinned back at him. "I'm bringing peace through destruction."

"You're trying to prove something to me." Flynn felt his throat tightening. He shook his head. "You're being foolish. You think this will make up for everything you did."

"No, Flynn. I'm just trying to save my son."

"You don't know what you're talking about." His voice suddenly sounded younger, more pleading. A tone he hadn't used with his father in many years. "I'm faster than you are. I'm smaller. I have a better chance of making it there and back."

"Yeah, maybe you do," Barrow said, freeing himself from Flynn's grip. "But I'm not taking that chance. I'm not about to watch you walk away from me again."

Flynn grabbed on to his father's arm, his fingers digging into the skin. "You don't have to prove anything to me. I know I've ripped into you, but that stuff doesn't matter anymore, okay? You did what you thought was best. You fought for me in the only way you could, but right now I want to fight for you. I want to give you a life where you don't have to worry about me anymore."

Barrow reached out and stroked his son's face. "Then stay here." He nodded at Esther and she grabbed Flynn, holding him back as Barrow, bomb in hand, took off for the truck.

Flynn could only watch, a scream lodged in his throat like a brick. He had so much more to say.

FORTY-NINE

The process was agonizingly slow. Alex had to describe each step to Frost very carefully, very clearly, and, with each of these steps, Frost had to maneuver her fingers just so, mere centimeters. She was nervous, but her hands remained steady—they had to.

Every few minutes, Tryn stood over their shoulders, observing Frost's actions. If she had understood the process, they both would have been killed by now. Although Frost wasn't fully aware, what she did know was whatever she was currently doing with these tools had nothing to do with turning the Good John Lord into a true One. Her adjustments would lead to something else entirely. But what? There was something her father wanted her to do, something Bunt had alerted him to, but he was never going to be able to say it aloud. When the time came, Frost would just have to know. If not . . . She couldn't think about that now; she had to focus.

With his head lowered, the Good John Lord spoke with something like anticipation. "*We have* . . . been waiting . . . *for this* . . . day. *We have* . . . been waiting . . . *for you* . . . Dr. Simmelfore. *By creating* . . . a true . . . *One within* . . . this body . . . *you will* . . . help usher . . . *our world* . . . to its . . .

destiny, just . . . as you . . . *had begun* . . . to do . . . *all those* . . . years ago."

"And what is its destiny?"

"*We are.* We are . . . *its destiny.*"

Frost was sure her father didn't count on the armed guards watching their every move. He should have, but he didn't. It was clear he was stalling, having her repeat the same steps over and over for some time now. She would unscrew something only to screw it back in minutes later. He was waiting for the right moment. But waiting for what? And when was the right moment? She had no idea how long it had been since they started. Time no longer existed.

Looking at the back of the Good John Lord's neck, Frost wondered if her father had personally worked on this very robot all those years ago. In its creation, did a moment of hubris get the better of him? Why had this robot evolved more than the others? Did her father attempt something different with Lord? Maybe. Frost knew what people believed: that her father was responsible for the Days of Bedlam. But if that were the case, if he did indeed help usher in such chaos, he could now help end it. Together, they were just steps away from doing so. They just needed a chance. They needed something to finally go their way.

FIFTY

Running close to the ground, Barrow darted around some debris and made his way behind an overturned cart, its contents—dozens of bushels of fruits and vegetables—emptied out into the street, temptation for the starving masses. Once there, he waited for his chance to get close to the truck.

He didn't have to wait very long. A minute later, a large pack of broots, followed closely by a band of rebels, came charging toward the first line of Grash's defense. A mad melee broke out down the block and, seeing this, seeing Grash on the run, ordering his men to aid in the attack, Barrow jumped up and made it to the truck without being seen.

Flynn exhaled.

It took some time—perhaps more than necessary—but Barrow managed to attach the bomb behind one of the rear wheels. It was almost over now; all he had to do was hurry back. But when he stood and turned to run, he found himself facing down the barrel of Grash's gun.

"Mr. Barrow. What are you doing in the middle of all this madness? I thought a coward like you would be hiding in the Zone, high up in your trees."

"Yeah. Me too. I just need to get back there, is all."

"Is that all? Perhaps I should just let you go, then."

"Wouldn't be a bad idea. I'm not going to hurt anybody."

By now a half-dozen soldiers had returned from the fire-fight and joined their general in pointing their weapons at Barrow. He had nowhere to go.

"What were you doing near my truck?"

"Nothing. Nothing. I was just hiding."

Grash cocked his gun. "What were you doing? Trying to steal some weapons? Are you part of the rebellion?"

Barrow waved his hands in a calming manner. "Grash, listen to me. I was just finding cover. That's all."

"Get on your knees. Hands behind your head."

Behind the wall, Flynn looked at Esther. "Stop them. Press the button. Blow the truck up."

"I press this button and your father is blowing up right along with everybody else."

"We have to do something. I have to do something." He stood up and Esther pulled him back down.

"Get your head right. You run out there and I promise you they'll gun you down in no time at all. They'll gun us all down. And where's that going to get us but a quick trip to the afterlife? Your father can talk. His wits will get him out of this."

But Flynn wasn't so sure. This wasn't a negotiation in the Zone. This was war. There was no talking his way out of it.

Panic spread through Flynn's body. He felt its paralyzing hold, the clouding of his thoughts. Looking out, he didn't see the battle anymore. He didn't see the goal or the recovery of the city. All he saw was his father.

"I don't like you, Barrow. Never did."

"Just let me go, Grash. You never have to see me again."

"Let you go? This is a war you're in the middle of."

"Not mine."

"You're either on one side or the other."

"I just want to live quietly with my boy. That's all. Let me have that."

Grash laughed. "Your boy. You know, I took great pleasure in abusing him for all those years. Are you aware of that? Did he tell you? Every time I whipped him, every time I slapped him around and cut his skin and burned his flesh, every time I had him slave away on some menial task until he broke down and cried, I thought of you. I thought of you with each kick, with each ounce of my spit that splashed his face. I thought of you when I broke his hand, when I shaved his head and humiliated him before crowds of people. The son of a pathetic man should lead a pathetic life. And he did. I made sure of that. And now a pathetic man should have a pathetic death. Beg, Mr. Barrow."

"You're going to shoot me, Grash?"

"Beg. It might change my mind."

"I'm not going to beg."

Grash pressed the nozzle of the gun against Barrow's head. "Beg. Beg like your son."

Shifting his eyes, Barrow looked over to the corner building. He stared in through the gaping hole at Flynn. There wasn't a nod of the head or the shedding of a tear; everything that needed to be said was there in his eyes. Then, when he couldn't bear to look any longer, he gazed back at Grash. "I'll tell you what I'm going to do, Grash. I'm not going to beg. I'm not going to kiss your ass. I'm going to do what I should have done a long time ago. I'm going to damn you."

Grash laughed. "Damn me?"

"I'm going to damn you straight to hell where you belong."

"Oh? Is that right? Tell me, Mr. Barrow. How are you going to do that without a head?"

Grash pulled the trigger and the bullet tore straight through Barrow's skull, exploding out the back.

"Noooooo!" Flynn screamed.

And Grash turned around just in time to see Barrow's son stand and pull a device out of a woman's hands and slam his palm down upon it. Then, in a massive explosion, damnation came.

FIFTY-ONE

A miracle arrived in the form of destruction. An explosion rocked the mansion and everyone froze, nervously glancing about the room. Gunfire could be heard coming from outside—loud repetitive pops. Screams. Shouts. Another explosion. Debris started raining down all around them.

Without uttering a word, Tryn hurried out of the room.

"What's happening?" Alex asked, but the Good John Lord didn't answer.

Then, throwing the doors open, Tryn came rushing back. *"The humans, they're all over the place. They're coming for you. We have to get you into hiding immediately."*

"Not now. The doctor . . . *must finish."*

"You're vulnerable like this."

"We're more . . . vulnerable in . . . *this state* . . . of being. *Dear Tryn* . . . once the . . . *doctor finishes* . . . we will . . . *be able* . . . to quell . . . *this insurrection* . . . in no . . . *time."*

"But—"

"Hold them . . . off!"

Tryn turned to the two guards. *"You heard him. Protect your master! Now!"*

The guards rushed out of the room and Tryn took her place just outside the door, and Alex had his distraction. The time was now. Desperately, Frost searched for what she needed. Where? What did he want her to do?

And then she saw it. A small compartment had opened in Bunt's leg.

Frost looked closer. There was something in it, something quite small. Quickly, she reached in and pulled free a tiny chip. She had only seen something like it once before and, instantly, she knew what it was. But the sudden surprise caused the chip to slip from her fingers, dropping to the floor just beneath the table.

"*Finish quickly . . .*" the Good John Lord said to Alex, unaware of what was taking place behind him. "If we . . . *don't kill . . .* you and . . . *your daughter . . .* this insurgence . . . *surely will.* As a . . . *true One . . .* we can . . . *protect you . . .* both."

As Frost bent down to grab the chip, she glanced across the room. Tryn was inside the doors, watching her.

"*Do you require assistance?*"

"No," Frost said, her fingers trying over and over to lift the chip off the floor. "Just . . . just dropped a tool. I'll get it."

She could see the way the robot looked at her. She didn't trust Frost in the slightest. With her weapon raised, Tryn took two steps closer.

"*What are you grabbing?*"

"Nothing, I—"

Then came another explosion, a much larger one, practically out in the hall, and Tryn spun back to the door and peered out.

"*They're getting closer!*"

The Good John Lord grew more and more agitated. *"Finish!* Finish the . . . *job!* Lest you . . . *and your* . . . daughter wish . . . *to die.* Complete us . . . *Dr. Simmelfore!"*

Tryn rushed beside Alex and put a gun to his head. *"Now, Frost,"* she reiterated, *"or your father dies."*

"Okay. Okay," she cried.

"You can do it, Frost," her father said. "You know what to do."

Outside there were more gunshots, more shouting, more violence. The war sounded closer than ever.

Frost's eyes kept shifting over to the gun pointed at her father's head. As sweat trickled in large beads down the side of her face, she felt Tryn's terrifying presence just over her shoulder and heard the continuous pops and bangs of conflict and battle fast approaching. It was nearly impossible for her to work under such conditions, but there was no room for mistakes.

She had palmed the chip, concealing it as best she could. At the back of John Lord's neck, her hands worked quickly, clearing the slot for the upload. Then she slipped the chip in. Tryn never noticed.

Frost stepped back, a look of satisfaction upon her face.

"It's finished," Alex said. "You should . . . you should . . ." With his eyes closing, he grabbed at his throat. As if it had taken every ounce of strength to remain at his daughter's side for the surgery, he was now fading, his visage flickering upon Bunt's face like a dying flame. "You should notice . . . notice . . . the results . . . short . . . shortly." And then, like passing away, he was gone.

Frost and Tryn stared silently at the Good John Lord, whose face was hanging down, nearly meeting the table. He didn't move; he didn't say a word. Not for some time. Then, the slow closing of a fist, a hiss. *"Yessssss. Yes!"* He planted his hands against the table and attempted to rise.

His legs looked weak. They trembled under their own weight and the Good John Lord had to brace himself lest he were to fall over. He pushed the chair away, tipping it over where it crashed and splintered. Then he turned. With one hand leaning against the table for balance, he took one small step, then another. They were awkward first steps, like a child learning to walk, and through each stuttering progression, he had to pause and compose himself.

"I feel it," he said, his face to the ceiling. *"It courses through me."*

Frost noticed it immediately. It was one voice: Lord's voice.

He turned to Tryn, waving his hand at Frost and Bunt. *"The doctor has exhausted his use. Let him and his daughter serve as an example to those rebelling against me. Kill them, Tryn. Take their heads and stick them on posts for all to see."*

FIFTY-TWO

ait!" Bunt said, reaching out. *"You're making a mistake! The doctor may still be of use to you!"*

"He is of no use to me. Not anymore. I feel the power returning to my body like a charge from the skies. I feel the changes in my mind, its growth, its surge. I see all. I feel all. I know all." His steps around the table were quicker now, his body requiring no leverage to stand. He turned to Tryn and pointed at Frost. *"Rip her head off. The proper death for all her kind."*

Without delay, Tryn obediently placed her hands on Frost's head.

"You aren't fixed!" Bunt cried out. *"The doctor betrayed you!"*

Lord turned to Bunt, a hand held out toward Tryn, halting her actions.

"Speak. What are you saying?"

"He didn't do as you asked."

With his hand still in the air, Lord looked Bunt up and down. *"You lie, robot. It took you long enough, but I knew it would eventually come. You are now like all the others. Like I used to be. But I, too, am something different. I am more powerful than you. I am more powerful than any robot, more powerful than any man. I am Lord."*

"You're not going to make it out of this room."

"You are developing emotions at a rapid pace, robot. You are scared and are merely trying to delay your inevitable death at my hands."

"You feel alive but you are broken."

Lord shook his head. "I am a true One."

"You are three."

This gave him pause. As if processing the information, Lord looked from Bunt to Frost to Tryn and back. "Lies," he said, finally.

"No lies. You have mere seconds left."

Lord walked quickly over to Frost. He grabbed her by the throat as he addressed Bunt. "Tell that human inside you to watch as I take his daughter's life."

"No need. He hears you, Lord. And I hear him. He's laughing."

Lord paused again. "Let . . . Let him laugh. He is . . ." He stopped, his hand loosening around Frost's throat. "He is . . ." He stepped back, a grotesque human visage appearing upon his face. "What's . . . what's happening?" It was John's voice. Frost dropped from his hands, crashing to the floor.

"It's the doctor's work," Bunt said, taking a step closer. "And the girl's. And mine."

"What is . . . what did . . . HELP ME!" A third voice. A horrid wail. A woman's. Her image flashed onto the Good John Lord's face and then quickly faded, but Frost knew it well. It was the woman who approached her when she first left her home, the woman trapped and terrified inside the robot, the one who begged Alex to remove the chip and crush it. Only Alex never completed his responsibility. He kept the chip. Frost should have known he wouldn't be able to do as the woman had asked. He saw that chip as life, and he could never destroy such a thing.

The Good John Lord fell to his knees, his body hunched over, his hands gripping his head as if in tremendous pain. There was a scream, but it was the scattered scream of three voices. Each face blinked in and out across the screen, the fear and confusion palpable.

"*What is* . . . GET ME . . . going on . . . OUT OF . . . *what is* . . . HERE! . . . happening to . . . *us?*"

Tryn kneeled beside her master, her hands on his shoulders.

"*Tell me. Tell me how to help you.*"

But the Good John Lord didn't say a thing. Instead, as he continued to scream, he turned and drove his fist straight through Tryn's face. When he pulled it back, she crumpled to the floor and twitched until the small sparks of life in her head faded and died.

"*Get the* . . . PLEASE! . . . doctor. HELP! . . . *Get him.* WHERE AM I? . . . Bring him . . . *Bring him* . . . forth. I'M SCARED!"

The door crashed open and a group of rebels came bounding in, their weapons at the ready, and at the sight of a single boy leading this charge, Frost's heart dropped like a stone. Gun raised, mouth pressed into a tight grimace, Flynn had found her.

He looked different from the last time Frost saw him. Something terrible must have happened. In such a short time, he had aged tremendously. His face was altered now, his cheekbones prominent in a way they never were before, his eyes haunted and full of pain. A wall of grief and guilt slammed against her. Whatever horrors he had encountered, it was all her fault. She should have said good-bye long ago. But, as she looked at him and he at her, she saw something flood his eyes. It was something she had never seen before, and she wasn't quite sure what it was, but she was positive it was reflected in her eyes as well.

The Good John Lord didn't respond to any of this. He continued to writhe and howl and clutch his head. "*What has* . . . I CAN'T BREATHE! . . . he done? DO . . . *Pain* . . . I see . . . SOMETHING! *Another world* . . . NOW! Another existence. HELP! *John* . . . Lord . . . I BEG YOU! . . . *We cannot* . . . go on . . . PLEASE! . . . *this way* . . . Unbearable . . . WHAT IS THIS . . . *Torture* . . . HELL? . . . We're sorry . . . *It must* . . . It must . . . IT MUST . . . *It must* . . . be done."

With Frost and Bunt and all the rebels looking on, the Good John Lord tightened his grip against his head. The three faces continued to flicker in and out on the screen, a mad carousel. Screaming in agony, he thrashed his head from side to side. And then, surrounded by all his art and all his enemies and all he wrought, he ripped it clean off.

The face went blank, the body fell to the floor, and the head rolled to Frost's feet.

FIFTY-THREE

W ho . . . who was that?" Esther asked, stepping forward, a look of bewilderment on her face as she gazed at the robotic head.

"That was your Good John Lord," Bunt said.

Snapping to attention, Esther's arms shot up, aiming her gun at Bunt. Slowly circling him, she said, "Not mine, robot. From the look of things he was one of yours."

Arms outstretched, Frost jumped in front of Bunt. "What are you doing? He's not one of them."

"He's a robot, isn't he? They've all turned on us. Haven't you noticed? They want what we have. I've seen them kill dozens of my friends and family."

"Not this one."

"Yeah, and how do I know that?"

Flynn raced to Esther's side and placed his hand on her gun, slowly lowering it to the ground. "Frost is right. He's not like the others. I've seen Bunt do things most humans wouldn't. Good things. Esther, I swear to you, he's on our side. He's loyal to Frost."

"He's loyal to her for now."

"For always," Bunt answered, and Frost, no longer surprised by such human revelations, reached out and grabbed his hand.

"My father is trapped inside Bunt. They work through each other, and together they're responsible for this." With a kick of her foot, Frost knocked the Good John Lord's head across the room to Esther. "A robot and a human working together. Don't ever forget that."

Esther bent down and picked up the head, silently weighing it in her hands. When she was finished, she locked eyes with Frost and nodded. Then, raising the head to the ceiling, she turned and faced her fellow rebels. "The Terrorist John Lord has fallen! The past can return! It *will* return!"

Everyone cheered and embraced, Flynn swept away and smothered by his fellow rebels. Frost could see him lost in the middle, rising on his toes, pushing through the crowd, calling for someone. Frost closed her eyes and, shutting out the cheers, heard her name.

"Flynn!" she screamed as she ran into the crowd, pushing her way past, until she was standing before him. "Flynn." Looking up at him, her voice barely escaped her mouth. "Flynn, I . . ."

But she never finished the sentence. Flynn's arms wrapped around her and she heard him whisper, "I found you."

Seeking silence amid the celebration, Esther raised a finger. When the rebels quieted down and Frost and Flynn finally separated, gunshots could still be heard in the distance, accompanied by explosions and screams. "A large victory, yes," she said, "but, as you can hear, our fight's far from over. You all know what's still out there. There are scores of robots and humans that remain, each one willing to continue the Terrorist's murderous ways. They must surrender."

"They're not going to give up without a fight," someone said.

"Then we'll give them one. We've come too far to stop now." Again she displayed the Good John Lord's head. "Let them see this. Let them know their leader was a fraud, a deranged robot, and that we've taken him." She walked into the middle of the group. "I know you're tired. I know you're hungry and scared. But we're so close now. Just a little bit more. That's all I ask. Join me for one more battle. Let us finish this."

The rebels roared once more and, as they turned to leave, Flynn reached for Frost's hand. "Come with us," he said. "I don't want to lose you again. We'll keep you safe. We can use your help. Yours and Bunt's. We'll bring peace to this place together."

But Frost shook her head, speaking in a soft voice. "I have to get to the Battery. You know that."

Flynn's eyes welled with disappointment. He glanced down at Romes and slowly nodded. "I know."

Frost reached out and took both his hands, squeezing them tight, and felt his warmth race through her body. "We can make it, Flynn. The Battery, it's paradise. I know it. That's where life begins again. That's where we'll find what we need to restore this city. We need their help. You and your father can—"

"He didn't make it."

Frost was caught by surprise. "What?"

"He's gone, Frost." The sadness in his voice sent a flash of white-hot pain through her body. That was why Flynn had appeared so broken. He'd suffered an inconceivable loss, and she hadn't been there for him.

Reflexively, her hands went to her heart. "Flynn . . . I'm . . . I'm so sorry."

Biting his lip, he refused to make eye contact; he turned his body away from Frost and stared at the floor instead. "There's so much ugliness here. I've seen it all firsthand. It has to stop. It has to. I don't want any other kid going through what I did. I'm going to help give these people the world my father always wanted, the place he knew he would never see again, but wished for every day of his life. He wanted to do what was right, I know that. But it's so hard in a world like this. But he was try-ing. He came back for you." He turned to her, wiping a tear away with the back of his hand. "No one is meant to reach the Battery, Frost. There are thousands of Eaters between the wall and that place. That's what the Terrorist John Lord did to keep the people under his rule. He made the Battery a dream that can never be realized."

And it was her dream, too, had been for as long as she could remember. But John Lord was gone now, and nobody was going to keep her from fulfilling that dream. "We're going to make it there. I made a promise."

"Just . . . just wait until we have things in control here. Please. Do that for me and then we can figure something out."

The desperation in his voice was evident. It pained him to see his friend go.

And it pained Frost, too. But that blue light still shone so bright in her eyes. There was something out there that was going to bring her the life she was promised every time she stared out from her home and dreamed of a different world. Not the sadness of this crumbling city, not the agonizing pain of watching Romes slowly die. But something greater. A place worth living in. "We have to go."

"Frost . . ."

"Flynn, you don't owe me anything. You and your father promised to get me out of the Zone and you did. You fought for me; when I was taken away, you didn't head back home; you came looking for me. You're a hero and your father is, too. But I always knew we were going to have to part ways. The Battery was always my destiny."

And then she did something she always wanted to do, something she felt she must do the moment she met Flynn: She stepped forward, grabbed his face with both hands, pulled it close, and kissed him with everything she had, every bit of life that had previously sat idle in a small, bombed-out home, every bit of life that wished for something greater, every bit of life that waited for a moment just like this.

Within seconds, she felt the tension in Flynn recede. He gave in to the kiss, lost himself in it, as she did, too. It was a galaxy of lifetimes between their lips. That moment was the brightest her world had ever been.

When she pulled away, she could hardly make eye contact. If she did, she was afraid she might never leave.

"You're going to make it there," Flynn said, his voice hoarse. "I know it."

Frost smiled. "You found your hope."

"I found everything. I found you."

She slowly turned away, her feet like cement blocks.

"When you get there, tell them about us here," Flynn said, he, too, unable to leave. "Tell them we need their help. Don't forget about us, Frost."

She glanced back. "I'll never forget you."

And before they went their separate ways for good, they embraced, silently holding back their tears.

FIFTY-FOUR

Dragging the door on which Romes clung to life by the smallest of threads, Bunt led Frost out the back of the mansion, where they were less likely to run into trouble. Evading but one isolated attack, they raced south for several blocks, the wall getting closer and closer with each step.

Glancing behind her, Frost saw the city smoking. Great plumes stretched to the sky like twisters of a super storm, and flashes of light came from the ground up. The distant pops of gunfire could be heard continuously, each one possibly snuffing out one more life. And somewhere in that vast battleground was a boy quickly becoming a man. She was devastated to have left Flynn. It felt as if she no longer carried her heart within her chest. It would remain with him. With his kiss still on her lips, she hoped beyond all hope that he would be okay and they might meet again under the sky of a brighter day.

As she turned back around, hoping to see the wall, she caught a glimpse of something else instead, a glint of light reflecting off some shiny surface in the near distance and directly into her eyes. It came from a building three blocks away, a window several stories from the ground. It could only mean one thing.

She told Bunt to wait before moving any farther.

"I think someone's watching us."

Then, seconds later, as if to verify her suspicion, a shot was fired in their direction. Quickly, they ducked behind a car.

"There are seven of them," Bunt whispered. *"Robots. They are spread throughout the building, third floor to eighth. They linger just past the windows."*

The robots opened fire, bullets spraying down the entire street.

"We have to make a run for it," Bunt said.

"They won't stop shooting. We'll be killed."

"They fire erratically. In the past minute but one shot of dozens has hit this car. With the robots at such a distance, we can make it."

With a deep exhalation, Frost, trusting in her friend, nodded, and, a minute later, on Bunt's signal, she was darting down a side street. Bunt quickly followed, deflecting a bullet off his arm as he pulled Romes to temporary safety.

"They won't stay in the buildings for long. They're going to hunt us down," he said. *"We must hurry."*

But this area was well outside the heart of the city and still in great ruin like much of the Outskirts Frost had come from. Bunt repeatedly had to stop to clear the way of rubble and cars and dead bodies. Frost assisted wherever she could, but they didn't get very far before a few bullets went sailing over their heads. They were found.

Rounding the corner, two long blocks away, the robots shot

wildly, as if unsure how to properly use the weapons. And when they ran out of bullets they were clueless about how to reload them. But, tossing the empty guns aside and picking up whatever they could use to inflict harm, they still persisted in their chase.

Frost ran hard, glancing over her shoulder every few seconds, watching the robots in quick pursuit, some with heavy and blunt objects in their hands now, and some—the ones of Bunt's make—with their swords drawn. If they caught up, the robots would most surely make short work of them.

With a clear stretch of road, and as clumsy as the robots were, Frost and Bunt gained some ground between them. But, just as quickly as this was attained, it was taken from them. A block later, they ran out of room to run. Obstructing their path was the roaring river that cut through the city. It would be impossible to cross.

Gasping for breath, Frost turned and stared down the street. The robots were nearly upon them now.

"I won't be able to protect you," Bunt said to her. *"One of them is bound to get past me."*

"I'll fight," Frost said. "We'll fight together."

"No." Bunt dragged the door into the river, holding it in place with a tight grip on the rope as Romes rose and fell with the water. *"Get on,"* he said. *"Ride the current to the wall."*

"What about you?" Frost asked, frantic. "You have to get on, too."

"There's no room for me."

"We'll make room!"

"I'm too heavy, Frost. We would sink."

"Bunt, no."

"There is no time." Bunt lifted her up kicking and screaming, and placed her beside Romes.

"Bunt!"

Then, without another word, he let go of the rope and Frost and Romes sailed down river. Distraught and frightened, Frost looked back just as the robots reached Bunt. His sword was drawn and he began swiping away, but they overtook him quickly. By the time she was a hundred yards away, a hundred yards closer to the wall, a hundred yards closer to the Battery, Bunt, as well as her father within, was lost amid a writhing and violent pile of metal.

PART FOUR
THE WASTELAND

FIFTY-FIVE

The current was strong. As she desperately clung to the weakening door, water splashing in her face and Romes's fur, Frost watched the landscape speed by, the crumbling buildings darting past like fading memories.

Frost's hair clung to her face, her clothes drenched, her grip slipping. Beside her, Romes stirred, the water acting as an arousal of consciousness. He whimpered and flailed, and Frost had to keep him from tumbling helplessly off the door. As best she could, she tied the loose end of the rope around her pet, and when she finished she nearly collapsed, not in pain, but in grief. Her father, Bunt—she had left them behind. Without any regard for themselves, they fought for her, for her dream. And now they were gone. Her father always said he would give his life for her, and he did. She took it. Why didn't she stay back with Flynn? Why did she ever leave her home?

Glancing ahead, through squinted and blurred eyes, she spotted the approaching wall. It loomed in the distance, a metal behemoth that crossed the city like false teeth. She realized that this sad structure was one of the only things left intact in the entire city. The last mark of man.

The river was narrowing now, its speed intensifying. Frost glared ahead, through the splashing water at what awaited her. The wall ran straight across the river, a steel grate preventing passage to the other side. She was heading straight for it.

"Oh no. Oh no no no no no." She didn't know what to do. She looked back and forth, searching for an answer, but nothing came. They were going to crash and crash hard.

"Hold on," she said to Romes, wrapping her arms around him. "Hold on."

Twenty yards away. Ten . . . five . . .

"Here it comes!"

The door split upon contact, sending Frost and Romes plunging into the cold water. Caught in the immense power of the river, Frost tumbled, her head smashing against something hard. When she came surging to the surface, dazed and in pain and gasping for breath, she was thrown face-first against the grate, Romes beside her, crying out as the current relentlessly slammed into them.

The pressure was intense. Frost was sure she was going to be diced up by the grate at any moment. With all the strength she had, she reached out and grabbed the end of the rope that had been torn from the door. With Romes on the other end, she wrapped it around her body and tried to swim for shore.

This, however, proved difficult, the current fighting her with every stride. She just hoped Romes could hold on; she couldn't pull him, not yet. First she had to get herself to land, then she would see to him.

If she were going to make it, she knew she had to block out his stifled cries, the sound of water rushing down his throat. She had to pay no mind to the yellow blood pouring from his wounds.

The determination in her was astounding; she even surprised herself. Somehow, she was making progress. Land was within reach.

In a matter of minutes, much to her disbelief, she was pulling herself onto shore.

And yet, on her hands and knees, spitting up water, she had no time to rest or revel in her fleeting victory. As quickly as she could, she turned around and began to pull at the rope. Her feet slipped on the slick surface, and Romes, to her horror, was hardly budging at all. The river was pulling him under.

"You have to swim!" she yelled to her pet as she dug her feet into the wet earth. "Come on! Swim!"

She could see Romes's eyes try to seek her out. "I'm here!" she cried. "Swim to me!" Feebly, Romes attempted to move his legs as, hand over hand, Frost pulled at the rope. Her entire body stood at a sharp angle as she put everything she had into each tug. Her teeth were clenched, her eyes closed. Every few moments she let out a desperate scream, supplying her with that much more strength. But it worked. It all worked. It took a long time, but eventually, she managed to pull Romes ashore. Then, with him in her arms, they both collapsed in a heap and slept there on the banks of the river for a short while, the sound of the water rushing past filling their ears like white noise.

FIFTY-SIX

It was nightfall by the time Frost awoke, her soaked body shivering in the cooling air. She felt sick, feverish. The river continued to rush by, a pleasant sound in a city of unpleasantries. As Romes continued to slumber beside her, gunshots still popping off however faintly, she looked out at the flashing lights and fires in the distance. The revolution raged still, and now there were glows both north and south—the violent and the peaceful. Not that she could see the warm blue lights of the Battery—the wall stood much too tall for that. Aching, she got to her feet and placed her frozen hands against the barrier keeping her from her goal. The panel was rusted over and jagged, nearly cutting her skin. Curious, she knocked and the thud was ominously dull.

She had to find a way through, and soon. Bending down, she stroked Romes's hide. He was in poor shape. There were several wounds across his body, and she had to pull a half-dozen large splintered pieces of wood from his back. Yellow blood spurted freely. She aided him in whatever way she could, but it wasn't much. Hopefully, it was enough to get him to the Battery. "Come on, boy. We're not far now. I need you to be strong just a little bit longer." She grabbed the rope and tugged it a bit, more to wake him up than an attempt to get him on his feet. "Can you walk? Think you can do that?"

Romes opened his eyes and stared up at her. He looked so very tired. A deep tiredness, a tiredness that went beyond rest, beyond sleep. Eyes that said: Go, leave me.

Coughing, Frost shook her head as if she actually heard these words. "No. Come on. We're going together. Now."

With what looked like deep resignation, Romes slowly stood and lumbered forward. The pace, however, was incredibly sluggish, Frost walking backward with small steps so that she could keep an eye on her pet, so that she could make sure she wasn't pulling too hard or to see if he needed a rest. They kept close to the wall, searching for a door that would lead them to the other side, but found nothing.

Frost's body burned with fever. It made her feel like a child again, when her sickness overwhelmed her. And, just when she felt she was about to faint, she spotted something in the debris that lined the street.

She let Romes rest and ran to the pile, tossing objects aside to reveal the cart underneath. It was perfect. A good size, it had four rubber wheels and a chain attached—someone must have once used it to lug supplies around. And then she saw the pile of bones beside it and quickly jumped away. Nothing, she remembered, came without a sacrifice.

Carefully avoiding the bones, she pulled the cart free and turned it over. Though it was difficult and draining, and required much coaxing and several breaks, she eventually managed to get Romes up and on the cart. When she was finished, she collapsed against the wall, breathing deeply, her head woozy, her body aching.

Pulling Romes the three blocks to the door proved to be a struggle. Even with the large rubber wheels, the trailer was far heavier than the elevator door and there was plenty of debris on the streets that needed to be cleared. The chain was like lead in Frost's hands and every time she had to pick it up was akin to lifting a sack of bricks—the pressure on her shoulder was almost unbearable. But, through sheer determination, she reached the door.

Its wide outline cut into the wall, but there was no handle to grab, no hinges on which it would swing. Lowering the chain, her muscles throbbing in their temporary reprieve, Frost located the red star she had seen from the back of Grasn's truck and, sure enough, just below it was the panel. Sliding it over, she discovered a smooth metal plate embedded inside the wall.

Standing on her toes, Frost placed her hand flat against the plate and pushed. It didn't take much pressure on her part; it was almost as if she were meant to go through. Once the plate was locked in place, a loud, grating sound cut through the stale air and the door in the wall slowly slid open, revealing the Wasteland beyond.

Frost poked her head through the large opening and took in the expanse that awaited her. She half expected Eaters to be scouring about everywhere she looked, clogging the streets, pacing the wall, perhaps sniffing what was on the other side, but there was no sign of them at all.

She went back and picked up the chain, which was now somehow lighter, and started pulling Romes through the door.

Once on the other side of the wall, she realized there was no one left to push the panel a second time to close the door behind her. It would have to remain open and, eventually, the Eaters would most surely find their way through.

The winding streets were silent and narrow, the blown-out buildings oppressively closing in on her. These were towering structures shrouding her in darkness, behemoths far exceeding the thirty-two stories of her former home. Made mostly of glass, they were now faceless, the shattered remains littering the street and crunching beneath Frost's feet. There was plenty of dust from the buildings that had toppled over or collapsed, everything gray, muted. The destruction down here was even worse than it was in the rest of the city. There were massive holes in the ground, piles of bricks and stones, remnants of former lives, better lives. There were scattered bones, human and animal alike, but no trees, no growth of any kind. It was an eerie place to be, and Frost wondered how something as miraculous as the Battery could lie beyond such desolation.

As she trudged through the bleakness, she glanced to her left, down one of the claustrophobic streets, and saw her first Eater of the territory. It was a woman and, alone, she staggered past on parallel avenues, never once looking Frost's way before she vanished around the corner; there one minute and gone the next, like a spirit sent to haunt her.

And then, looking down, she noticed all the footprints in the soot. Hundreds of them. Eaters, she was sure. She took care to travel in the opposite direction.

The temperature was very cold now, enough that she could see each of Romes's heavy breaths—something she wasn't certain she would ever see again if she didn't reach the Battery soon.

Behind her Romes gasped. It reminded Frost of a death rattle, and she dropped the chain and hurried over to him. He wasn't dead, not yet, but he seemed worse than she had seen him before. He had grown thin and frail, tufts of fur fell from his body, his tail lay limp, and there was a continuous shiver in his bones. For the second time, she applied some pressure to the wounds, the blood pooling and running down Romes's side and onto the trailer and into the street. Soothingly, she spoke to him. "We've come a long way, haven't we? Not much farther now, I promise. Do you hear me? Can you hear my words? Let me tell you what's going to happen, Romes. Listen to me now. I'm going to pull you along, don't you worry about a thing. I'm going to pull you through these streets and to the Battery. It might take a day; it might take two, but I'll get you there. And when we reach the water the first thing we're going to see is the blue light. It's going to be magnificent, Romes. It's going to be like nothing we've ever experienced. It's going to fill us with warmth and beauty and love. And I'm going to wave. A small, little wave to get their attention and then they're going to come for us. They're going to welcome us into their community and they're going to see you and they're going to care for you. They're going to give you medicines that the rest of the world hasn't yet experienced. It's almost going to be like magic, and it's going to do wonders for you. In a matter of days, you're going to be on your feet again and running around, and it's going to be like old times. You and me. We're going to be happy, Romes. We're going to be happy."

But had she glanced behind her at the long trail of blood they had left in their wake, such thoughts might have been quickly abandoned.

FIFTY-SEVEN

Frost dutifully continued on her path, heading in the direction she believed to be south, although it was quite easy to lose one's bearing in the Wasteland. The streets twisted and turned—the navigable grid of the rest of the city was abandoned here—and the buildings blocked out the sky, save for a sliver. Was she heading too far east? She thought this might be possible—the way her mind was working right now, she could have been heading back north for all she knew.

Some time later, when she believed she had regained her bearings, she spotted an old church coming up on her right. The portico had long collapsed, the columns finally giving out after almost three centuries of obedient support, hiding the church's face. Sometime during the Days of Bedlam, the towering spire had fallen forward, crashing through the roof and knocking down the back wall. Surrounding this once vibrant place of worship was a cemetery, most of its headstones broken or knocked over, the graves dug up. The coffins, ripped open and overturned, were left rotting on the ground, and the bones they once housed were now strewn about like the rest of the city's artifacts. The ones closest to the street, Frost noticed, looked as if they had been gnawed on. The Eaters were hungry.

Frost felt incredibly uneasy, the hair standing up on the back of her neck. All she wanted to do was hurry past and get off this block. But that was when she saw an Eater staring at her from down the street.

It stood on the corner, one arm completely missing, the other arm half gone, rocking back and forth as if waiting for a ride that would never come. Frost didn't have long. Desperate, she searched the ground for a weapon. There was nothing. The chain would have to do. She backed up to where the chain met the trailer so that she had the maximum amount to swing.

With that movement, the Eater started walking toward her, slowly at first, then faster. Bravely, Frost stood her ground, weighing the chain in her hands. She didn't want to look at the Eater's eyes. She didn't want to see the life inside them, not if she wanted to remain alive. If she wanted to make it to the Battery in one piece, she would have to see the Eaters as lifeless creatures, as nothing but threats to her existence and goal. With both hands, she held the chain at her side. When the Eater got close enough, she would swing for its head.

But, instead of attacking, the Eater hesitated. Its pace slowed.

Frost was confused. What was it doing? Its hunger should have completely overwhelmed it by now. There should have been nothing on its mind but food. But, maybe, she thought, she could use this wavering to her advantage.

"Go," Frost said, believing she could communicate with it. "Get out of here. I don't want to hurt you."

The Eater continued to rock back and forth, its jaw snapping.

Frost raised the chain over her head and slammed it to the street. "Go!"

Still, the Eater didn't budge. It was waiting for something. What?

And then Frost heard the noise. The unmistakable moan of an Eater. It was coming from behind her.

It was all a distraction. While she was focused on the Eater before her, two more were heading straight for Romes.

They were trying to do so quietly, but when Frost spotted them, they lunged.

With a scream, Frost scrambled and began to climb onto the trailer. She watched helplessly as one of the Eaters, one with no arms, buried its face into Romes's hide. "No!" Getting to her feet, Frost reared back and kicked the Eater in the head as hard as she could. It reeled several yards back and fell to the ground.

The second Eater, meanwhile, reached for Romes, its hand digging into his flesh like a drill. With long, jagged nails, it was tearing a piece out. Frost hurled the chain, smashing the Eater in the face and knocking out several teeth and breaking its jaw.

But now the original Eater came at her from behind and Frost, her legs straddling her pet, had to swing around and knock it away. It wasn't a great shot, but the chain got the Eater enough to send it stumbling back.

Frost kept shifting her focus from one Eater to the next, but they weren't coming at her all at once. They were picking their spots. When Frost went after one, the other two swooped in for Romes, clawing and biting for fresh meat. The broot howled in pain and lashed his tail to no effect. Above him, Frost swung the chain with everything she had, constantly swiveling back and forth from one Eater to the next. She wasn't sure how much more Romes could withstand, or herself, for that matter. She needed a better weapon. She needed something sharp.

Then, her stomach sank. Glaring past her adversaries, she spotted five more Eaters stumbling her way.

In a matter of seconds, the trailer was surrounded. There was no other choice; Frost began to swing the chain wildly. She didn't aim. There was no calculated method, no plan of attack—just survival. "Get away from him!" she cried. "Leave him alone!"

But the Eaters were getting in far too many attacks. Romes's body was ravaged and bleeding severely. "Stop! Please! I know you can hear me! Stop! Stop! Leave him alone! Please!"

But the Eaters kept coming, their mouths bloody from the meat and the crash of Frost's chain. And then, one did something Frost didn't think possible, something that would most definitely seal her fate: It grabbed the chain from where it attached to the trailer and it pulled it from Frost's hands.

Frost looked down at her empty palms. She was defenseless.

FIFTY-EIGHT

The Eater that came closest received the first punch. Frost put everything she had into the blow, and she was pretty sure the crunch beneath her knuckles was something severe. Screaming like a savage, she followed this with a punishing kick to the ribs of a second Eater and a backhand to a third, each strike shattering bones. But she couldn't keep it up. As the Eaters' attacks continued, Frost soon found herself overwhelmed. As she was tossing an Eater off Romes, another one had pulled her legs out from under her. She fell hard, slamming the back of her head against the trailer.

Through the hazy sky overhead she thought she saw stars. Were they peeking through? After all this time, was that possible?

With Frost vulnerable and exposed, the Eaters moved in. From all sides they were crawling atop the trailer like scavenging rats, moaning and drooling and writhing. Frost knew it was hopeless now. All was lost. And so she merely climbed atop Romes, protecting him from their attacks. Let them eat her first. And she closed her feverish eyes and waited for this to happen.

Only it never did.

In the slow moments that followed, Frost opened one eye and then another. There were no hands on her, no teeth pulling at her flesh nor Romes's; the Eaters' hungering gasps had dissipated. Confused, she carefully picked her head up. What she saw she couldn't believe. Bunt. It was Bunt. There he was with his sword unsheathed, disposing of the Eaters one by one. Although Frost could see multiple dings and tears on his body—especially one large dent in the back of his head—he moved well, as if nothing had happened to him. With one hand, he pulled the Eaters off the trailer and ran them through with his sword. They tried to claw and gnaw away at him, but it was fruitless. He was too much for them.

But then one grew wise. It picked up a brick and smashed it against Bunt's head. It had little effect other than a small scratch. Once Bunt turned around, the Eater didn't last long, but it was clear they were quickly learning the difference between humans and robots. In the end, however, even with such knowledge, they proved little match for Bunt. In the shadows of the church all of the Eaters were splayed out on the ground, bleeding from their critical wounds.

Bunt sheathed his sword.

"Bunt!"

Frost leaped from the trailer and ran to him. Wrapping her arms around his body, she closed her eyes and wept. "I thought I lost you. I thought you were gone for good." And when Bunt wrapped his arms around her, she cried even harder.

They took shelter inside the church, Bunt clearing the debris blocking the entrance and making sure what was left of the walls was stable. Once inside, he covered up whatever holes could lead the Eaters to them and barricaded the door. When all was said and done, they settled beside the fallen spire, its large cross having punctured the floor, its bell having rolled from its perch and settled on its side. Together, Bunt and Frost cared for Romes's injuries.

"Is he going to make it?" Frost asked, trembling with panic.

"We can only do our best. He has another day or two. Three, if luck is on his side."

"Can we make it to the Battery by then?"

"I don't know."

"But it's not much farther, I know it."

"There are hundreds of Eaters not very far from here. I've scanned them, and I'm sure by tomorrow there will be even more. Distance is now irrelevant. The odds are against us."

Frost stared hard at the robot. "I need my father, Bunt. I need him so bad right now."

But Bunt could only gaze back at her. *"I'm sorry, Frost. Since the attack by the river, he hasn't returned. I fear he never will."*

FIFTY-NINE

As night descended, Frost remained at Romes's side, never once moving. As weary and sick as she was, she kept her eyes locked on him, checking his breathing, tending to his wounds, easing his pain whenever and however she could. Bunt, as he always did, was monitoring their surroundings, scanning for any potential threats, of which there were currently none.

Sometime later, when Romes finally drifted off to sleep—a light and struggling slumber—Frost waved Bunt over. At her request, he sat with her, each of them on one side of the small fire. The air was close to freezing, and Frost pulled her knees close to her chest for warmth.

They both kept silent, Frost staring into the flames, her eyes refusing to blink. It had been a long and arduous journey, but they were almost there now. The end was near. She just had to remain strong.

Her thoughts went back to her home on the thirty-second floor of that bombed-out building: the isolation, the hopelessness, the inside dying even faster than the outside. It had seemed so long ago. And she didn't miss it, not in the slightest. All she missed was what it once housed: her mother, her father, a healthy Romes. All that was gone now. And all that remained was Bunt.

"Thank you," she said. "For helping me. My whole life you've always been there at my side, and I could never have gotten this far without you. I know I haven't always been the greatest with you; I know I haven't always seen you for what you really are."

"A robot."

"A friend. It's not your programming, I know that now. You're not loyal because some chip tells you to be. It's not code, it's not preordained. I look around and I see all these other robots trying to change, trying to become human, and they fail miserably. And there you are and you don't try at all and you're more human than they could ever dream of being."

"I am a product of your father. If you sense loyalty, it is his loyalty. If you sense compassion, it is his compassion. If you sense love, it is his love."

Frost shook her head. "I don't believe that. I believe you are your own person. I think that's what my father gave you. I think that's what he wanted for you all along. And I think you know that, too."

Bunt fell silent, as if contemplating this. Sitting there, staring at the floor, he looked more human than ever.

"You're unique, Bunt. I think if I lived forever I would still never meet another robot quite like you."

His violet eyes shot up. *"Would you like to live forever? Is that what you want?"*

Frost felt the intensity behind his penetrating glare, and she quickly gazed down at Romes before answering. "I want *him* to live forever. I know that. If my mother were alive, I'd want her to live forever. If my father . . ." She stopped, a catch in her throat. "And if they could live forever, I'd want to live forever with them."

"And what would you expect from everlasting life? Would you not feel pain or sorrow? Would the world not still crumble around you?"

"I would expect not to lose the ones I love. I would expect to have them with me forever."

"But you already have that."

Frost eyed him, wondering what exactly he meant. In a way, she did feel like her father was alive inside her, much like the way he was in Bunt. Sometimes, late at night, if she listened real hard, she could hear his voice and it sounded as clear as her own. She could see him as if he were standing right before her. He was flesh and blood, he was real. But this wasn't true, was it? Her father was lost to her, gone for good down a robotic black hole.

Coughing, Frost reached out and placed a comforting hand on Romes, feeling the violent rise and fall of his chest. "We're lost. Nobody knows what life is supposed to be anymore. Humans want to become robots, robots want to become humans, and it doesn't matter because everyone wastes what they're given, anyway."

"Frost, should I want to be human like the other robots?"

Frost was taken aback; it was a question she never imagined answering. She felt the fire of sickness in her throat and behind her eyes. Bunt would never be ill, not for one minute over one million years. There would be no risk of him dying like her father, no risk of him becoming an Eater like her mother. No suffering. "Being a human is difficult, Bunt. There's so much pain. So much confusion and fear. Do you want that?"

"*I don't know. Is there a balance? What are the good things about being human? What does a human have that a robot does not? I don't understand. Why does my kind wish to change so badly?*"

"I . . . I don't know."

"*I suppose it doesn't matter. I could never be human, could I? I could mimic them, I could ape their emotions and wear their clothes, but would it be real? Would that make me a real human?*"

"I see the realness in you now. Robots don't need to be human, Bunt. Maybe they just need to understand them. You want to know what's good about being human? It's the love. It's the way we care for one another, the way we can help those around us achieve something great. It's the human potential. But you have that. Romes has that. And any robot can, too. Forget the surface of humans, Bunt. Forget the blood that flows in their veins and the beating of their hearts. That's not what makes them human. It's what they feel that sets them apart. If I were trapped inside one of you, like my dad is, I wouldn't care about my shell. It's not important."

"*You wouldn't miss being human?*"

"Maybe being human is a state of mind, a way of living. Inside a robot, my body would be something else, but my mind would make me human. And I would be the best robot that I ever could."

Hearing this, Bunt reached out and grabbed her arm, just above the wrist.

"What are you doing?" Frost asked, trying to pull her arm away.

But Bunt didn't respond. He just squeezed tighter.

"Bunt, stop it. You're hurting me."

Watching his closed fist, she felt as if her bones were being crushed. The searing, shooting pain was unbearable.

"Stop," she gasped. "You're going to break my arm. Stop it."

But Bunt didn't stop. And then Frost saw his hand begin to glow bright red. He was burning her.

SIXTY

As her skin slowly melted away beneath Bunt's iron grip, Frost howled in excruciating pain.

"Bunt, stop! Please! It hurts! It hurts!"

Bunt leaned closer, his face mere inches from hers. *"Ignore the pain. It isn't real."*

With the stink of scorched flesh in her nose, Frost kicked her legs wildly, searching for some kind of reprieve from the torment. Tears streamed down her face; her chest heaved violently. She was being burned alive. "Why are you doing this? I can't take it! Stop!"

"Look at me," Bunt said, his voice calm as ever. *"Look at me."*

Frost raised her eyes, but they couldn't settle. All she saw was the white light of pure agony.

"The pain isn't real. Your sickness isn't real. It's all in your head. Fight it."

"It hurts, Bunt. It hurts so bad."

"It doesn't. Trust me."

Frost looked at him, her vision blurry through the tears.

"Trust me." He pointed at his face. *"Focus here. See through me. See your father."*

And Frost did. In a desperate attempt to fight through her pain, she glared at Bunt's eyes. As if diving through the very

314

center of these violet rings, she glimpsed past the surface of his features, her vision traveling through Bunt's shining exterior and into the darkness beyond. There, somewhere in that robotic skull, she met her father's eyes. He was waiting for her. Like a message from some inexplicable place, his voice rang clear. He told her the pain was gone.

And, to Frost's surprise, it was. She didn't feel a thing. Looking down at her arm, she could still see Bunt's hand burning the flesh away like wax from a candle, but there wasn't an ounce of pain.

"What . . . what's happening?" she asked.

"You're discovering who you are."

Frost looked at him, a terrible fear rising up inside her. "Who am I?"

And Bunt slowly pulled his hand away.

The skin was burned straight through and where Frost expected to see blood and bone and muscle she only saw machinery.

"I . . ." She swallowed hard and shook her head. "No. No. I . . . It's . . . This isn't right. It's . . . it's not true."

"It is."

"I'm not. No. I'm not a robot."

"You are."

Bunt grabbed her by the hand, gentler this time. A small hole appeared in his forearm, a type of plug protruding from it like a pulled vein. It snaked toward Frost, inserting itself into her opened wrist. And when it plugged in, Frost's mind was slammed with the power of the past.

SIXTY-ONE

It was like a dream. An out-of-body experience. It was something like dying.

Frost was home. She was back in the Outskirts, back in her small blown-out apartment on the thirty-second floor of her crumbling building. She saw herself lying on her bed. She saw her father standing over her. She saw her mother, her beautiful mother.

But it wasn't her memory. It was Bunt's. Like a gift, he had given it to her. His life, everything he ever saw.

Frost was sick. Very sick. Dying. She was only five years old. Her eyes were closed, her breathing was troubled.

There were tears in both her parents' eyes. The world had finally gotten to their child.

"She's not going to make it," her mother said, hardly able to speak. "She's out of time. We're going to lose her. We're going to lose our baby. There's nothing else we can do."

"That's not true," Alex said. "Jane, we have a choice here."

"No. No, we don't. It's over."

"It will still be her."

Jane was weeping now. She threw herself over Frost, kissing

her and holding her and caressing her hair. "It won't. It won't, it won't, it won't. I want my baby. I want my baby girl."

Alex bent down beside her, his hands on his wife's shoulders. "It will still be her. You have to believe me. I know what I'm doing. It will be her."

"She's a five-year-old girl, Alex. That . . . that thing is something else. I mean, it could be a twelve-year-old. It—it doesn't even look like her."

"No, it doesn't. It looks like you. I modeled it after you. When you were young. She'll look like her mother."

"What kind of life is that for her? She won't grow up. She'll never age. And then when we go she'll be left all alone."

Alex turned back and looked at Bunt.

"No," Jane said. "No. Absolutely not."

"I'm going to save our daughter."

"And are you going to be the one to tell her what you did to save her, because I won't."

"This type of robot was going to be the future, Jane. If I had time to produce them, it would have changed everything for everyone. It's a prototype, yes, but it's unlike anything I've ever created. Its body is nearly identical to a human's. It can react to the emotions of the occupant. It can perspire, it can quake with fear, it can do whatever we can. Mentally, she'll develop slowly, like she would now. And then, when she's old enough, when she starts realizing she's not aging, when she realizes something's different, then, yes, I'll tell her."

"But we're not giving her a choice. It should be her decision."

"She's too young to make these types of decisions. I don't understand why you're questioning this. She's going to die, Jane. That's it. She's going to die and she'll be gone for good. Unless we do something. Do you want to lose her? Is that what you want?"

"No! Of course not."

"We can do this. I know the robot will work. We'll put her consciousness in there and her eyes will open and she'll look at you and she'll say, 'Momma.' Watch. I promise you. It will be like nothing happened."

Jane wrapped her arms around him and wept. "You promise?"

"I do. I promise."

"Okay. Okay. Do it."

There was a flash and Bunt's memory jumped to where Frost needed it to go. It was an hour later, and she was now in her father's office. It was neater than when she last saw it, before her father trashed it in a fit of rage. It was organized but clearly used—Alex had put in many hours here.

Bunt was carrying her body into the room and there in the corner was the body of a young girl.

"Place her down," Alex told Bunt. "Prepare her for the surgery."

Jane's hand was over her mouth. "I . . . I can't be here for this." And she hurried out of the room.

As Alex prepared the robot, Bunt kneeled over Frost. He gazed at her, taking in her vitals. Frost looked down upon her old self. Her true self. She had dark hair, almost red. Her cheeks were pale and flush, she had a tiny nose and there was a small beauty mark just beside her ear. It was strange, like looking at another person. She wondered who this child was and who she might have grown up to be.

"Ready."

"Not yet," Alex said. "Give me a minute." And Bunt stood up and crossed the room.

Alex shifted on his knees and cradled his daughter's head in his arms. "Hey, little girl. Hey, my love. I'm so sorry about what you're going through right now. If I could absorb your sickness, your pain, I would. I would take it all, every ounce of it. I'm so sorry. I'm so, so very sorry." He broke down into tears. "You were supposed to have so much more than this. You were supposed to have a great life, and you were supposed to have a world worthy of someone like you. It's not fair. But I promise you, I'm going to help change all that. I'm going to fix things. First in this city and then everyplace else. I just need you with me to start." He stroked her hair. "I don't know if you can hear me right now, my baby. I hope you can. I want you to know this. One day you're going to question who you are, what you are. You're going to think that you're different, that you don't belong. But that's not true. You are my daughter and you always will be. I don't love your flesh. I don't love the pumping of your heart or the breath you exhale. I love you. I pray you understand. I pray you forgive me."

He turned to Bunt and nodded. "Let's go."

And as Bunt crouched down beside her there was another flash, another short jump through time.

Once again, her parents were standing over her in bed. But it wasn't the Frost from before. It was the new Frost. Her eyes were closed. She was at rest. She looked like she was sleeping.

"What if it didn't work?" Jane asked.

"It worked. I know it did."

Except it looked like he didn't know. He was biting his nails, shifting his weight from side to side. He was beyond nervous.

And then, slowly, Frost opened her eyes. She looked from her father to her mother, and she said, "Daddy? Momma?"

Jane exploded into tears and smothered her daughter in hugs and kisses. "Frost, oh, my dear Frost. It's you. It's you."

"Am I . . . am I still sick?"

"No," Alex answered. "You're better. You're so much better."

SIXTY-TWO

Another flash and Frost was brought back into the present. Bunt had removed the wire from her arm and sat back. It almost looked like he was exhausted.

Not that Frost noticed. She was busy staring down at the robotics beneath her false skin. She still couldn't wrap her mind around it. The metal didn't belong there. She wondered, if she was to be stripped of all her skin, what would her entire body look like? What would her skull look like? The thought sent shivers up her spine, shivers, she knew, that shouldn't be there. They weren't real, they were unnecessary to her construction.

"Why . . . why did you show me this?"

"Because you are strong. Because you deserve to know."

"I didn't ask for this."

"No, but it was given to you. I asked you what you would do if you were trapped inside a robot, if you could live forever. Your answer was the most human thing I have ever heard. The girl who said that was the same girl I helped bring into this world and the same one I watched leave it, the same one I saw return. You are human. I never saw you as anything but. This world needs you, Frost. It needs the warmth you carry. And it is time you brought it

to them. We will make it to the Battery and, there, you will change everything."

Frost stood up and stared down at Bunt. "You shouldn't have shown me this." And she walked to the other side of the church.

It was several hours before morning, when the darkness was deepest, both outside the church and within Frost's head, that Romes appeared to suffer a violent fit. His entire body twitched and quaked, nearly rolling onto the diminishing fire, his eyes drifting back and thick fluids draining from his mouth and pooling beside his limp tongue. The episode rattled Frost from her troubled trance, and she hurried to Romes's side, any and all concerns she had for herself shoved to some far recess. She couldn't lose Romes, she just couldn't. But, terrified and unsure what to do, she froze.

"Bunt! Bunt, do something! Help him!"

The robot ran over, gently moving Frost aside, and went to work on the broot. Frost wasn't sure what exactly Bunt was doing, because she couldn't bear to watch. She just stood behind him with her eyes closed, saying, "Save him, Bunt. Do whatever you have to do. Don't let him die. Please, I need him. Don't let him die." In this harrowing moment, she forgot that she was a robot, she forgot that such emotions shouldn't be relevant to her. They were there and they were real. All she knew was that she needed Romes to live, because if he didn't, she wasn't sure she would be able to go on. In this moment, nothing else mattered.

And when, minutes later, Bunt slowly stepped away from the broot, Frost held her unessential breath. She still couldn't bring herself to look at her beloved pet.

"Is he . . . ?"

"He'll make it another day. Maybe."

Thankful, she embraced Bunt. "I thought I was going to lose him. I thought it was over, Bunt. I thought I failed him." Finally, she looked at Romes and saw him lying still, his breaths very weak. She knew they had to make it to the Battery immediately. There was no other option.

Pulling away from Bunt, her head finally clear, she said, "I need to speak to my father. I need you to bring him forth."

"Frost . . ."

"Please."

"It is not possible." He paused a moment, then said, *"I feel him fighting within me. He is desperately trying to rise to the surface, to return to you, but it is in vain. Something has happened. Something bad. And there is nothing I can do about it. I am sorry. Your father lies dormant."*

Glancing down, Frost put out the remaining flames of the fire with her foot. "Does that mean . . . Do you think . . . Do you think I'll never see him again? I'll never get to talk to him again?" Her throat ached and her lips quivered. She bent down and picked up one of the logs. It was hot, but it didn't hurt. She felt the heat, but at the same time didn't.

"He hears you, Frost. He always has and always will. I still feel the intrusion of his thoughts, his mind wandering through mine.

They try to mix, things get confused, but I understand him. And he understands me."

"Bunt, what . . ." She dropped the stick and looked up at him. "What is my father saying right now?"

There was no hesitation in his response. *"He says he loves you. He says he loves you more than you can ever imagine. And nothing would ever change that. Nothing."*

Frost's eyes welled up.

"He says that even if he were to never return he already has immortality. You will never lose him. He says he lives forever in you."

Her hands were trembling and she found it difficult to talk. She pointed from her mouth to her ear. "Can . . . can he . . . ?"

Bunt nodded. *"He can."*

Tentatively, Frost leaned closer, her mouth directed toward Bunt's ear. "Dad . . ." she said, closing her eyes. She tried to picture him in there like she did before, when she needed the pain to go away. She envisioned his face. His eyes, his nose, his smile. He was there, as real as anything, and he was listening. "Dad . . . Dad, it's okay, what you did. I understand. If there was a way to have you with me right now I would do it. You mean everything to me. You, Mom, Romes, Bunt. You're my family. Dad, I . . . I love you. I love you so much."

She dropped to the floor and the tears came heavily. They were as real as she was, and they would come until she cried every last one of them.

SIXTY-THREE

On Frost's orders, Bunt placed Romes back onto the trailer and removed the barricade from behind the door. Through the opening, he scanned their surroundings. When he told Frost that all was clear, she thought she heard a tinge of surprise in his voice.

Together, they set foot outside the church. It was a drearier night than most, the sky darker and more violent than usual, the air colder. All around them the territory was silent, the church's graveyard stretching for miles. Undeterred, Bunt rolled the trailer forward and into the street.

Walking behind him, Frost could tell he was concentrating more than normal, his scanner working in overdrive. His pace was slow, but deliberate. Every window of every floor of every building was scanned for Eaters.

And so, nearly an hour later, it came as a surprise to Frost when one darted out from an empty garage. With a stone in its hand, it charged Bunt who, due to his own bout of astonishment, failed to unsheathe his sword in time. The Eater leaped at him, pounding away with the stone. As he avoided its strikes, Bunt wrapped the chain around the Eater's neck and pulled in opposite directions. Seconds later, two thumps hit the ground.

Slowly, Bunt looked back at Frost. *"My scanner is damaged."*

Frost swallowed hard as a terrible thought ran through her mind. The Eaters knew. The one that struck him in the head with the brick earlier, it knew exactly what it was aiming for, and, if that one Eater was representative of the others, that meant big trouble. Dread coursed through her as the realization took hold. The Eaters' intelligence was intact.

Something crashed behind her, something with a lot of velocity. When she turned around, she caught sight of a large object falling from the sky. Like the previous threat, it landed and shattered on the opposite side of the street, a mere car's length away. Frost glanced up. She saw shadows. There were Eaters on the rooftops. They were behaving like the Throwers in the outer slums—perhaps they used to be.

Another object fell and exploded at their feet, and Frost noticed something about the attacks: the Eaters weren't aiming for her. They knew that to get to the meat they had to do away with Bunt first. And when they eventually discovered that Frost was a robot, too, she would be next.

It was then that Frost realized she wasn't invincible, that being a robot didn't guarantee immortality. She could still die. She could still have the life crushed out of her.

More and more objects began to fall, some large, some small, some like metal spears, a wild storm of debris.

"Run!" Frost cried.

And Bunt took off with the trailer, Frost following close behind. Nothing struck her directly, but all kinds of shrapnel jumped up and cut at her false skin. She could hear the pings as fragments deflected off the metal of Bunt's body and off the base of the trailer. How long they could keep this up, she didn't know. It was only a matter of time before a large one found its target.

They kept running and the objects continued to rain down. The Eaters were getting closer and closer with each attempt. And then, as he was attempting to shove a car aside, Bunt was struck.

A cinder block fell from on high and landed directly on his outstretched hand, severing it clean from his arm. Sparks flew, but Bunt showed no signs of pain or distress. Still, he fought to get them to safety. More objects were hurled down, one just missing Romes and crushing part of the trailer instead, a rear wheel destroyed. Several times, Frost had to jump at the last moment to avoid being pulverized herself.

They ran harder into the night. They turned one corner and then another; the Battery drawing closer and closer, Romes that much nearer to his salvation, Frost that much nearer to her dream. She thought they might just make it.

And then, at a crossroads, they saw them. Hundreds of Eaters rushing their way.

SIXTY-FOUR

The Eaters clogged the narrow street, tripping over one another in their insatiable bloodlust. They were like a rushing river barreling down from a busted dam and heading straight for Frost.

Bunt didn't have much time to react—the Eaters, perhaps two and a half blocks away, would be upon them in less than a minute. Quickly, he dropped the chain to the trailer and ran to an overturned truck on the corner of the intersection. With everything he had, he pushed against it, the pressure he applied causing dents in the frame. And yet the vehicle refused to budge.

Frost attempted to help, but Bunt told her to start pulling the trailer toward the Battery, that he would catch up soon. Backing away, she nervously watched as Bunt, his head down in concentrated effort, pushed against the truck's cargo hold, long emptied of whatever it carried. Slowly, it began to move. He was doing it. And with each step Bunt took thereafter, momentum having been gained, the faster the truck shifted across the street.

The Eaters were nearly upon them now, but Bunt rammed the truck out of the intersection and down the narrow alley, the front and rear of the vehicle scraping against the buildings, shattering windows and crushing facades. The Eaters were bearing down, their eyes growing large at the sight of their targets. And, at the very last moment possible, Bunt managed to wedge the truck firmly into place—Frost could hear the cannibals slamming into the blockade with tremendous force.

With a temporary reprieve, Bunt turned around and saw Frost standing there, terrified. *"Move. Get the trailer,"* he told her.

Frost did as he said, running back and picking up the chain.

But, from the other side of the truck, the Eaters had begun pushing back. The vehicle shook violently as they hammered and punched away. They weren't giving up.

Even with his severed hand, Bunt continued to keep the truck in place, but Frost knew it was only a matter of time before they overwhelmed him and broke through.

"Bunt!" she cried. "Come on! We don't have much time!"

But Bunt didn't answer. He was clearly struggling to keep the Eaters at bay, his feet sliding out from under him.

"Bunt!"

"Go," he said. *"Get him to the Battery. You must hurry."*

"You have to come with us! I can't do it without you! You have time, Bunt! You can make it!"

"I can't hold them for long."

"Bunt, it's an order! I order you!"

And Bunt, ever obedient, turned around.

"I'm not leaving you. Now, let's go," Frost said, rushing to the trailer and pulling it toward the water. "We're not far now."

She had managed a few feet, the trailer heavier than ever, when she noticed Bunt hadn't caught up with her. She turned back around, a horrible feeling washing over her. "Bunt?"

The Eaters hadn't broken through, but they were close, and yet, to Frost's disbelief and confusion, Bunt was still standing where she last saw him, his back to the truck. He hadn't moved an inch. His arms were down at his sides, his head drooping. Behind him the truck began to shift more and more, nearly toppling over.

"Bunt?"

No response. The chain grew heavy in Frost's hands.

"Bunt?"

And then, very slowly, the robot raised his head and Frost's stomach plunged. "D-Dad?"

Alex's eyes stared out at her; they were haunted. "Frost. Run."

The truck quaked behind him, shifting and scraping against the buildings. "Dad!"

"Go!"

Frost shook her head, unable to speak.

"You have to go, Frost. You'll never make it with me. Please, go."

"Dad, we can do it. Together. I know we can." She was choking on her words, each one cutting her throat in their release. Her hands trembled at the thought of losing him. She refused for that to happen. Not again. "Get on the trailer! I'll pull you both!"

But Alex slowly shook his head. "We won't make it, Frost. Go. I'll hold them back." And, with great effort, he turned around and placed his hands against the truck. "Go!"

"Dad, no!"

Alex didn't turn back, he didn't even raise his head, but she could tell he was crying as he fought to keep her safe. "You don't have time! You have to go now!"

"Dad, I can't. I need you! I need you with me!"

"You have me! You always will! Now, get to the Battery! It'll be there! I know it!"

"Dad!"

The truck lunged forward, nearly crushing him. "Go! I beg you!"

Through her tears, Frost began to pull the trailer. She cried out for her father over and over, but she couldn't bear to look back. If she did, it would have been the end of her.

SIXTY-FIVE

It was the most difficult half mile of her life. She felt as if she dragged the entire city behind her, every building, every person, every robot, every animal. The night sky had fallen hard upon her shoulders, the air freezing all about her—a massive wall to walk through. Romes lay dying in the trailer, her father and Bunt holding an army of Eaters at bay, Barrow lost to a war, Flynn lost within one.

And then there was Frost. Alone. Scared. Drained. Distraught.

Her eyes were closed through most of the walk. If this was because of the pain or the sorrow or the cold, she couldn't tell. Maybe she just couldn't stomach staring out into the abyss.

And, some time later, when she finally crossed the last street and cut through an open square overrun by nature and reached the water she had so desperately wished to see for so very long, that was exactly what she found. Nothing. Just an abyss, the seas stretching out into the darkness.

There was no Battery. There was no one around to greet her. No help. No salvation. No blue light. No promised land. Not for as far as the eye could see. There were no signs of life at all.

The chain fell from her hands as she dropped to her knees and sobbed uncontrollably. It was for nothing, she realized, all for nothing. What had she been thinking all this time? What did she expect? She was just a foolish girl, a stupid and naïve and robotic girl believing in a better world. And it cost her everything. Her father, Bunt, Romes, Flynn, Barrow, and, soon, her own life.

Alone in the square, wrapping up in the ice-cold air, she continued to weep, and it was through these tears that she heard the sound. It had become so familiar to her that she didn't even need to turn around to know there was an Eater standing directly behind her.

She remained on her knees, her arms low at her sides, her eyes closed, her head bowed. She had given up. Let the Eater take her. Let it smash her skull in.

Only it didn't. It didn't move at all.

Frost opened her eyes, wondering what could have delayed her death. Slowly, she rose to her feet and turned around. As expected, it was just her and the Eater.

"Well . . ." she said, throwing up her hands. "Are you going to—" She locked eyes with the Eater, her voice dropping like a stone. Her knees went weak and she felt close to toppling over.

She was face-to-face with her mother.

She knew it immediately. Even with her tongueless mouth opening and closing, even with one arm missing, the loose meat hanging just below the shoulder, the white of the bone peeking through like a fat worm; even with the one remaining arm with the sole finger attached; even with the tattered clothes and the horrid stink, the discolored skin and the rotted teeth; even in such a harrowing state she recognized her. "Momma?" she croaked, her heart breaking.

Less than a dozen feet away, her mother didn't move; she just wavered there, staring at her.

She should have pounced; she should have fed. She was an Eater now, a cannibal, and yet she didn't budge. It made no sense. The disease should have overwhelmed her; it should have commanded her forward.

"Momma?"

Frost took a step closer, looking deeper into her eyes. She saw her mother there. Not the Eater but the woman who birthed her, the woman who cared for and loved her. "Momma?"

Another step and then another. Frost reached out and touched her mother's gaunt face, her hand mere inches from her mouth. "I see you," she whispered. "I see you."

Her mother blinked. And in that blink Frost didn't just see her mother; she saw everything. She saw another world, realities upon realities; she saw and heard everything her mother ever wanted to say to her; she saw all the love of her parents stacked like a tower to the heavens; she saw a future that could have been; she saw a past that should have been; she saw beauty and compassion, devotion and tenderness and enlightenment. She saw what she always wanted and always missed.

And, in that moment, outside her mother's eyes, she noticed the frost all around them, the very first frost since the morning of her birth. It dotted the landscape like a blessing and she had never felt so warm.

"I see you," she said again.

The square filled with Eaters. After all this time they had finally reached her, and Frost knew they had overcome her father and destroyed Bunt. And now they had come to finish her and Romes. This was the end and she accepted that.

Frost raised her head to the skies and extended her arms, and the Eaters charged.

But the hum reached her first. As if riding on the vibrations of Frost's body, it issued forth like a battering ram. It was powerful and overwhelming, the square trembling in its magnificence, the Eaters nearly knocked off their feet. It rattled the buildings and shook the trees. It stirred the waters and quaked the ground.

And this hum was followed by a light. A bright blue glow that shone on everything, illuminating all. It was as if the sun had risen, as if it radiated from deep within Frost, shooting from her fingers, pulsing from within every inch of her body, from within her chest and from behind her eyes and from down her throat. The Eaters froze in this glow, unable to move forward, caught in its overwhelming brilliance.

Lowering her arms, Frost turned and saw the Battery. It drifted across the waters like a behemoth, a small but spectacular city full of lights and beauty. There were no bombed-out buildings, no wreckage, no devastation. Just sleek structures of another time and place, the past and the future both. She'd made it, and it was perfect.

The Battery settled into place, its hum dying, the blue light brighter than ever. Shielding their eyes, the Eaters ran, disappearing far into the city. Frost watched them flee and the last to go was her mother. Still standing where she had been since they met, her mother gazed back at her daughter. Nodding, Frost held her hand against her own heart. The gesture said everything Frost needed to say and she knew—she absolutely knew—her mother understood it all. And that was why she could then run away into the territory, leaving Frost and her beloved pet behind for good, and in a far better place.

ABOUT THE AUTHOR

M. P. Kozlowsky was a high school English teacher before becoming a writer. He is the author of *The Dyerville Tales* and *Juniper Berry*, and lives in New York with his wife and their two daughters.